Totally Bound Publishing books by Robin Jeffrey

The Night
Hungry is the Night

D1594004

The Night

HUNGRY IS THE NIGHT

ROBIN JEFFREY

Hungry is the Night
ISBN # 978-1-80250-560-3
©Copyright Robin Jeffrey 2023
Cover Art by Kelly Martin ©Copyright August 2023
Interior text design by Claire Siemaszkiewicz
Totally Bound Publishing

HUNGRY IS THE NIGHT

Dedication

To Philip Allen
Thank you for teaching me
how to howl at the moon.

Chapter One

Marcus

I watched as Grace bit into a slice of rare steak with ravenous abandon, strands of filthy brown hair falling into her diamond-shaped face. She rolled her shoulders back as she chewed, her eyes flickering shut. Sweat shone on the exposed plane of her chest, the thin gray hoodie she wore doing little to hide the fact that she was naked beneath it. Leaning against the back of the vinyl booth, knife and fork gripped tight in her hands, she breathed deep through her nose, face held up to the sky as she swallowed.

Thirty years, and she was still the most beautiful woman I had ever seen. As I slid into the booth across the table from her, it took everything I had to keep a tremor out of my voice as I queried, "Rough night?"

Grace's hands seized around her utensils. Her eyes shot open, but she didn't look over at me right away. Her surprise surprised me—she should have smelled me from a mile away. She was slipping, getting sloppy.

Smacking her lips, she answered, "I suppose you could say that."

When I didn't respond, she tipped her head back down to look at me at last. Her gaze was cold, revealing nothing of what she might have felt. "Been a long time, Marcus. What are you doing here?"

I smiled at her, my left hand fiddling with the thin gold chain wrapped around my right wrist. "Looking for you, of course."

Grace slid farther down in her seat, baggy sweatpants slipping up her hips. Her gaze roamed over me unchecked, every place it passed breaking out in goosebumps. "You found me."

I clasped my hands together on top of the table, examining her in kind. I swallowed hard, trying and failing to muster up a smile. "You look good."

Grace blinked. She took in a deep breath and let it out slowly. Shaking her head, she pulled her gaze away from me and focused on her plate, cutting off another hunk of steak. "You look exactly the same."

I was silent as she lifted the bite to her mouth. The sounds of the five a.m. weekday Waffle House washed over us...the scratching of cheap silverware against cheaper ceramic and the clatter of cup against counter, the old trucker at the bar, red cap perched back on his forehead, slurping his fifth cup of coffee as he worked through his third plate of pancakes, the muted murmuring of a pregnant woman and her partner, seated in a faraway corner, splitting an order of chili fries, the shuffling of two waitstaff workers and the short order cook, bored out of their minds, but too tired to gossip.

"How's the job?" I asked at last, desperate to try to carry on a normal conversation, as if nothing had happened, as if the intervening thirty years were so much smoke between us.

Grace glared at me as she chewed. "The job is fine," she said around her mouthful of meat. She took a large gulp of milk, tangled hair falling away from her face. "Did you really come all this way to chit-chat with me, Marcus?"

The blood drained from my face. My smile faded. "You can't fathom for a moment that maybe I missed you?"

Grace stared into my eyes, her own expression stubbornly blank. She put down her knife and fork and scratched the side of her nose.

Breaking under the weight of her gaze, I collapsed back into the seat, hands sliding off the tabletop and into my lap. "I need to talk to Mama, all right?"

Grace snorted a laugh and cut another piece of steak free from the whole. "So you come to me?" She lifted her fork and gestured with the hunk of flesh. "You must have heard by now — the last time Mama and I came face to face, we nearly ripped each other's throats out."

My smile returned, one corner of my lips pulling up over my stark, white teeth. "God, I wish I'd been there to see that."

"My point is," continued Grace, shoveling the meat into her mouth, "you're barking up the wrong tree." She winced. "Pardon the expression."

"Grace, you're my only way in." I shifted in my seat, pulling my suit jacket tight over my chest. "None of the other Nameless will even talk to me."

Grace chuckled again, but this time it was a laugh devoid of mirth. She tossed back the last swallow of her drink. "Well, yeah. The last time one of us talked to you, it didn't end well, did it?"

9

"Grace. This is serious." I stabbed the smooth plastic tabletop with my finger. "This isn't just me asking. This is the Feóndulf. We need to talk with Mama."

With slow deliberate movements, Grace picked up her napkin, wiped the grease off her lips and dropped the crumpled paper onto her dirty plate. She met my eyes, gripped the edge of the table and leaned in. "I am done with Mama." Sliding out of the booth and standing, she jabbed her finger into my chest. "I'm done with you, and with the dens, and with all of that shit. I'm not sure what you expected to happen here, Marcus, but the past is the past. I'm focused on my future."

Looking from her finger to her face, I let out a strangled sigh. "You know it's not that simple, Grace."

Grace scoffed and straightened, tugging her pants further up her waist. "I'd love to stay and shoot the shit, Marcus, but I've got work in a few hours and I need a shower." She turned and walked toward the cash register at the front of the restaurant, wiggling her fingers in an insincere goodbye. "Wish I could say this has been nice."

Digging my cell phone out of my trouser pocket, I muttered, "So do I."

I scrolled through my contacts until I found the number I was looking for and hit 'call', holding the phone up to my ear. I only half-listened to the ringing, the rest of me preoccupied with watching Grace pay for her meal and exit the Waffle House, my gaze intent as she pushed open the door and disappeared into the dim parking lot. As I rubbed at my chin with my free hand, the sound of the other line picking up brought me out of my memories and back to reality.

"Yes, sir. I found her." I shook my head. "No, she won't help." Sighing, I slid down in my seat until the back of my head hit the top of the booth, screwing my eyes shut. "I did, sir. Yes, I did. I think we'll have to try something else."

* * * *

Grace

Seven a.m. found me pushing my fingers through my sopping wet hair, shivering under the onslaught of ice-cold shower water. I listened as the mournful cry of a distant freight train floated through the open bathroom window and closed my eyes, scrubbing off the dirt, sweat and blood. I couldn't go into work smelling like roadkill. It was fine for the customers, but the employees were held to higher standards. Squeezing another dollop of soap onto my rough loofah, I attacked my raw, red skin with vigor.

I wouldn't think of him. I wouldn't think of him. I wouldn't think of him.

But trying so hard not to think of him was, in a way, thinking of him — wasn't it?

I held the loofah up to my face and breathed in deep. Still, the scent of him, real or imagined, lingered.

With a sigh, I went back to washing myself, paying special attention to the bottom of my feet, my knees and my hands, all places I knew from long experience where forest filth liked to stick and hide.

The summer was still young in Southeast Oregon, stretching its legs out into the nineties as the days tripped their way through July. Already, I had had enough of the heat. In Seattle, it had been a near-apocalyptic event for the thermometer to register above eighty. Here it was the norm.

The one-bedroom home I had rented in the small, rural town of Klamath Falls had no air conditioning and no shade. I'd invested in an army of fans that were useful in pushing the hot air from one room to the other. The only real relief from the heat came at night, when I could lie, starfished and naked, beside my open windows, or when showering, when I could douse myself in cold water.

Mindful of my sky-high utility bills, however, I turned off the shower and stepped out onto the worn red towel that served as a bathmat. Standing in the brightening dawn, water dripping from me, I thought about Marcus.

How had he found me? There was only one person who knew where I had ended up, and I couldn't understand why Lily would break a confidence like that, especially to a stranger like Marcus. If he had found me, would other wolves come sniffing around as well?

Was it really so terrible to be found by him?

Hadn't I missed him?

I met my eyes in the square bathroom mirror that hung over the pedestal sink. I dragged my hands down my face and watched the skin stretch and snap back into place.

Timing was everything and, as usual, Marcus' timing couldn't be worse. It had only been a year since I'd left the Nameless behind, a year since I'd told Mama and Seattle goodbye. I wasn't about to go crawling back because Marcus had batted his eyelashes at me. I'd worked too hard to get out.

Grabbing my towel off the rack, I rubbed myself dry, still lost in thought. The whole thing was strange. Thirty years of silence, then a sudden reappearance…a sudden, desperate need to see a woman who would most certainly kill him if she ever laid eyes on him again. What were the Feóndulf up to? What had the Nameless done this time?

I walked into the bedroom, heedless of the open windows, and tossed my towel onto my bed. Taking in a deep breath, I shook my head in an attempt to clear it.

These were questions from another lifetime, for another Grace who still concerned herself with such things. This Grace's biggest worry was what to wear to work today. That felt good. That felt normal.

My closet stood open, and I pawed through my clothes without really looking at them, considering the day ahead of me. At least work was air conditioned.

I plucked out a knee-length red summer dress and considered it. Looking down at my bare legs, I groaned. I had forgotten to shave again.

The light cotton fell over my head and onto my hips with feather touches. I shook my wet hair out across my shoulders and examined the effect in the full-length mirror. I took another deep, centering breath and let it out slowly. I smiled, testing the expression. It had been a long night. But I could get through the day. I always had.

* * * *

The bank where I worked was not really a bank, but a credit union. There was more than a cursory distinction, I assured the customers who daily sat in front of me in my cubicle, anxious to open up checking accounts and apply for home and car loans, but leery of giving their hard-earned cash over to strangers.

"A credit union," I explained to the plump young lady across the desk from me, "is a non-profit organization. We're not in the business of making money, but taking care of yours. A bank — well, profit is the top thing on their agenda. That's why we offer lower interest rates on loans, higher interest rates on savings accounts, financial literacy resources, and we welcome more members through our doors!"

I smiled wide, hands clasped on top of the cheap plywood desk. The ten-year-old desktop computer to my right whirred and hummed as it struggled to run the basic software I needed to do my job. I resisted the urge to kick the tower on the floor until it stopped making noise.

"So, can I get you signed up as a member? Then we can work on getting your application ready for that new motorcycle loan."

"I don't know..." The young woman cast a glance around the regulation bland office space. "I mean, maybe I should just put all my cash in a safety deposit box, you know? Like a safe?"

I just managed to stop myself from rolling my eyes. Instead, I nodded, hands sliding off the desk and into my lap. "You could do that, yes, but you should know that anything that you put in a safety deposit box is not insured."

"What?" The woman widened her eyes. She straightened in her worn chair. "But what if you guys get robbed or something?"

"Well, first, the First Citizens Credit Union has been at this location for over twenty years, and we've never been robbed, so keep that in mind," I said. "Second, for safety and security reasons, our employees don't know what is in the safety deposit boxes. So, we can't insure what we don't know is in there. You see what I mean? That's why it'd really be better for you to open a savings account and put the money in there."

The young woman grimaced. "I don't really want the government to know how much money I have."

"Forgive me," I said after a moment. "But...aren't you enlisted with the Air National Guard here at Kingsley Base?"

"Yeah, so?"

"So...they pay you. The government pays you." I blinked once, then again. "They already know how much money you have. They...they gave it to you."

The young woman thought about this for a moment, furrowing her brow. "Oh."

The rest of my day passed in similar fashion. The members of First Citizens Credit Union were, on the whole, a cautious, some might even say paranoid, pack of people but, I assured myself several times a day, their hearts were in the right place. Finance was not my passion. It was a talent, a knack, and it had proved easiest to get a bachelor's degree in finance online while keeping Mama and the den in the dark as to what I was doing. It had taken me six years, two years longer than a traditional student. With Mama keeping a close eye on me, I could only manage to take one or two classes at once, even though I was doing my schooling online. But now that I was here, out in the real world, with a real job, all the late nights at the computer, all the hiding of my textbooks, all the breathless moments when I was almost found out—it was all worth it.

Even if the mundanity of my day-to-day tasks and the endless mathematics and paperwork sometimes made me want to put my eyes out.

I finished entering the last pieces of information for a member's home loan application and looked down at the clock on the computer. Five more minutes and I was done for the day. With a groan, I bent over in my chair, reaching into the knapsack by my feet and feeling around for my phone. I was half under the desk when a voice from my cubicle door queried, "How would I go about opening an account here?"

I jerked up without thinking, the back of my head cracking against the underside of the desk. Hands clutching my now-throbbing skull and teeth digging into the tip of my tongue to keep from cursing aloud, I straightened in my desk chair and fixed Marcus with a stare that would've murdered a human man on the spot.

"What are you still doing here?"

Marcus stepped inside my tiny office, his hands slung lazily in his trouser pockets, and settled himself into the chair in front of my desk. "I told you," he said, his face the very picture of innocence. "I need to talk to Mama."

"And I told you. I don't care. Go talk to her." I tossed my head upwards and raised a brow. "You know she's not here."

Marcus fixed me with a reproachful look. "I'd waltz in without an invitation, but I'm attached to my genitals."

I gripped the bridge of my nose and squeezed my eyes shut. "You're smarter than you look, then."

"Listen." Marcus rested his elbows on top of the shaky plywood and leaned over the desk. "Grace—"

"No. No, Marcus, you listen." I pushed myself up onto my feet, my words coming out in a low hiss. "I've spent all my life neck deep in this bullshit. From the day I was born, I had Mama on my back, whispering in my ear, telling me how I was going to live my life." Placing my hands on the desk on either side of him, my face inches above his own, I shook my head. "Well, not anymore. I'm out. And I'm not letting you drag me back in because the Feóndulf have a bug up their asses about something. You hear me?"

Marcus stared up at me, his ice-blue eyes wide, his pink lips parted slightly. "I've forgotten how beautiful you look when you're angry."

My jaw clenched, along with my fists. "Then I'm about to be goddamn breathtaking, buddy."

"Phew, I am ready to get out of here tonight!" said Tim, rounding the corner into my cubicle. His arms were stretched over his head, his face screwed up as he worked out tight muscles. "I don't know about you, but I had some real interesting folks — oh." Tim hesitated on the office threshold when he saw Marcus sitting in front of him. "Sorry, I didn't realize you were still with someone."

"Hi, Tim." I relaxed my fists one finger at a time, my eyes never leaving Marcus' flushed face. "I'm not."

"Uh, you're not?"

I ran my tongue along my teeth and took a step back both physically and mentally. "No. He's not a member. He's just…"

Turning my attention to my gregarious coworker at last, I caught the curious look the young man threw Marcus, who had straightened up in his chair and was smiling back at him with warmth. I closed my eyes and swallowed before tossing my hand out toward Marcus.

"Tim, this is Marcus. Marcus, this is Tim." I froze, realizing that this introduction, while factual, might not prove sufficient. "Uh, Marcus is… He's — "

"I'm an old friend from university." Marcus stood and proffered his hand to the gangly man opposite him, shaking firmly. "Pleasure to meet you, Tim."

Tim beamed, his brows lifting high over his rimless glasses. "Wow — I haven't had the chance to meet any of Grace's friends yet. Do I detect an accent there? British?"

"Welsh," answered Marcus.

"Cool, cool." Tim pivoted so he could look at both me and my so-called friend at the same time, clasping his hands together. "So, you two went to school together, huh? Are you in finance as well, Marcus?"

"Wouldn't that be something? No, I'm a detective with the South Wales Police, actually."

Tim's jaw dropped. "You're kidding."

Marcus shook his head and reached into the breast pocket of his sport jacket, slipping out a thin leather wallet. "Got a badge and everything," he said, offering Tim his credentials.

Tim handled the wallet with care, examining the officially branded documents, typed out in both Welsh and English. "So cool! I've never met a real detective before. Your job must be fascinating."

"It's not," I interjected, my arms crossed high over my chest. "Actually, Marcus was just leaving, so—"

"Yes, I was. But I'll see you tonight, though, yeah?" Marcus reached forward and rubbed my arm. "For our date?"

Shocked into silence at the very suggestion, I was a few seconds too slow to denounce Marcus' lie for what it was. Tim's brown eyes grew even wider, his head snapping up.

"A date? Wow!" His smile was stark against his brown skin, broad but slightly pained. I wanted to hurt Marcus all the more. Instead, I crouched down and began to gather up my things, wincing at the excitement in Tim's voice as he asked, "Where are you guys going?"

Marcus leaned against my desk, lips drawing down into a frown. "Hadn't decided yet—got any recommendations?"

"Rooster's is one of the nicest restaurants in town," said Tim, handing Marcus' credentials back to him. "Great atmosphere, I'd bet you'd love it."

Marcus nodded, tucking the wallet back into his pocket. "Rooster's it is then."

I stood, heaving my bag onto my shoulder.

Marcus swung around to face me, his arms outstretched. "Oh, you leaving now? Let me walk you to your car."

A glare was my answer. I strode out from behind my desk and stopped just shy of kicking my way out of the credit union's glass double doors.

I power-walked through the empty parking lot, my hair whipping off my shoulders and around my face. I curled my fists so tight my close-clipped nails left crescent moons in my palms, pounding my shoes against the pavement, sticking every now and again on a patch of heat-melted tar. I was sweating, and it wasn't from the ninety-four-degree heat.

"Grace!"

I bit down hard on the inside of my cheek and ignored him, refusing to give him the satisfaction of my anger and any more of my time.

"Grace, Grace, Grace, hold on a second—"

Marcus' hand cupped my bare shoulder. I jerked away from the contact as if it were a hot brand, hissing, "Stay the hell away from me, Marcus."

With satisfaction, I listened as he stopped in his tracks. I kept walking and was within feet of my car's driver's side door when Marcus' voice broke through the silence once more.

"Grace, Colquhoun's dead."

I rolled my eyes and reached for the door handle. "Bullshit."

My fingers brushed the metal, but I didn't pull back on the latch. What Marcus said took a moment to sink in, but when it did, it sank all the way to the bottom of my stomach.

My resolve weakening, I risked a glance back at him.

Marcus stood several feet behind me, arms hanging limp at his sides. He met my gaze, his lips a thin, grim line, and raised his brow.

"Bullshit," I repeated, slower this time, awe creeping into the word. I retracted my hand and shielded my eyes from the sun, my gaze falling to the asphalt just in front of Marcus' feet.

Marcus took a cautious step forward. "Now will you listen to me?"

I slid my hand down to cup my cheek, looking back up at Marcus with wide eyes. "How did it happen?"

Licking his lips, Marcus glanced around us. Deserted as the parking lot was, he lowered his voice anyway. "Is there somewhere else we could talk about this? Someplace more private? Your place, maybe?"

I blushed at the suggestion, but tried to hide my discomfort behind a scoff. "Like hell." I took a step back and swallowed, eyeing him up and down, weighing my curiosity against my desire to be rid of him and get back to my new, normal life.

Marcus seemed to allow me this moment of consideration, slipping his hands into his pockets and leaning back onto his heels.

I rolled my eyes heavenward and gestured to the passenger side of the sedan. "Come on, get in. I've got a place in mind."

Chapter Two

Marcus

The Basin Martini Bar was as swanky a place as a person could find in a rural outpost of a few thousand people like Klamath Falls. I learned that since its opening it had proven to be a popular hotspot with the trendsetters of the town. The lights were kept low, and the plastic discs that dripped off the electric chandeliers threw muted illumination into each high-backed, velvet-padded booth. Beaded curtains hung from the ceiling at odd intervals, dancing in the breeze of recirculated air.

I eyed the undulating strings of plastic baubles above our table with some concern, twisting the cherry in my drink around the rim of my glass. "When you said we were going to a bar, this was not what I pictured."

"Too bad," said Grace, taking a large sip of her chocolatini. She licked a smear of syrup off her bottom lip and sat back, sliding her fingers up and down the stem of her glass. "So...Colquhoun is dead. Wow." She shuddered and sneered. "Couldn't have happened to a nicer guy."

Holding my cherry up by its stem, I shot her a disapproving look. "Oh, I don't know if that's entirely fair."

"Come on. Colquhoun was a bastard through and through, you know that. Loved to keep people in their place, wherever he thought that happened to be." She shook her head, taking up her drink once more. "Bet Aidan is dancing on his old man's grave. He was always hungry for advancement. I doubt he'll be any less of a despot, though."

"Aidan's dead, too." I popped the cherry off its stem with my teeth, chewing the alcohol-soaked orb with relish.

Grace froze, her mouth still full of the mixture of vanilla vodka and liqueur. She stared at me, and I met her gaze evenly. When she swallowed, her brow furrowed. "What are you talking about?"

"Yeah." I paused a moment to pluck the cherry pit out from between my teeth, tossing it onto the table. "About seven months ago." I picked up my drink and sipped my whiskey. "Then his old man a few weeks back."

Grace shook her head, her eyes wide. "Well. Sounds like you've got a hunter problem on your hands."

"It would seem that way, wouldn't it."

Grace narrowed her eyes. As intended, my flippant tone was like a thousand red flags flying in front of her face all at once. She waved a hand over the table, sipping her drink. "But...?"

I grimaced, turning my tumbler this way and that. "There was some...time taken. With Aidan and with Colquhoun. Before they were killed."

"A hunter with a bone to pick, then," said Grace after a moment of silence, licking her lips clean.

I leaned forward, resting my arms on the table. "Now do you see why I need to talk to Mama?"

She mimicked my posture. "Not really, no."

I scoffed. "If there's a hunter out there that can get to our den leader and his heir, what's to say he's not going to come gunning for one of the other dens next?"

"What's to say he will?" Grace relaxed back into her seat, swirling what was left of her drink around its glass. "And I'm sure Mama will be touched by the Feóndulf's concern, given that the two dens haven't had any official relations since 1562."

I lifted my pointer finger. "Not for lack of effort on our part—you know that."

Grace's face flushed pink. She pulled her arms tight around herself and rolled her eyes. "Oh please, Marcus," she said. "Colquhoun and the rest of the Council never seriously expected you to succeed as an Ambassador to the Nameless. You said as much yourself. If they had, they never would've chosen someone who was bitten, like you. And they would've sent someone to replace you instead of going silent for thirty years. So don't go pretending that the Feóndulf have been the wronged party all this time, offering olive branches that the Nameless have been too proud to accept."

My smile disappeared. My grip on my drink tightened. "Because no one could ever accuse any of the Nameless of the sin of pride, is that it?"

Grace looked down her nose at me. Her hands flexed into fists. "Better to have too much than none at all." She adopted an air of mock curiosity. "With both Colquhoun and Aidan dead, whose leash are you on these days, anyway?"

I stared at her, jaw clenching so tight I could feel each of my bottom teeth pressing against their top mates. Some color rose in her face, a flush of embarrassment, of shame. She could tell she had gone too far. I hated that she could do this to me, could get to me so easily after all these years. I sat back in my seat and tried in vain to hide the hurt, but my voice was quiet and pregnant with pain when I replied, "I answer to the Council, Grace. I always have."

Swallowing hard, Grace shook her head, looking away from my face. "There's something you're not telling me, Marcus. What is it?"

A shrug was my answer to her accusation. "You wanted to be out, remember?"

"Yeah." She blinked and sat upright. "Yeah. I did. And I am."

Digging into her knapsack, Grace pulled her wallet out and tossed enough money onto the table to cover the cost of both drinks and a generous tip. "I better get going, things to do." She stood and stuck her pointer finger out at me. "You should be getting ready, too — I don't want to wake up in the morning and hear a bunch of horror stories with your name written all over them."

"Yeah." I rolled my shoulders back. "Yeah, yes. You're right, of course." I drained the last of my drink. "The night does beckon, and all that." I looked up at Grace, one brow cocked. "What about Mama?"

Grace caught the tip of her tongue between her teeth. She shook her head, tearing her eyes away from me with some difficulty. "Listen, Marcus, whatever this is really about... Just stay away from Mama, okay?"

"Orders are orders, Grace." Sliding out of the booth, I adjusted my jacket, pulling it down over my shoulders. "I have my instructions."

"Loyal to a fault, aren't you? What good is your loyalty if you're dead?"

I caught the note of concern in her voice and my expression softened. In a hesitant, jerky motion, I reached out to her, the tips of my fingers ghosting over her elbow. "Mama can't still be angry."

Grace closed her eyes. "Yes," she said. "She can."

It wasn't the first time I had considered what the intervening thirty years must have been like for her. It wasn't the first time I had wondered if our separation had carved her apart in the same way it had me, had burrowed into her chest like a parasite and festered there. It wasn't the first time I thought about what she must have gone through, alone in that house with Mama after what we had done had come to light.

It was just the first time I could see in her face that all of what I had feared was true.

She took a step back from me, her hands up. "Do what you want. Just...don't say I didn't warn you."

"Grace—" I tried.

But she was already snatching her bag from the booth before her name was out of my mouth, and she didn't spare me a glance as she walked out of the bar. I gave her a few minutes' head-start before gathering myself and following her out, careful to make sure she was unaware of the fact that I was dogging her steps.

I winced a little as the evening sun hit my unprotected eyes, but didn't slow my stride as I walked back up the block to where her car was parked. I glanced around the corner and watched as Grace stood beside her beat-up sedan, looking down at her phone in her hand. I likewise slid my phone out of my pocket and checked the time, doing some quick math in my head. It was half past five. That meant three hours until sundown. Plenty of time for her to get to the butte, get the tent set up and get ready.

Confident that I would be able to track her in the woods around Harriette Lake, I called a local taxi and waited for it to arrive to take me back to the credit union where I had left my car. The night was coming on fast, and we both had to be ready for it.

Chapter Three

Grace

When I had first moved to Klamath Falls, I had worried I wouldn't be able to find a location to match my somewhat unique needs. Several internet searches and some local chatter had put me on the trail of Aspen Butte, the high point of the Mountain Lakes Wilderness, and from the first day I had scouted the area, I had known it was perfect.

Stamped by a large caldera, the wilderness was filled with a series of small lakes, several of which had places for overnight camping. One small campground sat beside Harriette Lake, bordered on the other side by a sparsely traveled, dusty service road. I had heard some people compared camping at Harriette to camping in a gravel parking lot.

I loved it. I had a standing reservation for the whole season, my campsite the one closest to the woods, farthest from the lake. No one else had seemed to want it.

When I drove in, the setting sun reflecting off my rearview mirrors, I returned the neighborly waves of some of the other camp regulars, fishermen who all had sites much closer to the water. I had stopped by the house on the way out of town to change into something more appropriate. I stepped out onto the packed dirt campsite in worn khaki pants and a baggy, sweat-stained T-shirt.

Conscious these days of the passage of time, I wasted little of it on taking in my surroundings. Instead, I immediately set about making camp. Even though it was all for show, it had to look convincing, just in case one of my fellow campers got curious and decided to come over and check on me.

The small, dark green tent took shape under my practiced hands, poles fitting together tightly as they moved under the fabric of the structure. I staked it to the ground with ease, and moved on to building the fire. I had purchased the logs from the closest ranger station, which was a comfortable thirty miles away. I would throw them away unburned in the morning, but for now, I stacked them together into a pile of kindling.

Brushing off my hands, I took a look at my work and gave a satisfied nod. I walked back to my car and emptied my pockets out into the trunk. I pulled my favorite set of sweatpants and gray zip-up hoodie out of the duffle bag, wrapped them around a bottle of water, and placed the bundle in the tent. After checking that the car was locked, I tossed my keys inside the canvas tent as well.

With a glance at the lowering sun, and one last look around to make sure no one was watching me, I strode off into the woods behind my tent.

Tennis shoes crunching into the flora-covered earth, I hiked for an hour, careful to avoid any trails or footpaths that cut through the forest. Twilight crept beside me. It wasn't long before the night animals began to call, signaling the end of day, and I felt the old, familiar tug at the back of my mind that told me the time was coming.

Pausing to sit on a fallen tree, I removed my shoes one at a time, tucking my socks into them before tossing them away into the undergrowth. I sniffed at my shirt and grimaced before pulling it off as well, balling it up and throwing it behind myself. Yawning, I stood up and undid my khaki pants, pulling them down and off my legs.

Standing naked in the growing dark, I scratched the top of my breast and considered my options. Kicking a few sticks and leaves out of the way, I cleared a spot on the ground beneath where I stood and folded myself down until I sat, cross-legged, onto the earth.

There was nothing left to do now but wait.

My thoughts drifted to Marcus. I wondered if he had been able to find a secluded place for the night. I hadn't even asked or offered to help. Not that his welfare was any of my concern, I reminded myself, frowning. Not anymore. Still, if someone got hurt, I would feel partially responsible...

I was just beginning to worry in earnest when pain hit me like a baseball bat to the stomach. If I hadn't already been on the ground, I would've collapsed under the shock. Instead, I doubled over, the top of my head pressed hard into the dirt, my arms wrapped tight around my abdomen. I gritted my teeth together as cramp after cramp wracked my body, the pain radiating out across my back, shoulders, buttocks and legs.

Soon I was vomiting uncontrollably. Eyes watering, legs shaking... For a few seconds, all that existed was the pain of my abdominal walls contracting, and the sensation of being unable to breathe as the last few bits of lunch came pouring out of me. My steak breakfast followed moments after, then nothing but bile, thick and yellow.

As I jerked up onto my knees, my skin stung, like I was covered in biting fire ants from the top of my head to the bottom of my feet. Clutching, grasping, pulling, my hands skittered over my body, tugging at every piece of flesh they could reach until the skin began to come free. Slow at first, sticky, like peeling off a Band-Aid, my skin came loose, and soon great swathes of it tore off in my hands like tissue paper, revealing raw, shiny, vein-covered flesh beneath it.

I tried to cry out, but was silenced as I choked, not on bile, but new muscles and ligaments that crowded my throat. Pushing them out like unwanted guests, I spat my teeth out of my mouth with the blood, my elongating tongue twitching around brand-new fangs.

The color began to drain from the world and I closed my eyes, my twisting, cracking body falling to the ground. My fingernails and toenails scattered around me like confetti. I braced myself on hands a foot in length, retractable claws flexing into the dirt. The front of my skull began to flatten and grow long, rushing out to accommodate my crowded mouth. My spine followed suit, thickening and lengthening as it attempted to become equal to the task of holding up a pair of massive ribs and powerful hips.

The fur grew last, as it always did, sprouting thick and brown over my blood-flushed new skin like spring flowers over a meadow. At last, struggling upright on unsteady back paws, new muscles rippling under fresh fur, I lifted my muzzle to the sky and howled at the rising moon, the sound of my cries echoing in my stiff, pointed ears.

The warm night air pulsed out of my large nostrils, and the world blossomed in my blank mind as the scents flooded in. I could smell the campground, the sweet stench of humanity wafting through the air like smoke. I forced myself to ignore it and refocused on what the wilderness around me had to offer. All the wildlife of the forest had left its marks around me, from the fresh pellets of feasting owls, to the droppings of a mountain lion.

A mile away, by a small rocky creek, a buck, hooves pawing at the dirt in search of fibrous roots and tubers to fill its belly, released a rich musk that caught my attention.

Hunger coiled in my gut, and I let out a low growl. The mind of the wolf was a mind of endless appetite, and the scent of the deer drew a haze across my other senses that felt giddy and familiar.

It was time to hunt.

I crouched, the tips of my long fingers brushing the ground as I readied to burst into a run, when the sound of cracking branches broke through my intense focus. As I turned with a snarl, my honed claws glinted in the growing moonlight.

At first, even my sharp eyes could see nothing in the surrounding darkness. I sniffed the air, and the smell of him overwhelmed me. Shaking my head with a snort, I stumbled back.

He emerged from the forest in front of me like a shadow, his ice-blue eyes shimmering in the dim light. Covered from head to toe in thick fur the color of black ink, Marcus stepped toward me on his hind paws, large head cocked to one side.

I bared my teeth and snarled, circling away from him, my body lowering into a defensive posture. Marcus paused his advance, his eyes fixed on me. Leaned forward, he took a large sniff of air, then another, as if testing the waters in a lake. My tongue flicked across my exposed teeth, a low rumble emitting from deep within my chest, a warning.

Marcus took a single step forward.

It was all the provocation I needed. With a roar, I launched myself at Marcus, barreling into him and knocking him to the ground. Baying and barking, we wrestled in the dirt for several minutes, jaws snapping, legs and hands blocking and striking in turn, with me on top one moment, and Marcus on top in the next. All the while, my rage grew until it felt like I was going to burst through my skin all over again.

Waiting until my back was to the sky, I pushed myself up and away from Marcus, yanking my right arm free from his grip before slashing at his chest. He twisted to one side and the blow hit high, my claws ripping down into the top of his shoulder. Howling, he shoved me off with his good arm and his legs, sending me several feet up into the air.

I hit the ground hard, my shoulder breaking through the rotting trunk I had been sitting on prior to my transformation. Splinters flew in every direction, but I was on my feet again in moments, turning, ready to fend off Marcus' next attack.

But the attack never came. Instead, I spun around, blood still dripping from my hand, to find the other werewolf prone. A high whine curled up from his clenched jaws. He rolled so his injured shoulder was spared from rubbing into the leaves and dirt.

I barked and snapped at him, swiping at the air in front of him. Curled into a ball, one hairy hand gripping his wound, Marcus stared at me and gave a small, pitiful yelp in response.

Confusion gripped me. The hair that ran down my spine began to flatten back against my body, my ears following suit. When I sniffed, the scent of him once more filled my mind, but mixed with it now was the scent of blood and the unexpected stench of fear.

Teeth sheathed within my muzzle, I gave a tentative whine in response, crouching down onto all fours and shuffling forward. Marcus pulled away, but I continued to advance, whining, hands lifting and reaching toward him.

Marcus let loose a soft yowl when my hands, claws withdrawn, touched his wounded shoulder. Chest heaving as he panted, Marcus began to relax when I dipped my head and began licking the blood clean from the gashes. My soft, warm tongue probed against the wounds I had inflicted, my padded hands gripping him tight. Marcus rested his head against my back, the huffing of his breath sending my fur swaying.

We stayed that way until the bleeding stopped. As I retreated, Marcus risked a lick at the corner of my mouth. Something warm and soft coiled in the pit of my stomach and I returned his gesture of affection with one of my own, swiping my muzzle across his own.

He began to reach for me, but stopped as I rose back up onto my hind legs, my nose held high. I started taking in huge breaths of air, my head swiveling back and forth. Marcus mimicked my stance, and soon we had both caught the scent of the buck again, now almost two miles away, pacing through the forest on careful, delicate hooves. He was healthy and young — he would be hard to catch.

Exchanging a few rough barks with my companion, I took off deeper into the forest, running as fast as my strong legs could carry me. Soon, Marcus was keeping pace at my side, ready to help in any way he could.

Chapter Four

Marcus

I woke to the soft patter of rain against my skin. Eyes easing open, I found myself deep in the woods. I stretched my sore legs out from my body, the scraping of sticks and leaves joining the symphony of sounds that surrounded me. I turned over onto my back, buttocks pressing into the hard ground, and stared up into the sky, squinting as the light mist fell into my eyes. The first rays of sunlight glowed behind a blanket of clouds, but despite the coming dawn, the canopy above me was so thick that the surrounding forest was still draped in darkness.

With a groan, I sat up. I brought my hand to my forehead and took in a shaky breath, hazy mind piecing together incoherent images and sensations from the previous night. The last night of the full moon was always the worst. I didn't know why, but in the last almost eighty years, I had yet to be proven wrong. It was like the wolf knew that this was its last chance to make mischief for another month, and it pulled out all the stops.

I always found being back in a human body a bit like being back on dry land after a tour of duty at sea. The only thing for it was to force the body to adjust, so I pushed myself up onto my feet, despite the knocking of my knees. My normally kempt hair was tangled and matted with brambles and mud, and I spent a few seconds trying to knock some of the nature out of it before giving up. I looked with some interest at the four horizontal raised scars which wrapped around my left shoulder, surprised to find the area free of blood.

I stuck out my tongue, running it along my lips. I could taste the dried blood that was smeared there, and my mind worked faster. I worked hard to tamp down the instinctive panic that blood always inspired in me and took another, deliberate lick. Deer. Yes, that was right. We had hunted down a deer.

Oh. *We.*

Before I could look for her properly, the sound of a great crashing behind me made me jump. I spun around to see Grace explode into the patch of woods in which I stood, pushing branches and bushes out of her way as she strode toward me, shouting. "Goddammit, Marcus!" Her long, bedraggled hair swung around her reddening face. "I knew you were reckless, but I never thought you were straight-up suicidal!"

I took several quick steps back, but not before Grace closed the distance between us, landing a hard shove on my chest and demanding, "What the hell were you thinking, following me out here?"

Stumbling, I tripped over my own unsteady feet, landing flat on my backside, my hands splayed behind me for support. Grace stood over me, chest heaving, fists clenched.

I looked up at her, and shook my head, not a trace of my usual smile on my face. "You can't fathom for a moment that maybe I missed you?"

She stared down at me, and I could see the anger drain from her like so much muddy water down a bathtub drain. Rain dripped off her forehead and into her eyes, but she didn't move to wipe it away. "I...I could've killed you," she managed at last.

"But you didn't." I sat up straight, tongue coming out to wet my lips. "Grace, you have to believe me. When I heard you were out, I wanted to come see you, I wanted to—"

"But you didn't," said Grace quietly.

The drizzle slowed then stopped. A robin began singing in a tree branch above us. Grace swallowed hard and looked away, offering her hand to me without making eye contact. "Come on. We need to get out of here before some poor ranger finds us."

I considered her hand for a few moments before taking it, pulling myself up and falling into step just behind her as we trooped naked through the forest. In less than an hour we arrived back at her campsite, where doubtless she had homed in on the scent of her clothes or other belongings like a beacon, a common enough practice in our community. Pausing for a moment at the tree line, we waited to see if any other campers were up and about this morning, but no one appeared. Crouching low, we scurried to the front of Grace's tent and crawled inside.

I sat in the far corner of the tent and forced myself to remain silent while Grace threw on her clothes. As I watched, she unscrewed the cap from a plastic bottle of water and took several long, deep drinks from it, swishing the lukewarm liquid around her mouth. Then, after pouring a small puddle of water into her hand, she placed it on the ground so she could splash the water over her face, scrubbing as hard as her sensitive skin would allow. Having gotten the base layer of blood and dirt off her, she passed the bottle to me. I took it with a sickly half-smile and a nod.

"Stay put," she said, watching me chug the rest of the water in a few gulps. "I'll go get you some clothes."

A nod was my answer, but she didn't wait for me to give her one. She was out of the tent and heading for her car in a split second, moving quickly, keeping as low to the ground as she could. For my part, I settled down in the corner of the tent, toying with the now empty plastic bottle. Last night had been sheer idiocy. But I had to know. Had to know if the wolf inside her felt the same way about me as the woman did. Things were more complicated between us than she or I wished to admit. That would make what had to happen next...uncomfortable, to say the least.

How much should I tell her? How much can I tell her?

I looked up when Grace shoved her way into the tent, throwing on a casual smile and waving the empty water bottle at her.

"These things are terrible for the environment, you know."

Grace rolled her eyes and dropped an unzipped duffle bag in the center of the tent. "Here."

I crawled forward on my hands and knees and dug out a pair of blue jeans and a plain black T-shirt. I held up the jeans, prodding at the holes that dotted each leg. "Not my usual style, but I suppose they'll do."

Grace lowered herself onto her knees and got out a package of wet wipes. She yanked a damp white square free from the rest and offered it to me. I stared back at her, hands still holding up my borrowed clothes. Grace swallowed, gesturing to my body, gaze flickering over me. "You've got..." She licked her lips, shaking the wipe insistently. "There's blood."

"Oh," I said. I looked down at myself and caught sight of the edge of a stain that ran down my chest and, presumably, up under my neck. I dropped the clothes to take the wipe and began rubbing at my skin. "Thank you."

Shoving her bare feet into her tennis shoes, Grace nodded in response before heading back outside. In her absence, the questions that had plagued me since my dispatch to the States returned to the forefront of my mind. My message was for Mama. Grace was out. But didn't she have a right to know? I shook my head from side to side and tossed the blood-caked wipe to one side to begin dressing. She probably wouldn't believe me, anyway. She hated me.

Grace poked her head back into the tent to find me standing hunched over, buttoning the fly of my jeans, bare toes wiggling against the tent's canvas bottom.

"Hurry it up," she said, leaning into the small space to grab up the discarded wet wipes and shove them into her now empty duffel. "I've got to get packed up and back into town."

"Right." I scooted past her out of the tent. "Your job."

Grace stayed frozen half in and half out of the tent. Her grip on the handles of the bag tightened. Tongue probing the inside of her cheek, she looked over her shoulder at me, glaring. "Why did you say it like that?"

Still walking toward her car, I turned and blinked at her, careful to keep my eyes wide and innocent.

Grace straightened and, putting on her worst Welsh accent, rolled her eyes up into her head. "'Your job'," she repeated. "What, you've got something you want to say?"

"Not at all." I grimaced and scratched the back of my neck. "I mean, it is a little..." I trailed off, the start of a smirk twisting my lips. "I just never thought of you as the banking type, I suppose! Counting other people's money all day, punching numbers into a computer. I don't know. I would've thought you wanted to do something a little more...exciting. Seems a bit dull for you."

With a derisive snort, Grace began dismantling the tent, folding it as she went. "Shows how much you know about banks." Then, not quite under her breath, she added, "And me."

The smile faded from my face as quickly as it had appeared. I dropped my gaze and worked my hands into the tight pants pockets. "I suppose." With my toe, I began to draw patterns in the loose dirt under my feet. "I'm proud of you, you know."

Grace stopped mid-fold, looking up to stare at me, the collapsed tent pressed against her body.

I sighed and shook my head. "Which is why I hate to sound like a broken record and all, but...have you given any more thought to what we talked about?"

Grace furrowed her brow. She rolled the tent up the rest of the way and crossed by me, moving toward her trunk, muttering, "I don't remember much talking..."

Now it was my turn to stare. I flattened my hand against my chest. "Me. Mama. Meeting." I risked another smile, brows drawing up to a point. "Will you help me, Grace?"

"Marcus..." Grace looked heavenward as she tossed the tent into the trunk. She turned to me, her hands on her hips. "No. No, I'm not going to help you."

My face fell.

Grace slammed the trunk shut and moved toward me, hands outstretched. "You have to understand, Marcus. Getting away from Mama, from the dens—it was one of the hardest things I've ever done in my life. It's only been a year, but it's been a good year. Really good." She placed her hesitant hand on my shoulder. "I have a real chance out here. If you still care about me at all, you won't...you won't make me give that up."

I nodded, meeting her gaze. Shrugging, effectively loosening myself from Grace's grip, I tried and failed to recover my fake joviality. "Well. Guess an old dog can learn new tricks."

Grace rolled her eyes, but smiled all the same. She waved me off, backing up toward her sedan. "Ah, you don't really need me, Marcus. You'll find another way. You always do." She had walked to the driver's side of the automobile and reached for the door handle before stopping, a thought seeming to occur to her. She glanced around. "Where's your car?"

I shook my head, wincing. "It's, uh, parked up at the ranger station."

"Get in," said Grace, popping her door open. "I'll give you a lift."

"No, thanks, Grace." I gave a mirthless, tired smile. "I'll make my own way there."

Grace leaned on the roof of her car, stretching her arms out over the dirty metal. "It's thirty miles. And you don't have shoes. Get in."

* * * *

Grace

As I drove down the deserted two-lane highway that led to the ranger station, we sat together in a silence that was not awkward, but not comfortable either. I kept sneaking glances at Marcus every time I checked the rearview mirror, tensing and relaxing my hands around the steering wheel. Marcus sat half curled up in the passenger seat, one bare foot perched on the lip of the seat, his elbow resting on his knee as his fingers toyed with his bottom lip.

Staring out at the road, I found myself compulsively rewinding and reviewing the incidents from the last night, picking apart the actions of the wolf and examining them for some hint of meaning. The wolf was a creature of desire and instinct. But its impulses were ones I had, for the most part, learned to control. If I hadn't, I would still be hunting humans. Of course, Marcus following me had been unexpected. I had been caught unprepared. Given our history, I couldn't pretend to be surprised that the wolf's first reaction had been violent. The disturbing part was how little persuasion it had taken to turn the wolf from that course of action. Not that I wanted Marcus' death on my conscience. It was just that I could've done without the memory of my tongue on his flesh, his blood in my mouth, the tickle of his breath against my fur, the smell of him filling me until the only thought in my head was of him.

The car hit a pothole and I jumped at the sudden jolt. Marcus cast a sideways glance in my direction, but wisely remained silent. I cleared my throat and refocused my attention on the road, turning my windshield wipers up as the rain returned, this time with more intensity. It didn't matter. It was over. The three days of the full moon were over for another month. Marcus would go back to Cardiff. He'd be an ocean away, and I could get on with my life.

I could play at being normal again. I winced at the thought. 'Playing at being normal'. That was what Mama had called it when I had announced my plans to leave them all behind. Like normality was some kind of silly game rather than a worthy goal, a childish waste of time, a pursuit that was beneath me. I hadn't bothered to explain to her what a normal life would mean to me. Mama couldn't have possibly understood.

For six years, I had pursued my dream in secret. Then, a year ago, I'd cut off all contact with my den, gotten a real job and moved out of Seattle and into a place of my own. I'd finally begun living a life that was mine and mine alone. There were yet to be friends, but I had anticipated that relationships would be challenging, and I was pacing myself accordingly.

Then Marcus had to show up. I slumped in my seat, tongue probing the inside of my cheek. Out of everyone the Feóndulf could have picked, they had chosen Marcus. Again. And why? Did he even know himself?

"Why'd they send you?" I asked aloud.

"Hm?" Marcus lowered his foot to the floor and faced me, his brow furrowing. "What?"

I grimaced at the appearance of a pickup truck on the road behind me, its brights turned on full, but I saved the majority of my attention for the conversation at hand. "The Feóndulf—why did they send you? Why not a member of the Council?"

"With both the Colquhouns dead, the Council is tied up in knots working out what to do next." Marcus sniffed and rolled his shoulders. "Also, I volunteered. I—"

"Have a death wish?"

Marcus closed his mouth and glared at me. "It's important that Mama get this message."

Straightening in my seat, my interest piqued. "What message?"

"What I have to say is for Mama's ears only. I'm sorry, Grace. I have my instructions." Marcus heaved a sigh, his fingers rubbing at his wrist where his bracelet should have been. "Besides, I don't want you any deeper in this..."

"Any deeper?" I stressed the last word, taking one hand off the wheel to adjust the rearview mirror, the glare from the truck's headlights behind me almost blinding. "Deeper than what? Than I already am? Am I deep in anything?" Volume rising along with my temper, I turned away from the road to face my companion, shaking a finger at him. "I swear to God, Marcus, if you—"

The truck rammed my sedan's rear bumper, and the steering wheel was pulled out of my hands. We both jerked forward in our seats with a shout, our seatbelts alone stopping us from making hard contact with the dashboard. I scrambled for the wheel, my breath shallow, and looked up just in time to see the truck pulling up alongside us. The tinted windows stared back at me for a split second before the vehicle fell back several feet.

The truck used its massive front to body-check my small sedan off the road and into a drainage ditch. The last thing I remembered before passing out was the explosive pop of the airbag into my face.

* * * *

I awoke in slow stages, my return to consciousness hampered by the blindfold cinched tight around my head. Ropes bit into my wrists and ankles, but I soon discovered that the restraints were purely precautionary, as I was unable to twitch a single finger or toe, let alone move my arms and legs.

This realization brought on the first wave of real panic. I wanted to thrash around, to cry out and demand release, and my mouth hinged open to do just that, but the words stuck in my throat and melted there. Drawing in a breath to scream had also meant drawing in a breath to taste, to smell, and what I had detected had given me pause. The air around me was wet, damp and cold. Stale and still. I could tell I was indoors now and, if my sense of smell were any good at all, someplace near a natural body of water. At first, I thought that I had been taken back to Harriette Lake, but there were no indoor structures around that lake. Crater Lake or Upper Klamath Lake were far more likely options. I took in another deep breath. Yes, there was the algae. Definitely Upper Klamath Lake then. I was practically back in town. Probably in a boat shed or warehouse was my best guess. Which meant I'd been out for some time.

What I didn't smell was Marcus. My stomach dropped. I did my best to think back to the crash, but could only recall the sounds of crunching metal and shattering safety glass, the smell of airbags and blood and a vague sensation of being dragged along asphalt. If he wasn't here, he could still be out there, on the side of the road, hurt—or worse.

I needed to find him. And to do that, I needed to get out of here.

I took in a deep breath and held it, focusing on the two senses that were still of some use to me. My keen ears picked out the whoosh of someone breathing. They sounded close, closer than I cared for them to be. But why couldn't I smell them? There was a scent in the air, under all the freshwater, algae and dust. But it wasn't the smell of a person—it was heavy, floral and chemical.

I swallowed the stale oxygen in my mouth. "Hello?"

There was shuffling to my left, and I turned my head toward the sound.

"Hello?" I cleared my throat and hoped for the best. "I think I'm hurt. I can't move my arms or legs."

A voice, high and bright, like the tinkling of bells, broke the silence. "That would be the wolfsbane." There was a smile in its tone, a bored amusement, to which I took an instant dislike. "It'll wear off in a few hours. Or it would, if you were still going to be alive by then."

"Ah." I nodded, my stomach lurching. The metal chair in which I sat was beginning to bite into my back, but I was powerless to shift into a more comfortable position. "That would explain it then. Thanks." I tried to sound stern. "Where's Marcus?"

"Was that his name? I wondered." There was a sigh. "I assume he's dead."

My mouth went dry. I gulped, and it was like swallowing powdered glass. He couldn't be dead. It wasn't true.

It wasn't true.

I could feel my heart still beating in my chest, but all the warmth had been stolen from my blood. Inside the darkness of the blindfold, the world began to spin. He couldn't be dead. If he was dead, I... Well, I would kill him.

I seized on the thought, and found a kind of solace in it. That was right. If he was dead, I had to kill him. Which meant getting out of here. Which meant staying alive.

"I'll admit, you surprised me," the voice continued. My ears keyed into the sound of rustling clothing then the flick of a lighter. "Never thought I'd live to see the day...a Nameless and a Feóndulf rubbing shoulders. Does Mama know?"

I cleared my throat and lifted my brows above the blindfold. "Not that it's any of your business, but no, she doesn't."

Silence descended once more. Anxious to keep a bead on my kidnapper, I licked my lips and asked, "I suppose there's going to be torture, yeah? When do we start? Or is the talking part of it?"

I might have been unable to move my limbs, but they weren't numb. I could feel the warmth of a slight, sharp backside sliding across my thighs and onto my lap. I could feel arms drape themselves around my neck and shoulders. I could smell the lit cigarette dangling from my captor's lips.

"There doesn't have to be any unpleasantness," the voice said.

My hair was woven around invisible fingers. I leaned my head back and looked in what I hoped was the direction of the person's face. "Oh. Really?"

A puff of warm smoke hit me in the face. I coughed.

"Of course. Tell me what I want to know, and I'll kill you quickly."

I shook my head from side to side, trying to clear the cigarette smoke out of my sinuses. "Did Aidan Colquhoun get the same offer?"

"Of course he did." The woman slid off my lap and back onto her feet, walking behind my chair. "He came around to my way of thinking. In the end."

I let my head fall back until my face was level with the ceiling. "Well? What do you want to know?"

"Mama."

I tried to shrug before I remembered I couldn't. "Yes?"

A hand fell on the back of my chair, making it vibrate. "Tell me how to get to her. I need to know when she's alone. Vulnerable."

I shook my head. "Listen, if you knew Mama, then you'd know. She's always alone. And she's never vulnerable."

The tip of the cigarette ate into the flesh of my collarbone like it was dipped in acid. I bit back a scream of pain as my tormentor ground the cigarette out on my skin. I tried to ignore the smell of my own burning flesh while I sat, unable to flinch beyond jerking my head from one side to the other.

After a few agonizing seconds, the cigarette was removed. There was a moment of silence, then another flick of a lighter. A slow inhale, then I was assaulted by another cloud of smoke.

"Don't get cute," counseled the high voice.

I nodded several times, gritting my teeth as the aftershocks of pain rippled through me. "This doesn't have to get ugly," I hissed. "We have more in common than you might think."

Footsteps echoed around me, the sounds of my attacker moving around to the front of the chair. "Really?"

I turned toward the voice. "You don't seem to be a fan of Mama. I'm not either."

"She's your blood." I jerked away when I felt a finger draw itself down my jaw. "Doesn't it go that blood is thicker than water?"

"It's 'the blood of the covenant is thicker than the water of the womb'." I shook my head. "Anyway, I gave up blood a long time ago."

"I'd heard rumors." The voice sounded interested. "You don't take the sacrament."

I licked my lips. "That's right. Not for some time now."

Hot ash bit into my skin once again, a few inches to the left of the first burn. "Weak."

"Goddammit!" I shouted, the muscles in my neck and head convulsing. At length the cigarette was tossed away like the other, and I took in and let out several heavy breaths. "You're a tough bitch to please, aren't you?"

The voice twittered out a laugh. Once more there was the flick of a lighter, but this time I could feel the full heat of the flame next to my cheek. "The only thing that will give me pleasure is you and Mama dead."

I took in a deep breath, pulling away from the flame as much as I could, but preparing myself all the same. I would scream. I wasn't proud.

Before the flame could eat away at my skin, there was a crash, followed by a loud bang. Smoke immediately clogged my nostrils and mouth. Coughing, I tucked my head to my chest at the sound of gunshots ricocheting around me, sending up a short prayer that whoever was shooting was using lead and not silver. There were shouts and the sounds of running. Soon, I felt footsteps rushing toward me, the tread vibrating up through the floor and into the legs of my chair. The blindfold was lifted off, and I winced my open eyes shut against the glare of floodlights that surrounded me.

Chapter Five

Marcus

"Hold on, Grace," I said, moving so my body was between her and the lights. "I've got you."

She peered up at me from where she sat in the middle of the small empty boatshed. Four floodlights were set up around her, their electric cords snaking off into darkness. Her red-rimmed brown eyes fought to make me out against the sudden change from dark to light. "Marcus?" she shouted. "What the hell — what is going on? Who's with you? Who's —" She flinched at the sound of more gunshots. "Who in the hell is shooting?"

"Ah." I stepped back and fumbled my hand into my jacket pocket, pulling out my cell phone. I shook it with a smile. "Amazing what sort of audio you can find on YouTube, isn't it?"

Grace stared up at me, her mouth gaping. "You —"

"I'll explain everything later," I promised, switching the phone off. Kneeling down, I began to examine the ropes that secured Grace to the chair. "First, let's get you out of here."

Closing her mouth with a snap, Grace nodded. "I can't move my arms or legs. She dosed me with wolfsbane."

"Right, because of course they did." Even with my enhanced strength, the recalcitrant knots were proving problematic. I stood and retreated toward a table that sat a few feet behind me, picking up a large Bowie knife from an array of other torture implements. "Don't worry, won't be a minute."

When Grace's ankles and wrists were free of restraints, I tossed the knife away and stood, scooping her off the steel chair and into my arms. Grace flopped about awkwardly for a few moments, arms drooping as I found firm grips around her knees and shoulders. When I was confident that I wasn't going to drop her, I nodded down at her, my brows drawn up to a point. "You ready?"

"More than. Let's go."

With Grace cradled in my arms, I ran out of the building through the boatshed door, which hung on a single hinge where I had kicked it open. The boatshed, a half-falling-down, ramshackle excuse for a building, backed onto the muddy shore of the lake. The land around the building was uneven and overgrown with weeds, and a few hundred feet away I could just make out the depressed foundations of where a house must have once been.

My black rental car waited on the lip of the dirt driveway, the engine running, passenger- and driver-side doors open. I slid Grace upright into the passenger seat, stopping for only a moment to fasten her seatbelt. We peeled away from the abandoned plot of land and bumped down a dirt road in serious need of repair. I kept my attention fixed on the rearview mirror for several minutes, awaiting the reappearance of the pickup truck. But when no one appeared, I relaxed my vigil, my attention turning to the woman in the car beside me.

It was with a start that I found her staring at me, grimacing openly in concern. I had forgotten how rough I must've looked after crawling my way out of her wrecked sedan. I had sustained a large bruise on the right side of my forehead, at the center of which was a raised bump. On the same side of my face, just below my eye, a cut ran vertically down my cheek. My lip was split and the top of a diagonal, rectangular bruise that ran from my shoulder blade across my chest under my shirt was just visible.

"My God, Marcus, are you all right?"

I let out a bark of crazed laughter and stared at her. "Me, am I all right? Are you all right?" I looked her over as best as I could while driving, eyes widening as I spotted the two circular burns on her collarbone. "No, you're not," I half whispered, half groaned. "Damn it, Grace, I'm sorry I didn't get there faster."

"How did you get there at all?"

"Please," I said, rolling my shoulders back against my seat. "I'm a detective and a werewolf—what do you think?"

Grace stared at me in answer, and shook her head. I cleared my throat and shrugged. "I'll admit, the crash left me a little worse for wear. But a very nice cattle truck driver stopped to make sure I was all right, and gave me a lift to the ranger station. They patched me up, and I slipped out while they were making arrangements to contact the local authorities. Then it was just a matter of getting back to the crash site and following my nose from there."

"Oh God, cops." Grace moaned, letting her head fall back against the headrest. "Just what I needed."

I gave an oversized nod. "Yes, I assume they will be contacting you at some point about your mangled Taurus, why you left the scene of an accident, who I am and all kinds of lovely questions."

She screwed her eyes shut. "How am I going to explain all this?" Grace's eyes flew open, her head vacillating from side to side. "I don't even know what this is!" She turned a fearsome glare on me. "And why aren't you surprised?"

I did a double-take, her accusatory tone taking me by surprise. "What?"

"We were attacked! I was kidnapped! And you're not freaking out!" Grace shouted at full volume. "Did you know that this was going to happen?"

"No, of course not!" I sputtered. I flexed my hands around the steering wheel. "I mean, I was concerned that something like this might happen, but — "

Grace cut me off, her voice a rough, hoarse whisper, her eyes boring holes into the side of my head. "You are so lucky I can't move my arms or legs right now, or else I would be seriously kicking your ass."

I rolled my eyes. "Grace, I'm sorry, but you have to believe me. For once, this isn't actually my fault. I'm trying to help here." I sliced my hand through the air. "I need to talk to Mama. Once I do that, hopefully some of this will start making sense."

"Then go talk to her!" howled Grace, her eyes heavenward.

"You know it's not that simple!" I shouted back, banging my fist against the steering wheel.

"Damn it, Marcus, I'm scared!"

For a moment, the only sounds were the tires trundling against the hard-packed dirt beneath the car. Grace closed her eyes. She took a deep breath. She let it out. "Marcus, I can't go back there. Please. I'm scared."

The car bounced onto asphalt and we were once again cruising down a paved highway. I wet my lips and, hesitating once, reached over and gripped Grace's hand, not knowing whether she could feel it or not. "It won't be like last time, Grace." I squeezed her hand tight. "You're different. Stronger. I can see it. You can do this."

Grace looked down at my hand holding hers. She opened her mouth to speak, but nothing came out. After a moment, she blinked twice and looked out through the window. I took this as a signal to withdraw my hand, swallowing hard. If only she knew how scared I was, scared for her. Maybe then she'd understand why I had volunteered to carry this message.

Grace wrinkled her forehead and scoffed in thought. "Was...was that a smoke bomb you used back there?"

I let out a breathy laugh, rubbing my chin. "Uh, yeah. Yeah, it was."

"Did you sneak that in your carry-on, or...?"

I straightened in my seat. "The local ammo shops here are very accommodating."

Now it was Grace's turn to laugh, her brow clearing. "What, they just had one in stock?"

"Believe it or not."

"I terrifyingly believe it," she assured me, smiling. "Where are we going anyway?"

"My hotel. I don't think it's a good idea to go back to your place just yet." I glanced at her then back at the road. "We'll go there, wait for the wolfsbane to wear off and then figure out what to do next."

I had a point, and I could tell that it annoyed Grace. Her head fell back and hit the seat with a muffled thud. "I hate waiting."

I grinned and let out a quiet laugh. "But you love making other people wait."

Grace turned her head to glare at me, her brow raised in both question and accusation. I shook my pointer finger at her, a smile still on my face. "You made me wait seven years to take you out for a drink. And even then, you were late."

The sudden rush of memories surged over me like a wave on the beach, and caused me to lose my footing, if only for a moment. I welcomed the distraction from the aching pain of my injuries, and let myself revel in the sight of Grace breaking out into a nostalgic grin herself. "I almost didn't come at all, you know."

"I don't believe that for a second," I said with a firm shake of my head. "You weren't about to stand me up."

"Oh ho! Sure of yourself, aren't you?"

I glanced at her from the corner of my eye, my smile widening to a mischievous grin. "You don't think that I didn't know, do you?"

Grace's eyes narrowed. "Know what?"

"That every time I came to the house, you would spy on me."

"I wouldn't!" The denial shot out of her mouth in a high-pitched squeal before she could compose herself enough to offer a more measured response.

"Yes, you would!" I pressed. "I'd wait at the front desk to get the inevitable brush-off from Mama, and I could feel you watching me. You were very clever, hiding up on the balcony or in the living room, but I knew you were there. I never forgot your scent after the first time we met."

Grace's face flushed. I couldn't help but think back to that first meeting. It wasn't my first visit to the den house. I'd been coming for a few years, trying to get a meeting with Mama, ostensibly to discuss the reopening of relations between the Nameless and the Feóndulf. I'd never gotten past the front desk, of course.

She'd picked her moment to approach me carefully, anxious that we not be interrupted. She'd had questions for the Feóndulf stranger, and she'd intended to get her answers, den rules be damned.

How could we have known then what a mistake we were making?

"I was just too damn curious for my own good," said Grace, her words echoing my own thoughts.

I pushed a hand through my mussed hair. "Well, who can blame you? It's not like you'd ever seen a Feóndulf before."

Grimacing, Grace shook her head. "That wasn't it."

"It wasn't?"

She swung her head around and studied my profile. "No. I just…didn't meet many wolves who were bitten. Let alone ones who admitted they missed being human. Do you remember? When we first met, I asked you if you missed it. And you said yes. I must have asked that question to a half dozen other wolves, and none of them had ever said yes. You were…fascinating.

And honest." Grace's face grew somber. "But all that was a lifetime ago."

I clicked the tip of my tongue off the roof of my mouth, letting my head fall to one side. "Feels like yesterday." I flexed my hands around the steering wheel. "I stand by my answer, by the way."

"You still miss it? Being human?"

"Sometimes. Not that being a werewolf doesn't have its advantages, of course," I said. "Hard to complain about super speed, strength, smell, rapid healing and, oh, let's not forget about the exceedingly long life and slow aging."

Grace pursed her lips and nodded. "There's just that pesky person turning into a gigantic monster that craves raw meat three times every month."

"Drawback. Admittedly, a drawback."

She stared at me. "Don't you ever wish you could just be normal again?"

I furrowed my brow. "What makes you think I was ever normal?" Throwing up my hand, I glanced at her, frowning. "Normal — what does that even mean?"

"Nothing. Forget that I asked," said Grace. She returned to looking out of the window. "We should be hitting town in a few minutes."

Chapter Six

Grace

The winding highway did eventually spit us back out on the outskirts of Klamath Falls proper. Fifteen minutes later, Marcus drove into the parking lot of the Olympic Inn. I let out an impressed murmur. "The Olympic, huh?"

"Oh yes," answered Marcus, pulling into a parking spot as close to the back entrance as he could find. "The Feóndulf spared no expense." He switched the car off and swiveled in his seat, looking me up and down. "How are we going to do this?"

"It's an upscale hotel at" — I glanced at the dashboard clock — "Three-seventeen in the afternoon on a Friday." I let out a deep breath through my nose. "We're going to run into people, aren't we?"

"The likelihood is high."

I smacked my lips together and smiled ruefully. "Well...let's play it drunk."

Marcus lowered his brow and stared at me. "It's three-seventeen in the afternoon."

"So I have a problem. You have any better ideas?"

A shrug was Marcus' answer. He got out of the car and walked around to my side, bundling me out and up into his arms as quickly and efficiently as he had loaded me in. Face flushed bright red, I nestled my forehead against Marcus' neck and launched into a muffled, slurred rendition of *Hooked on a Feeling*. I kept my eyes closed, half to sell the drunk bit, and half out of deep embarrassment, but I could feel Marcus walk across the parking lot and push open the back door. I heard the ding and swish of elevator doors, the soft twitter of laughter that followed us as we walked down a long, plush-carpeted hallway. Marcus jostled me briefly as he tried to both support my legs and reach into his pocket for his room key.

I opened my eyes at the sound of the door unlocking, pulling away from Marcus as much as I could under the circumstances. The room was, in fact, a suite, complete with a small living room and a walk-in closet, all done in tasteful eggshell white and deep, dark wood. Marcus strode through the spacious quarters heading for the bed, a California king. He deposited me on the mattress gently, stretching me out with my head flat on the plush pillows and my heels pressed into the silk comforter.

"We should be safe enough for now." Marcus switched on the lamp on the bedside table before crossing the room to the large windows. He drew back the privacy curtains and looked out onto the quiet street. "I doubt they'll try another grab like that in broad daylight." Marcus let the curtain fall back into place and rubbed his hands together, spinning in a slow circle. "Your body should bounce back in a few hours, depending on the dose of wolfsbane you were given."

"It must have been intravenous." I wiggled my head back and forth. "I didn't taste anything in my mouth when I woke up."

"Needles. Nasty." Lunging toward the worktable in the corner, Marcus grabbed hold of the office chair, rolled it to the edge of the bed and fell into it. "Do you think you'd know this fellow again if you saw him? Smelled him?"

"No. Except he's a she." I felt exhaustion start to work its way up my body, starting at the pads of my feet and lapping upwards, like waves working their way inland after an outgoing tide. "She kept me blindfolded the whole time, and she was drenched in some kind of perfume. I couldn't get a good read on her."

"A female hunter." Marcus leaned back in the chair, his feet coming up to rest on the mattress. "That's refreshing."

I rolled my head over to look at Marcus. "I don't think she's a hunter."

Marcus lifted a brow. "What makes you say that?"

"What she was doing, the way she was talking, it was…" I wet my lips, trying to get the taste of the word I was searching for. "…it was personal." I nodded. "Whoever they were, they didn't care about the sacrament either. Seemed offended that I refused to partake, as a matter of fact."

Marcus made a non-committal sound at the back of his throat.

I glared at him. "Once again, your lack of surprise irritates me."

"I'm sorry." Marcus dropped his feet to the floor and sighed. "After the day we've had, I don't have much energy for effusive displays."

"Sure." I closed my eyes, frowning. "Be that way."

"Listen, Grace," said Marcus, standing. "Give me your address — I'll stop by your place and pick up a few things for you. Change of clothes, things like that. You stay here and rest."

"314 North Laguna Street." I struggled to lift my head, my brows knitting together. "But, um, Marcus?"

Marcus froze, his hand halfway through his thick hair. He looked down at me, a question in his eyes.

"Would you…stay? For a little bit?"

A single lift of his brow was his answer.

I let out a huff of air, my tongue sliding along my teeth. "I, I can't move, you know? And I'm terrified I'm going to choke on my own spit or need to be rolled over or something."

Half smiling, Marcus resumed his seat, pulling himself closer to the head of the bed. "Who am I to say no to a lady in her hour of need?"

The muscles that could relax in my body did so, and I turned my face toward the ceiling, settling back into the pillows with a sigh. "Thanks, Marcus." I closed my eyes, hoping sleep would come quickly. "I owe you one."

"As usual, Grace, you don't owe me a thing."

I fell into a deep sleep within ten minutes, slipping away into unconsciousness without even realizing it. Maybe it was the physical strain of what I had been through in the last twenty-four hours, or maybe it was Marcus' presence alone. But my mind, unbidden and unwanted, began to dredge up the sensations of the last time I had seen Marcus in Seattle. I hadn't dreamed of that in some time, but the nightmare began as it always did — with the smell of blood.

I pushed open the door to Mama's sitting room and the stench of blood hit me like a fist to the gut. But it was nothing compared to the sight that assaulted me.

Mama's ivory nightdress was flecked and smeared with bright red blood, so fresh it still glistened on the surface of the fabric. More blood dripped from her knuckles and fingernails and onto the marble floor, where it pooled around her feet in little puddles, like wax from burning votive candles. One hand was clenched in a fist, raised to strike. The other was wrapped tight in the back of Marcus' shirt. She held him up off the floor, the only thing that seemed to be keeping him from collapsing into a boneless heap. His legs were splayed under him at unnatural angles, his head lolling loose on his shoulders, his face unrecognizable under a heavy layer of blood and torn skin.

"Marcus!"

I ran forward, but came to a jarring halt when Kassandra, the head of Nameless security, stepped in front of me. I tried to bolt around the large woman, but found myself pulled back by her strong arms, one holding my left arm to my side, the other wrapped around my shoulders.

"How dare you?" spat Mama. She thrust Marcus forward, but kept a hold of him, sliding his limp body across the marble floor toward me. "How dare you associate yourself with this Feóndulf mongrel?"

I looked up into Kassandra's face, but Kassandra stared forward, as if she wasn't restraining me at all. I pushed against her again, but it was like pushing against a wall. I shook my head, the words sticking in my throat. "Mama, I —"

Mama brought up her free hand, seemingly oblivious to the fact that it was dripping with blood. "Don't even think about denying it." She pulled the barely conscious man back to her side, giving him a shake for good measure. "Security caught him trying to sneak onto the grounds and brought him to me. The second he stepped foot in front of me, I recognized his stench. It was all over you this morning." Mama's face contorted as if she were the one in pain. "Consorting with a flea-bitten, turned Feóndulf? Grace, have you lost your mind?"

"Grace…" The name did not so much fall, as bubble out of Marcus' blood-filled mouth. The sound of it made me whimper aloud, straining against Kassandra's arms, while Mama shuddered with rage.

"Shut up!" Mama heaved the werewolf up by his collar and swung another punch into his stomach.

Marcus folded in on himself as much as he was able, blood splattering across the floor.

Mama rattled him back and forth like he was nothing more than a ragdoll, shouting, "You keep that name out of your filthy mouth!"

"Mama!" I screamed, hot tears now flowing freely down my cheeks, collecting at the tip of my chin and smearing themselves across Kassandra's sleeve.

"Give me one good reason I shouldn't rip this pathetic creature limb from limb right now." Mama lifted Marcus up into the air with one hand, as if preparing to fling him down. Her head snapped back to face me as she snarled out my name. "Grace!"

I stared at Marcus, and the words burst from me like fireworks. "You kill him and I'm gone."

Mama's eyes widened. She lowered Marcus back down, his limp feet hitting the ground with a thud. "What?"

"I mean it, Mama." I shook myself free of Kassandra's grip, which took most of my strength. Standing on my own, I met Mama's stare. "I'll leave. You'll never see me again. You can say goodbye to your precious heir, goodbye to all *your dreams of succession, of carrying on the bloodline for millennia."*

Mama released Marcus, and he fell to the ground in a heap. She took a large step toward me, her bloody hands clenched at her sides. "You think I can't keep you here?" I let out a hissing sigh from between my clenched teeth. "Try. Kill him, and I will spend every moment of my life running from you." Looking past the older woman's shoulder to the crumpled wreck of a man on the floor, I took in a deep breath, my fists loosening. "But...let him go and I'll stay. I'll stay here with you and I'll – I'll be exactly the kind of granddaughter you've always wanted me to be."

The room was silent. So silent that I could hear the wheezing of air struggling in and out of Marcus' body. I found myself wondering, with odd detachment, if a rib had punctured his lung.

With a suddenness that demanded attention, Mama spun around and returned to the spot where Marcus lay. Kneeling down, she heaved his body up into her lap.

"If you ever come back here again" – whispered Mama, her face pressed against the top of Marcus' sweat and blood drenched head – "I will personally eat your heart out of your chest."

A garbled whimper was Marcus' response. Mama jolted him back to the floor, rising to her feet and shaking off her blood-covered hands. She nodded to Kassandra. "Get the rest of your people in here. Put this thing on the next flight back to where it came from."

Kassandra moved with the military efficiency for which she was famous, abandoning me and striding toward the crumpled male wolf on the floor. Like clockwork, several more members of Nameless security marched into the room and surrounded Marcus until he was hidden from my view. I closed my eyes when Mama's wet, warm hand clasped my shoulder.

"One day," said the Nameless matriarch. "You'll thank me for this, Grace."

Tears still flowing freely down my cheeks and onto my neck, I bit back a sob. The only thing that stopped me from collapsing to the ground was the knowledge that I had just made a promise that I had no intention of keeping.

A loud crack split the shell of the dream. In Marcus' hotel room, I jerked awake, jolting upright despite the creaking protest of my spine and shoulders.

I awoke to a room shrouded in darkness, full of shadow-like half-shapes that hulked and loomed at me. For a moment I had no context for where I found myself. The shuffling sound of footsteps drew my eyes toward the door to the hotel suite, and I saw the hunched figure who stood inside the closed portal.

"Sorry about the door," said Marcus, walking the rest of the way into the room, his face hidden in gloom. "I was trying not to wake you."

My heartbeat began to slow. I let out a huff of stale air and held a quivering hand to my forehead, my hand sliding across the sweat slicked skin.

Marcus crossed the living room to the curtains, balancing the cardboard drink carrier he was holding in one hand as he pushed the blinds open. Waning sunlight spilled into the space. I swung my legs over the edge of the mattress and sat upright, switching on the lamp beside me. My purple gym bag was hanging from Marcus' shoulder, and I was about to stand and help him with his load, when I also noticed the green paper cups he was carrying.

Still blinking my vision clear, I pursed my lips into an 'o'. "Is that...is that coffee?"

"Yes." Marcus stopped in front of me and placed both cups on the bedside table, sliding my gym bag off and onto the floor. He tapped the lid of the cup closest to the bed. "You like it with about twenty sugars in it, if I remember correctly."

I took hold of the warm beverage with both hands and gulped at it greedily. Marcus watched me closely as he sipped his own drink. "Good to see you up and about again."

I shook my head and swallowed. "Wolfsbane — I wouldn't recommend it." Leaning down, I heaved my duffle bag onto the bed and unzipped it, exploring its contents with one hand. "Did you have any trouble getting into my place?"

"Not much. Your home security could use some work, if you don't mind me saying." Marcus reached into his jacket pocket and extracted two small pieces of paper. "These were wedged in your front door."

My practically empty stomach churned at the sight of the very official business card from someone named "Thomas Garber," who was evidently a member of the Oregon State Patrol. On the back, written in red ink and all caps were two words.

CALL ME.

"Shit."

The second piece of paper was the torn corner of a newspaper, across which someone had scrawled a message.

Covered for you today. State Patrol looking for you. Everything okay? Call please.

It was signed with the initials TZ. My eyes widened even further. I shot to my feet, spilling a few drops of coffee onto my hand. "Ah, shit, work!" Head swiveling, I looked around the room for a phone. "I've got to call Tim now, before I get myself fired."

"I took the liberty of putting in a call to him while you were asleep."

My eyes narrowed into thin slits. I plopped back down onto the mattress. "You did? What did you say?"

Marcus fixed me with a bored stare. "That you'd been involved in a minor traffic collision, and would need to take some time off to recuperate."

"Oh." My face slackened in surprise. "That's…that's good. Thank you, Marcus."

"As for the State Patrol officer, you're on your own there. I mean, I could try talking to him, law enforcement professional to law enforcement professional, but—"

"No, no." I waved him silent. "You've done enough. Thanks."

Marcus started to reach for me, but seemed to reconsider it, instead sitting down in the desk chair that was still stationed by the bed. "Grace. What are you going to do?"

I let out a long breath through my nose, gaze falling to the tops of my feet. It'd been a rough couple of days. I considered my options. I could stay here in Klamath Falls and try to explain what happened to the State Patrol. Hell, I could even try being honest with them, or mostly honest anyway. I'd been driving back from a camping trip, a truck had sideswiped me, the person inside the truck had kidnapped me and I had barely escaped with all my body parts intact. Maybe they would help. But as soon as the thought entered my head, I knew I was being naïve. Telling the truth would just bring up more questions, questions to which I didn't have any good answers, and I'd end up in either an insane asylum, jail or on the run. Still, it wasn't a problem that was going to just go away.

The woman who took me would try to take me again.

The thought made me close my eyes. I couldn't be on guard every second of every day. I didn't have the resources or the skill. I'd get sloppy. Then I'd be dead.

I looked up at Marcus, meeting his patient gaze.

He knew more than he was telling me. I was certain of it. But I wasn't going to be able to charm or beat the information out of him. Something was going on, something important enough to make him cross an ocean, track me down and risk his own life to see the woman who had promised to kill him.

There was only one way I would find out what that something was. Only one way I would be able to get clear of all this and back to my new life.

The muscles in my jaw tightened. My head dropped low between my tense shoulders. "Hell. It's Friday night. I have nothing better to do with my weekend. I might as well go and ruin my life." I drained the rest of my coffee in a few large gulps and tossed the empty paper cup into the nearest trash bin. "When do you want to go?"

Marcus' brow furrowed. "Go?"

"Do you want to see Mama or not?"

His face lit up, his blue eyes sparkling as his smile reached them. "You'll help me?"

I hated the relief in his voice, hated the gratitude in his glance. "I'll help me," I said with a sharp shrug. "If you won't tell me what's going on, maybe Mama will."

I pushed my hand back through my tangle of hair. "Now, when do you want to go?"

"As soon as possible."

I threw up my hands and brought them down onto the mattress, shoving myself up onto my feet. "Right, okay then. I'm going to grab a quick shower, get into some fresh clothes and then we'll head out. You can handle the flight arrangements?"

"Course." Marcus stood up, still grinning. "Grace? Than—"

"Don't thank me." I cut him off with a warning shake of my pointer finger. "There's still a fifty-fifty chance this little visit will get us both killed."

"It'll be fine," he said, scrunching up his nose at me. "You worry too much."

A snort was my only response to this. I unzipped my stinking, filthy hoodie and dropped it to the floor as I walked into the bathroom, calling behind myself as I went. "By the way, I need to make a stop before we see Mama."

"It can't wait?" Marcus shouted.

"No," I insisted, raising my voice over the cacophony of falling water as I switched on the shower. "It can't wait. And before you ask"—I poked my head around the doorframe, lips a firm line—"I'd prefer to go alone."

His brows shot up, but Marcus shrugged, careful to keep his gaze on the floor. "All right, suit yourself. As long as it doesn't take too long."

Chapter Seven

Marcus

Getting in and out of Klamath Falls was more difficult than one might imagine. Medford, the closest 'big city' and location of the nearest commercial airport, was an hour and half drive west through the mountains. The road was single-laned in either direction, steep and winding, with no shoulder. In winter, the road would become impassable, packed with snow and ice several feet high, and residents of the basin were trapped for weeks at a time.

However, given the right conditions, the drive could also be a breathtaking one. As Grace and I headed out into the evening, the sky turned the colors of melting sherbet and the pine trees showed off the luscious bright greens of fresh growth. The sun, drifting ever lower, glowed orange like a dying ember and long shadows began to creep out of the deep forest.

It had been thirty years since I'd left Seattle under a cloud, no joke intended. It was a city I had grown fond of during my visits over the years prior to my disgrace, but, if I were being honest, the main reason for that fondness was sitting right next to me here in the Medford Airport.

I had never met anyone like Grace. At first, I had attributed it to the fact that she was born, not bitten, but gradually I began to see that Grace was unique, and looked at the world in a way few others ever could. During our annual meetings, she would interrogate me on everything, from my own personal history and experiences before being turned, to world politics, economics and the latest trends in music and art. I had something to say about everything, and Grace listened voraciously, especially when it came to her favorite topic…being human.

During the third year of our arrangement, while she was pushing me to describe in greater detail the men with which I had served in the last world war, I leaned back, throwing one arm over the back of my chair, smiling at the entranced expression on Grace's face. "You've really got a thing for humans, haven't you?"

Grace blushed and hunched over her martini. "Well, I've never been one." She stirred her olives around the glass of gin and vermouth. "And I almost never get to interact with any of them. Except the butcher."

Forehead wrinkling, I brought my own drink up to my lips, head falling to one side. "Come again?"

"The den has an arrangement with a local man, for those who can't, or don't, partake in the sacrament. He's a butcher. He provides fresh meat for those of us who need it." She gazed into the middle distance, smiling warmly. "He's got a sweet

little girl, too. I've gotten to know them both pretty well since Mama put me in charge of our dealings with him."

"Should I be jealous?" I asked, only half-joking.

Grace guffawed and shook her head. She plucked one of the olives off the toothpick with her teeth, and chewed it contemplatively, shaking the rest of them at me. "I should take you by his place sometime so you can meet him. I think you'd like him."

I did not respond, opting instead to sip at my drink. "Do you indulge?"

Grace looked at me with wide-eyed confusion.

"In the sacrament, I mean," I said, by way of explanation.

Grace wrinkled her nose and nodded. "Of course, it's expected."

I let out a sharp sigh, looking her up and down with a critical eye. "You know, just because it's expected, doesn't mean you have to do it."

The undercurrent of reproach in my tone caught her just under the chin, and she drew back, surprised. Grace straightened and her smile shrank. She took a drink of her martini. "Don't you?"

"Never have. Never been tempted." I stared into what was left of my drink. "Just because I turn into a monster, doesn't mean I have to act like one."

"We..."

I heard the hurt in her voice and looked up. Her brow furrowed, she held her hand up to her throat, petting herself. She shook her head. "We don't turn into monsters, Marcus. How can you say that?"

I leaned across the table, one hand outstretched. "What would you call a ten-foot wolf that stands up on its hind legs and is impervious to harm? A pet?"

"It's just..." Grace looked around us, then pressed her hand to her collarbone. "It's what I am."

"But it's not who you are." I pointed to the tabletop. *"Even when we're the wolf, we're still in the driver's seat — if we want to be. We don't have to take more lives."*

"What about the hunger?"

"It can be controlled. With practice." I leaned back, gesturing up into the air. *"Besides, there's always animals to hunt."*

Grace nodded, her lips a thin, firm line. "I never really thought about it that much." She reached across the table and took my hand, squeezing it once then releasing it. *"Thank you, Marcus."*

I smiled, skin tingling where our hands had touched. "For what?"

"For making me think."

As the boarding call for our flight echoed over the airport loudspeakers, I considered the memory. I was no fool. I knew that had been the source of our mutual attraction at first. We made each other think. We had challenged each other in ways no one else ever had. Grace was fun to talk to, to be around, and even though I was younger than her, Grace said that it often felt like I had lived so much more. Who wouldn't want to go back and have a relationship like that again? A real friendship. But then we had gone and ruined it, spoiled it all by falling in love with each other.

And that was the real problem with going back to Seattle, with sitting on this plane with her now. I couldn't be sure if she was still in love with me after all this time. I stared harder at the seat back in front of me. I wasn't sure that I wanted to know.

* * * *

74

Grace

The airport and flight were messy blurs of checkpoints, flat soda and jostling commuters. Seattle, which had seemed a world away in Klamath Falls, was reached with shocking speed and ease. I had a distinct sense of whiplash as I stood alone under a streetlight on a dark Seattle avenue, staring at the familiar and welcoming sight of the butcher shop window across the street.

The painted mural on the glass featured a stoned-looking heifer dancing on her hind legs in a field of flowers. A searing yellow sun hung suspended in an aquamarine sky. Directly above the cow's bulbous head, in bright orange letters, were the words — "OUR MEAT CAN'T BE BEAT."

I admired Lily's handiwork. The woman had been painting the same advertisement on her shop windows for almost twenty years now. The heifer had become an unofficial mascot of the neighborhood. Small details changed with the seasons. In winter, the cow would sport a stylish Santa hat. In fall, the field of flowers would become a pumpkin patch. But through it all, the slogan remained the same — "OUR MEAT CAN'T BE BEAT."

Lily Donovan held a place of special significance in the werewolf community of Seattle. Just as a Jewish community came to rely on a handful of local, Kosher butchers, Lily Donovan was relied upon to feed the hungry bellies of those members of the Nameless who did not partake in the so-called sacrament of the flesh, all while keeping their existence secret from the world at large.

The relationship was mutually beneficial, of course. The regular monthly orders to fulfill the metabolic requirements of the werewolves of Seattle kept Lily's business afloat. In this modern industrial age, there wasn't much call for artisanal, fresh-killed meat anymore. Not unless a butcher happened to know the right people.

I had known Lily since the day she was born. As a friend of her father's, from whom Lily would eventually inherit the business, I first viewed Lily through a lens of scientific fascination. I was obsessed with all things human, including her. And little Lily felt the same about me, enchanted by the visits from the woman who never grew old. In time, Lily grew into adulthood herself, becoming fiercely opinionated, independent and wise beyond her years.

When things got too much for me with the Nameless, I knew there would always be a place for me at Lily's. Over the years, we became as close as any sisters. I told Lily everything about the Nameless, more than any human should have known. It was Lily who had convinced me to finally get out. It was Lily who had pulled money out of her savings to help me. It was Lily alone with whom I had trusted my plans.

Plans that had now taken a significant detour.

I looked both ways before crossing the street. I shouldered the glass door open, and stepped inside the fluorescent-lit shop, my sense of smell awash with the unmistakable scent of raw meat and spices. It was a small establishment, modest in outward appearance. There was a single counter and display case that ran the length of the entire room, with various scales, wrappers and containers scattered on top. The cash register sat on the far end and, above it all, a chalkboard was screwed into the brick wall that listed all the items in the case and their prices.

The door chimed as I entered. Before the electronic bell had finished sounding, a shout came from the doorless back room behind the counter. "Sorry," boomed the deep voice. "But we were just closing up for the night. Could you maybe—"

Struck dumb as soon as she stepped out of her prep area, Lily froze halfway through the doorframe, her viscera-covered hands held close to her chest. "Gracie?"

I smiled, tucking my wild hair behind my ears. "Did I come at a bad time?"

"Gracie!" Lily shouted. She let loose a sharp, barking laugh, a smile splitting her face. "Any time you decide to visit me is a great time!"

The fifty-year-old woman dug a stained rag out of her apron pocket, and scrubbed her hands clean as she lumbered forward. I hurried to meet her, my own arms outstretched, and we embraced.

My eyes flickered shut as I squeezed my friend tight. "It is so, so good to see you, Lily."

Lily patted and rubbed my back, her strong, thick hands warm through my thin long-sleeved shirt. The older-looking woman then leaned back to examine my tired face. "Is it?" She furrowed her brow. "Could've fooled me." She took a step away, sliding her hands down to grip my arms. She peered at me over the rim of her gold, half-rimmed glasses. "What's wrong? What are you doing here? I thought we agreed that the next time we saw each other, it'd be down in Klamath Falls? I was looking forward to visiting you in your new place."

Swallowing, I mimicked Lily's posture, my long fingers digging into Lily's muscular upper arms. "Why?"

The furrow in Lily's brow deepened. She opened her mouth to respond, but I cut her off, pressing, "Why did you tell Marcus Bowen where I was?"

Lily's oak-brown eyes widened as her face cleared. "Ah."

I released her. Lily's hands dropped to her sides. She pursed her lips and nodded. "Yes. Yes, I did do that."

I shook my head and looked down at the shorter, stouter woman in expectation. Lily turned away from my stare, striding back behind the counter as she pulled at the knot that kept her leather apron closed. "Let's go upstairs. Have you had dinner yet?" She lifted the apron up over her head and wadded it into a ball, before tossing it under the counter. "I've got some of Uncle Del's chili left over. I can heat it up for you — cornbread, too. Come on."

Knowing better than to push my friend, I followed Lily into the back room. On the other side of the wall, Lily paused to hit a few switches, turning off the lights in the main part of the shop and engaging the lock on the front door. Shop secured, we wandered past the sealed walk-in fridges and freezers that dominated the area.

Lily's family had lived over the butcher's shop since her grandfather had first opened it. The fact that the two-story building had remained undeveloped so close to Seattle Center was a miracle in and of itself, though it had less to do with heavenly intervention, and more to do with the Nameless protecting their interests.

The two-bedroom apartment on the second floor was as simple and unassuming in appearance as the shop below. It retained its original white and red wallpaper, although brown shag carpet had been put in sometime in the seventies. Small tables, crammed full of photographs and knickknacks, could be found in every room, even the bathroom and the kitchen. Although Lily herself had no children, she had a large extended family who never forgot her.

Lily walked straight to the kitchen, hoisting a large black pot out of her old fridge and placing it on the gas stove. A few squares of cornbread, wrapped in tinfoil, were popped into the oven to warm.

I made myself at home as I always did, sitting at the small round table in the kitchen. I watched my friend, taking inventory of her.

Lily turned from the stove, ladle in her hand. "How hungry are you?"

I straightened in my chair and tried on a weak smile. "I'll just take a small bowl, thanks."

Lily slid a worn blue bowl in front of me, a wedge of cornbread resting on top of the steaming, mouthwatering chili. "You look like hell, girl. Bad moon?"

"It was a tough few days, yeah," I said between spoonfuls of chili. I ripped off a piece of cornbread and popped it into my already-full mouth. Leaning back in the wicker chair, I fixed Lily with a reproachful stare as I chewed. "Marcus being around didn't help."

Lily grimaced as she settled into the chair opposite. "Yeah. Look, I'm sorry about that, Gracie. But — "

"You knew I wanted a clean break from everything, Lily," I said, stirring the thick concoction around my bowl.

Lily fixed me with a blank stare. "Even Marcus?"

I shoveled another heap of chili into my maw and put down my spoon. "Especially Marcus," I mumbled.

Silence. I looked across the table to find Lily staring at me, her eyes narrowed, one brow raised. Chewing faster, I shook my head. "Don't—don't give me that look."

Lily's stare intensified, her arms coming up across her chest. I sucked a breath in through my nose and slashed my hand through the air. "Lil, I'm serious. Don't."

"Was it good to see him?" Lily held up her hand preemptively. "And don't bother lying to me."

I slunk down in my chair, my fingers coming up to poke at my bread. "That's not the point." I rolled a crumb between my thumb and pointer finger. "He always makes things...complicated."

"I thought you liked that about him," Lily said, picking at the fraying placemat in front of her.

I frowned, but didn't respond, avoiding Lily's probing gaze by hunching over my food. "He needs to see Mama."

"I know." Lily shook her head, her beaded earrings clicking against themselves. "Why else do you think I would tell him where you were?"

As I lifted my head, my eyes brightened with sudden curiosity. "Oh. What did he say to you, exactly?"

Lily shrugged. "He said he needed to see Mama. That you were in danger."

"Who?" I leaned over the bowl, my elbows on the table. "The Nameless?"

"No, Gracie." Lily's face was grave. She pointed across the table. "Not the den—you." She tilted her head to one side, her brows drawing together. "He didn't tell you?"

"No," I said, my attention drifting over Lily's shoulder. "He didn't."

"Well, I'll tell you, that man was beside himself when he came here, damn near tearing his hair out. Kept saying that he had to find you and make sure you were all right." Lily sighed, her tongue caught between her teeth. "You know... He really cares about you..."

"I don't want to hear it," I snapped, my eyes flickering back to Lily's face. My lips firmed into a thin line. "Why wouldn't he just tell me?"

Lily sat back, rolling her eyes. "Maybe he didn't want you to worry," she said. "Or maybe he didn't think you'd believe him." Lily ran her hand back and forth over her shaved head. "When are you going to see Mama?"

I stabbed at the chili with my spoon. "In the morning."

"She's not going to be happy to see you. Either of you."

"We'll be okay." I put on my best reassuring smile. "Family just gets a little complicated sometimes, doesn't it?"

"You said it." Lily watched as I devoured the last few mouthfuls of chili. "Where are you staying tonight? Do you need a place to crash?"

"No." I wiped sauce off my bottom lip with my thumb. "Marcus has got us a couple of rooms at the Maxwell."

"Well, whatever happens tomorrow, check in with me afterwards." Lily stood and removed the empty bowl from in front of me. "I want to know that you're okay. Both of you."

Chapter Eight

Marcus

Early the next morning, I started knocking on the connecting door that linked my and Grace's hotel rooms together after I heard the sink start going in the other room. I started out soft, but when it became clear that I was being ignored, I had no problem ramping things up.

My pounding became so intense that the framed pictures on my walls began to rattle. I stopped when I heard the thud of striding feet, and I stood back from the door as the lock flipped from engaged to disengaged. The door flung open into Grace's room, and Grace stood in the frame, mouth foamy, toothbrush gripped tight in her free hand. "What?"

I held a thin silver and black tie aloft in one hand, holding it against my crisp black suit jacket and white dress shirt. "Is a tie too much?"

Grace jammed the bristly end of the brush back to her molars and stared at me. "It'll give them something to hang you with, I guess."

"Hm." I examined the tie a moment longer then shrugged. I popped my shirt's collar and slipped the strip of fabric around my neck.

Rolling her eyes, Grace walked away into the bathroom. She spat in the sink, grimacing as the sound of my voice reached her.

"You're not really going in that, are you?" I frowned at her ensemble — an ultra-casual collection of loose, faded blue jeans and a light green T-shirt that had the logo of the credit union where she worked emblazoned across the chest.

Toothbrush clattering onto the marble counter, Grace used both hands to shake out her mane of earth-brown hair. "I'm a loan officer at a small, rural credit union," she said, meeting her gaze evenly in the bathroom mirror. "How else am I supposed to dress?"

"Are you trying to antagonize her?"

"Just worry about yourself, Marcus." Grace stepped back around the corner to find me standing in front of her room's full-length mirror, struggling to knot my tie. She rested her hands on her hips. "You better hope she thinks that what you have to say is as important as the Feóndulf think it is, or she'll have you in pieces. And I won't be able to stop her this time."

"Won't be able to?" I mumbled, my chin pressed to my chest as my fingers fumbled with the twirling pieces of fabric. "Or won't want to?"

I glanced up at her reflection just in time to see the hurt expression that skittered across her face, before she could hide it behind manufactured annoyance. Sighing, Grace closed the distance between us, flapping her hands at me. "Just—just let me, let me do it, will you?"

I turned at her approach, ready to deliver another smart remark, but pain still lingered at the edges of her eyes, and I thought better of baiting her. I dropped my hands obediently, lifting my chin and allowing Grace to twist and loop the tie into submission, all while trying and failing to keep my gaze fixed just over her head.

Grace stared at my throat, a small smile playing around her lips. "Over a hundred, and you still can't tie a damn tie." She furrowed her brow and looked through me, clearly thinking of a time long ago and far away. She finished the knot and slid it up to the base of my neck, shaking her head. "I don't want you dead, Marcus. Hell, you're one of the only friends I've got left."

Her hand began to fall to her side, but I caught hold of it and squeezed it tight, holding it in both of my own. "Is that what we are?" I said, my voice gentle and urgent. "Friends?"

All at once I was aware of how close we were to each other, of the heat of her hand inside mine, of the way her attention had drifted to my lips. I wanted to reach out and bury my hand in her hair. I wanted to lean forward and hold her to me, bringing the familiar scent of her deep into my lungs.

It would be so easy.

But I waited too long. The moment passed, unseized, and instead Grace glanced at our clasped hands, blinking as if waking from a dream.

"We..." I cleared my throat and tried again, my voice sounding much stronger as I returned Grace's hand to her. "We should get going, yeah?"

Grace nodded hard, shaking out her hands. "Right. Right?" She walked to the hotel room door and leaned down to slide her feet into her already-tied tennis shoes. After a moment of wiggling and pulling, she straightened, breathing in deep through her nose. "Ready?"

I cracked my neck, first one side, then the other. "As I'll ever be."

* * * *

The Nameless had called Seattle home since the beginning of the twentieth century. They had been drawn there by the flow of travelers who frequented the area, humans eager to reap the promised rewards of the Yukon Gold Rush. The city had turned out to be a perfect base of operations for the den. Seattle offered a bustling urban environment, replete with all the modern luxuries and vices that a shadowy organization could exploit, while at the same time being in close proximity to vast swathes of wilderness. The house on Queen Anne Hill, which served as the den's headquarters, had been built in 1902. It reflected the style and sensibility of that era. White walls rose three stories high, and wide windows dotted the structure to absorb as much of the elusive northwest sunshine as could be found. Balconies opened out toward the downtown area, and given that the home was built on a jutting rock promontory, the view of the city was spectacular, unmarred by other structures. Surrounded by a cobblestone courtyard and a low dark stone and wrought-iron wall, the only vehicle access to the house was through a twelve-foot-tall gate.

I pulled up in front of the house. I smoothed down the front of my suit with one hand. Grace winced at the forced nonchalance in my voice when I asked, "So... How do you want to do this?"

"I'll go first," she said, unbuckling herself. She popped the car door open and stepped out. "You find someplace on the street to park and follow me in. I'll leave the gate unlocked for you."

I nodded.

Grace

I shut the car door, watching Marcus drive up the hill. I walked toward the gate. When I reached the closed portal, I looked at the tall brick pillar to my left, which housed the buzzer, speaker and fingerprint scanner embedded in the wall. I reached for the scanner, then stopped. Looking up at the house, I considered how well I knew every inch of every room, every corner, every crystal on every chandelier, every faucet, every door. I knew how it felt to stand outside on the second-floor balcony and look out over the city, bright and alive in the dead of night. I knew how my favorite meal smelled sizzling on the stove in the massive kitchen. I knew how it sounded to cry in the living room, the sound swallowed up by the heavy velvet curtains. I knew every nick in the burnished wood railing for the staircase, and I could mark my progress up and down the flight of stairs by touch alone.

I knew how it felt to be trapped for years and years and years, with no hope of ever getting out.

I slammed my thumb against the scanner. With a beep and a click, the gate opened. I strode through, my head held high, leaving the gate gaping open behind me.

The front door was built into the side of the house. Polished wooden double doors sat recessed between two gleaming white pillars at the top of a short flight of stairs. Moving quickly lest I lost my nerve, I hopped up the stairs, twisted the handle and entered.

The entryway had been built to show off the owner's wealth and status. A golden three-tiered chandelier hung from the high ceiling, dripping with crystals. The light it caught bounced off the waxed marble floors. The marble was a deep, verdant green, the color of freshly minted money. Fifty feet inside the space, a half-circle reception desk had been set up, black and shiny, holding nothing more than a computer and a phone. Behind that lay the stairs, a wide wooden affair that stretched up to a landing that housed a reading nook and floor-to-ceiling stained-glass windows.

At the desk stood a young woman, blonde, her hair pulled back in a tight, professional bun. Around her neck hung several strings of pink and white pearls, which matched the pink and white dress suit that clung to her every curve. She looked up when I entered, a bored expression giving way to a raucous grin.

"Grace," said Sylvia, all smiles, her voice dripping with honey. "Welcome back." She waited until I came to a stop in front of the desk, then leaned forward, her tone becoming that of a conspiratorial whisper. "We had a pool going, you know. How long you'd make it out there in the real world. I gave you six months."

"I'm not back."

Sylvia drew away, her hand coming up to her throat. "Oh?"

The door opened behind me, and I turned to watch Marcus saunter in, spinning his car keys around his finger. Stopping in the middle of the entryway, he smiled. "Sylvia," he said, giving a small bow. "Good to see you. You're looking as lovely as ever."

The woman's friendly veneer vanished like condensation wiped from a window. A look of disgust contorted Sylvia's perfect face, and she drew herself up tall, hands clenched into fists on top of her workstation. "You brought a Feóndulf here?" The words struggled out from between her clenched white teeth. "And Marcus Bowen? Out of all of them? Grace, are you out of your goddamn mind?"

I rested my forearms on top of the reception desk. "He needs to see Mama."

Sylvia's eyes widened, her mouth falling open. She shuddered and lunged for her phone. "I'm calling security."

"Sylvia, wait —" Lifting myself onto my tiptoes, I thrust out my hand and pressed down hard on the phone's plunger.

Sylvia glared at me, handset held up to her ear.

I placed my free hand flat against my collarbone. "Listen, I'll vouch for him."

"Which means almost nothing."

"But it still means something, right?" Brows raised, I rested back down on my heels, my fingers coming off the phone. "Call Mama. Make it her decision. Everything else is."

Still scowling, Sylvia dialed a four-digit extension and waited while the phone rang. I took a step back to stand behind Marcus, who surprised me by reaching out to squeeze my hand. I half-listened as Sylvia relayed events down the telephone line, my heart in my throat. After a few terse yesses and nos, Sylvia replaced the handset on the cradle.

"Mama will see you." A cruel smile split her ruby-red lips. "She's in the sunroom."

We started forward and Sylvia's hand shot up. "Ah ah!" She pointed to Marcus, eyes narrowing. "He's supposed to wait right here."

I only realized we were still holding hands the moment I had to let go. Marcus gave a reassuring smile, sliding his hands into his trouser pockets. I tried to return the same, before marching behind the desk and up the stairs.

To the human eye, Mama would've appeared to be a very healthy seventy-year-old — the kind of seventy-year-old who worked out with a private trainer, ate organic meals prepared by a private chef and every night dutifully applied a facial cream made from the placenta of some exotic animal. Werewolves, however, given their unique relationship with aging and time, did not judge a person's age strictly on sight. Like many things in their lives, it came down to smell. The longer a person had been roaming around the planet, the more complex their scent became.

Mama's scent was unlike anything else on earth. The truth was, no one knew exactly how old she was. She was old enough to remember a time before the Nameless had ever existed, old enough to remember when all the dens of the so-called civilized world could be counted on one hand. For centuries, she had ruled over the affairs of the Nameless, defeating, from time to time, various challengers who had sought to oppose her rule. None had lived to recount the experience.

When I entered the sunroom, I was relieved to find that I would not be alone with my grandmother. Like all great rulers, Mama was often attended by a group of powerful counselors, confidants and sycophants. Today, the group of hangers-on consisted of four well-dressed women of various shapes, sizes and ethnicities, sitting on the eight-piece sofa on the far side of the large room, drinking coffee and eating breakfast pastries. They looked up as a group when I entered, following my steps with the same intense interest that a dog had for a bouncing ball.

Mama stood at one of the large bay windows that looked out over the city, her breakfast cooling on a small table beside her. She was already dressed for the day, her rose-patterned blouse open down to her breasts, the skirt she wore so long it trailed onto the floor.

I came to a stop a few feet behind my grandmother. I clasped my hands behind my back and focused my attention out of the window, watching as the early morning pleasure boaters began taking their vessels out on the water. I felt Mama shift to look at me, but remained intent on the scenery, dreading the moment I would have to once again look into the fearsome woman's face.

"Grace." Mama's serene voice oozed into my ear like ice water. "Back with your tail between your legs, I see."

I tilted my head to one side, my gaze darting to the older woman. "I'm not back."

"Oh?" Mama raised a single pencil thin brow. "Am I suffering from some kind of hallucination then?"

"I'm just doing a favor for a friend."

Sighing, Mama drew a bony hand down her face, turning to look out over the city once more. "Feóndulf are not our friends, Grace. How many times do I have to teach you this lesson?"

"I really don't give a shit about den politics anymore, Mama. Feóndulf, Nameless, Sangre Sagrada, Yè Láng, Čeljusti Smrti—" Forcing a smile, I unclasped my hands. "You can keep them all. I'm out."

"Out?" The word dropped from Mama's mouth like it was a rotten piece of fruit. Her eyes narrowed, and she came away from the window, skirt swishing against the smooth marble floor as she walked. "You think that what's inside you is something you can just walk away from? Is that what your mother died for?"

I let out a long breath through my nose. "It's not my fault you only had one daughter, Mama."

"But it is your fault she's dead." The old woman scowled at me, her bottom lip trembling.

Rocking back and forth on my heels, I repeated my side of the argument that my grandmother and I had rehashed a hundred times. "She knew the risks. Carrying a wolf child to term is dangerous, even in this day and age, let alone in the eighteen-hundreds. She did it anyway." I jabbed a finger into my chest, meeting Mama's gaze. "I didn't ask to be born."

Mama took in a deep breath and let it out, wrinkled face contorting. She began circling me, her low-heeled shoes clicking against the floor. "Your mother understood the importance of continuing the bloodline."

I shook my head, my hands clenching and relaxing at my sides. "You bullied her, the same way you bully everyone."

"I," said Mama, her volume rising, "am the leader of this den, and everything I do is in the den's best interest!"

"Eating humans?" I shouted in return. "That's in the den's best interest?"

"The sacrament of the flesh is our birthright!"

"I—" I swallowed my words with difficulty, the muscles in my neck and shoulders tight and throbbing. I held out my palms and closed my eyes. "I didn't come here to fight, Mama. I just came to help deliver a message."

"Then let's hear this message." Mama crossed back to the small table by the window and stooped down to pick up the phone that sat next to her coffee cup. Unlocking it with a swipe, she stabbed at the screen and held it to her ear. "Yes. Send him in."

The room was silent except for the sounds of cups finding saucers, and bodies shifting against cushions. Stomach churning, I stared at my grandmother. The last time the three of us had been in a room together, there had been blood. This time I was determined not to cry. I would not give the woman the satisfaction of seeing me beg ever again.

Chapter Nine

Marcus

I walked into the sunroom with a smile, my hands in my pockets.

"Ladies." I nodded to a quartet of women gathered on a sectional sofa nearby, looking them over as I passed. I came to a stop beside Grace, gave her a nod, then, as if it were the most natural thing in the world, I knelt, my head bowed, my hands folded on top of my knee. "Mama. It is an honor to be brought before you."

Mama smiled. She tossed her head to one side, a sheaf of silver hair fluttering away from her face. "Marcus Bowen."

She closed the gap between us in a few steps. She placed her hands on my shoulders, squeezing them gently. I tilted my head back to look up at her, and Mama's smile widened. "Your manners have always been exceptional, Mr. Bowen, especially for someone who was bitten and not born."

Grip firming, Mama jerked me forward, bringing her knee up at the same time. She slammed my face into her knee with tremendous force, and a sickening crunch echoed through the room. I bounced off her kneecap like a tennis ball off a racket. She sent me backward with an additional shove. I slid against the cold stone floor and was about to turn onto my side when Mama's foot landed in the center of my chest, pressing down hard.

One of the women on the sofa giggled. Grace watched, but said nothing, her jaw clenching.

Still smiling, Mama leaned down, resting her forearm on top of her thigh. "I believe the last time we met, Mr. Bowen, I told you that if I ever saw you again, I would personally tear you limb from limb, and eat your heart out of your chest."

I gagged and coughed, turning my head to one side to spit out a mouthful of blood onto the marble. Rolling my head back to face forward, I gave a sharp nod, face contorted in pain. "Yes, Mama."

Mama ground the flat of her shoe into my collarbone, her head tilting to one side. "Was I in any way unclear?"

I writhed under her foot, and my next two words came out in a wheezy whisper. "No, Mama."

The older woman straightened and let out a long sigh. After a moment, she stepped back and off me. Shaking out her skirt, she moved to return to her place at the window. "I understand you have a message for me."

Propping myself up, I wiped blood from my face with the back of my hand. "Just for you, Mama," I said, voice wavering as I struggled to get my breath back.

Mama waved a limp hand toward the women on the sofa. "Leave us."

Taking final sips of coffee and last bites of food, the entourage got to their feet and drifted out of the room, whispering among themselves. I struggled to my feet, blood dripping from my face and staining my white dress shirt.

Grace made a beeline for the empty sofa and threw herself onto it, sprawling across the cushions in as unladylike a fashion as she could manage. "I'm staying."

Mama's hand came up to pinch the bridge of her nose. "Grace—"

"I'm staying," Grace repeated, crossing her arms over her chest. She fastened an empty glare onto me. "This has something to do with what happened to me, am I right?"

Frowning, I opened my mouth to speak, but Mama cut me off, turning to face her granddaughter with a furrowed brow. "What happened to you? What are you talking about?"

"Just a slight kidnapping. And some torture." Grace narrowed her eyes. "I'd like to know why, though."

"My darling girl!" Mama flattened a hand against her chest, her mouth open in horror. "Dear God, are you all right?"

"I'll be better after I get some answers." Grace leaned back. "So, Marcus, I got you to Mama—what's the message?"

Looking between the two women, I could already feel what were sure to be dark red bruises blossoming under my eyes. Shaking my head, I readjusted my suit jacket before beginning. "Three weeks ago, Dylan Colquhoun was killed in his home in London."

"I know. He was shot in the heart. Silver bullet." Mama took a few steps toward her breakfast. She lifted her coffee to her lips and took a sip. "I shall wipe away a tear."

"Then you'll also know that seven months ago, his son, Aidan Colquhoun, was also killed."

Mama ran a finger along the edge of her coffee cup. "I'm getting bored, Mr. Bowen."

"Both men were tortured, prior to being killed."

I watched as Mama's shoulders tightened underneath her thin blouse. The older woman took another sip of her coffee, then tossed me the cloth napkin that sat folded beside her plate. "Tortured, you say?"

I caught the napkin one-handed, using it first to wipe off my hand, then to dab at my face and nose. "There may only be a few ways to kill a werewolf," I said. "But having your fingernails ripped out and cigarettes put out on you hurts, no matter how quickly you heal. Just ask Grace."

"It's not an experience I'd recommend," Grace confirmed.

Mama's cup clattered into its saucer, and she turned to face me fully for the first time since I began talking. "How were they restrained? Silver?"

"Wolfsbane." I crumpled the stained napkin in one hand then, lacking anywhere else to put it, shoved it into my trouser pocket. "We think they're being injected with it."

"You've got a hunter problem on your hands, Mr. Bowen." Brows raised, Mama crossed the room and settled on the couch next to Grace. "A particularly nasty one, it sounds like. The Feóndulf should be on guard."

"I'm afraid it's no longer just our problem, Mama." I followed the matriarch to the sofa, standing in front of the pair of women, inclining my head toward Grace. "What happened to your granddaughter is proof of that."

"What makes you think the hunter was targeting her specifically? Maybe they were going after you, and got her instead." Mama smiled. "It wouldn't be the first time you got her hurt."

Outwardly, I shrugged off the dig, but inside I felt it land in my gut like a fist.

"It seems while under duress, Colquhoun gave up the access codes to his personal safe," I said. "All the records of den business were kept offsite, thankfully, but his personal records, his diaries going back hundreds of years were...rifled through. Pages torn out. Anything that referenced the Nameless was taken."

"And you think that the perpetrator intends to use this information to, what exactly? Murder us all in our beds?"

"We do have special reason to believe that you and Grace may be next." I reached into my jacket's breast pocket and withdrew an envelope. I held it out to Mama, reaching over Grace to do so, while taking one last look at the writing on the envelope's face — *Sélène Holtz*.

From the way Grace straightened in her seat, I could tell that she had spotted the name. I couldn't imagine how many years it had been since she had seen her grandmother's real name written in someone else's hand.

"We found this in Colquhoun's desk," I said by way of explanation.

Mama looked at the envelope as if I had just offered her a silver dagger, her jaw clenching. She swiped it from my hand and worked open the stiff flap, which had been tucked inside the envelope rather than sealed shut. Inside was a single piece of paper, folded once, scrawled on in a tight, cramped hand.

Glaring, she began to read. Grace and I waited, watching as the color drained from the older woman's cheeks. Her eyes widened. Rising, Mama began to pace.

"Jesus Christ, Marcus," said Grace from the corner of her mouth. "Why didn't you just tell me I had a target on my back?"

My face a picture of bloody misery, I shrugged my shoulders. "I couldn't, Grace. I had my orders."

At last, Mama swung back to face us, the letter held out in her hand. "You've read this?" she asked me.

I nodded.

Mama slapped me across the face, the back of her ringed hand connecting with my cheek and jaw so hard that I stumbled.

Standing, Grace placed herself between us, facing her grandmother. "What does it say?"

Rage was etched onto every line of Mama's face and, for a second, I thought Grace was about to be struck as well. But the older woman took in a deep breath and let it out, her hands clenching at her sides. At last she turned away, folding the paper and tucking it back into the envelope. "It's from Dylan Colquhoun," she said. "A warning. This person intends to end the bloodlines and bring both the Feóndulf and the Nameless to ruin. We're next." She folded the envelope several times before tucking the tight square into her bosom, her tone becoming light and conversational. "It also expresses his wish that, given the death of his son and heir, you assume control of the Feóndulf den."

Grace laughed aloud. "What?"

Grinning, she looked at me. I stared at the floor. Still burbling with laughter, she returned her gaze to Mama. Head tilted to one side, the matriarch of the Nameless watched her, the smallest of smiles playing around her thin lips.

The sight of Mama smiling squashed all sense of humor in Grace like the wheels of an eighteen-wheeler would squash a slow-moving toad. "What?" Grace repeated, her voice flat. She took a step back. She shook her head. Her mouth opened and closed, then opened again. "That's ridiculous. That's unheard of. He's insane. There's been a mistake."

Mama shook her head. "He's quite clear. He feels it's time for our two dens to be united, and that your leadership is the way to do it."

"But I'm not—" Regaining herself in a rush, Grace scoffed aloud, throwing her hands up into the air. "Well, that's just too bad! I'm not going to do it. So there." The tip of her tongue darted out and wetted her bottom lip. "And how did Colquhoun know we were next on the list of this psycho? What does he say, exactly?"

The older woman lifted her head, shaking her hair back out of her face. She strode toward the bay windows. "Under the circumstances, do you really think that is what's important?"

Grace dogged her grandmother's steps, her arms swinging. "Ah, yeah, I think his knowledge of our imminent painful deaths is pretty damn important."

Mama turned without warning, her teeth clenched. "The world is shifting under our feet," she hissed. "Our very existence is threatened, and still, all you want to do is bicker with me?"

"Whatever is really in that letter," said Grace, hazel eyes flashing. "I will find out. Either you'll tell me" — Grace stepped back, breathing heavily, and pointed at me — "or he will."

They stared at each other, matching one another in fury and stubbornness the way only two women from the same family could. The hair on my arms and neck began to bristle. If it came to a fight, I had no doubt who would win, but I was loath to think it, let alone say it out loud.

Mama relented first, however, her brow unfurrowing, her shoulders relaxing. She unclenched her fists and pushed her hands back through her hair as she turned away, her voice laced with exhaustion. "Perhaps it is only right that he tells you. He is one of your den members now."

"Oh, Christ." Grace's face blanched. "Don't say that."

Mama cleared her throat and addressed me. "Who from the Feóndulf is looking into this matter?"

I drew myself up, chin lifting. "I have been directed to do so, Mama."

"And Grace is your master now?"

As I winced, my shoulders fell, but I managed to keep my tone even. "I'm answering to the Feóndulf Council for the moment, until a new leader is...confirmed."

Grace and Mama could only imagine the turmoil the Council was in at this very moment. Feóndulf women weren't allowed to work, to have a say in den matters, to go out in public without an escort, to even be on the Council — the thought of having one lead the Feóndulf, and an outsider at that, was tying the Council in knots. They were desperate to try to figure out a way to elect someone else to head the den without blatantly spitting in the face of their leader's dying wish.

"I will contact them, and let them know that Colquhoun's final message was received and understood," said Mama, folding her hands in front of her waist. "I will also inform them that you will be continuing your investigation here, under my protection."

I blinked and leaned forward. "Pardon?"

"What?" said Grace, her mouth falling open.

Mama lifted her eyebrows and spread her hands in front of her. "With the attack on Grace, it's been proven that we are indeed the next target for this lunatic. Whoever they may be, they are almost definitely in the city by now, don't you think? Your best chance of catching them is to find them here, before they strike again."

My lips parted, I glanced at the sickened Grace, stumbling over my words. "I—I don't disagree, Mama, but I have no jurisdiction here. And all, all my files, my work, it's all—"

"I'm sure we can get your things sent here without too much trouble," Mama said, dismissing my concerns with a wave. "And you'll be working with my authority at your back, so that should do away with any red tape you may encounter. Besides"—she smiled wide, fiddling with her rings—"Grace will assist you."

The sound of her name jolted her out of her surprised stupor, and Grace let loose a mirthless laugh. "Like hell I will," she exclaimed, backing away. "I've done my part. I'm going home."

"You are home, child." Mama tutted, and shook her head. "And you have a responsibility now, to the Feóndulf. They need you to lead them, to guide —"

"You think they want me guiding fuck all? I'm a Nameless!" Grace swallowed, her throat raw from shouting. "And I'm not even that anymore. No, no, I'm going back to Klamath Falls, back to my job, back to my life!"

"And if this hunter strikes again?"

"I'm almost two hundred, Mama. I'm not a child. I can take care of myself." She spun on her heels, her hands outstretched, and headed for the door, moving faster with every step. "I'm leaving. There's nothing here for me anymore, nothing I want to be a part of."

"What about the butcher girl? Lily?"

Grace stopped on the threshold of the room, her hand on the doorframe.

"I had wondered who provided you with the collateral to leave the city." Mama heaved a sigh, examining her fingernails for dirt. "Humans. Unfortunate, but necessary. Not all of them, though."

"No."

The word came out from between Grace's lips so quietly that at first I wasn't sure if she had said it aloud, or if the word had just risen in her throat and died there, too desperate to be spoken.

"Perhaps it is time that she is bitten."

Grace clenched her fists, her chin falling to her chest. "No."

"Or simply...replaced."

She spun on her heels and my heart broke to see tears welling at the corner of her eyes. Her fists shook at her side. "Stop it, Mama!"

With a touch that in any other context might have been construed as tender, Mama placed her hand on Grace's shoulder, leaning so that her mouth was beside her granddaughter's ear. "This life that you're so proud of, Grace, exists only because I allow it." She tightened her fingers around Grace's shoulder. "I can take it all away from you, piece by piece, bite by bite. Never forget that." Mama stroked Grace's long hair with her other hand. "Go with Marcus. Find out who's doing this to us. Kill them. Then both dens will belong to us, as they should have from the beginning."

Chapter Ten

Grace

We walked out of the den house unmolested. Even Sylvia was missing from her usual place at the front desk. Outside, the day was shaping up to be a beautiful one — a cloudless sky overhead, a soft cool breeze playing among the trees planted along the street. Marcus led the way to the car, parked a block up from the house on a side street.

I sat, folded in the passenger seat of the pristine rental, looking out of the window. I held my arms tight against my body, splaying my legs out in front of me. I tensed when I felt Marcus watching me from the driver's side.

There was a jingle as Marcus dropped his keys into his lap. He sighed. "Grace, I am so, so sorry. I—"

"Oh, shut up, Marcus." I shook the whole car when I kicked the floor. I pushed my hair out of my face with both hands and let out a shaky breath. "How the hell did she find out about Lily?"

"She didn't hear about her from me, I promise you."

"And you." I glared at him, fury writ on every line of my face. "You should have told me. About the letter. You should have told me what Colquhoun did."

"I couldn't, Grace."

I held up a quivering hand, my brows falling into a hard line. "If you're going to say that you had your orders one more time, I'm going to stick my foot so far up your ass, you'll be tasting rubber for a month." I doubled over, hugging myself. "I was out. Do you understand that? I had a life. It wasn't much of one, but it was mine. And then you had to come along..."

"You think I wanted this?" Marcus shifted in his seat so his back pressed against the driver's side door, one hand gripping the headrest, the other wrapping around the steering wheel. "You think I wanted this to happen?"

"I think you're delighted," I said, my voice cracking.

"I wanted to keep you out of this, Grace!" He flung his hands up in the air, and fell back into his seat with a thud. "I just wanted you safe! Jesus Christ, don't you think that I, of all people, know how important being normal is to you?"

"Then why didn't you say no?" I looked up through the windshield and into the clear blue sky. "When the Feóndulf told you to find me, to deliver this message to Mama, why didn't you say no?"

"They would've sent someone else," said Marcus, his voice hushed. "And I wanted to keep you safe." Swallowing, he reached up as if he was about to pinch the bridge of his nose, but stopped himself just before touching his swollen face. "Besides, I couldn't. You could've, but not me. It doesn't work that way for people like me."

"Not this bitten versus born shit again." I collapsed back into my seat, jabbing a finger into Marcus' arm. "You know the only person holding you down is you, Marcus."

"That might be the stupidest thing to ever come out of your mouth, and that's saying something." Marcus' eyes were wide. "Do you have any idea what it's like to be treated like a second-class citizen by your own damn family?"

"Then don't let them treat you that way!"

"Oh right, right! Why didn't I think of that?" He laughed, shouting. "I can tear down an entire social system that prioritizes the voices and well-being of one group over another, just by insisting they treat me a little nicer. Of course, genius!" He leaned into my half of the car, forcing me to look him in the eyes. "And they're just going to listen to me, are they?" Throwing himself back into his seat, he grabbed the steering wheel, throttling it with both hands. "I will always, always be a tool to them, Grace. The best I can hope for is to be a useful tool."

"You're a tool, all right," I muttered, crossing my arms high over my chest, and tucking my chin.

Marcus stared at me for several long, quiet moments, his jaw clenched. He looked away, drawing a hand down his chin. "Okay. Okay. Listen, you're upset." He threw his hand up toward his face. "I've got a broken fucking nose." He retrieved his keys from between his legs and forced them into the ignition. "Let's go back to the hotel, clean up then we can talk about what to do next, all right?"

I shouldered open the passenger-side door, got out and slammed it shut behind me.

Marcus got out of the car and stood watching me pound my way down the street. "Grace!"

I crossed the road without looking for traffic, turned the corner and was gone.

Without giving much thought to where I was headed, I marched through Queen Anne toward Seattle Center, my feet taking over as my head and heart were adrift in a hurricane of thoughts and feelings.

I pushed open the door to the butcher shop, a rush of cold, blood-scented air greeting me. Lily stood behind the counter, wrapping a large flank steak in a parcel of brown paper, and chatting with a small Asian woman. The woman appeared to be in her mid-forties, but smelled closer to four or five hundred years old.

"Hey there," said Lily in her customer service tone. "Welcome — be with you in a minute."

The woman turned when I entered, her dark brown eyes widening, her smile disappearing. She looked away as if she had just caught sight of something obscene. Hunching over, she brought her handbag closer to her body.

Lily finished wrapping the meat with sure, steady hands, and passed the package over with a nod. "There you go, Mrs. Kimura. Cook that like I said, and it should come out bloody like you want."

Mrs. Kimura murmured something, returning the nod and clutching the meat to her chest. With a final worried glance at me, she scurried for the door.

I waited for the other werewolf to leave, listening for the chime on the door as it swung shut. When it sang out, I leaned my forearms on top of the display case, resting my chin on my wrists. "Got any lunch plans?"

Arms akimbo, Lily lifted a brow. "I have a feeling I do now."

It was a forty-minute walk from the shop to Pike Place Market, but it'd been a year since I'd been in town, and I was craving the fresh delights of Mee Sum Pastry. Lily and I waited patiently in the lunch rush line outside the simple red storefront, sandwiched between a group of businessmen on a break from a conference and a family of tourists from Florida. The Mee Sum Pastry staff were, however, more than equipped to handle the crowd in their usual quick and personable manner, and before long, we were sitting on a bench in front of Victor Steinbrueck Park, food in hand.

Telling the story of the morning took considerably less time than living it. I did my best not to overwhelm Lily with details, giving us both time to eat, digest and insert personal comments where appropriate. I left out the part where Mama had threatened her, deciding internally that was something of which my friend need not be aware.

I bit into the fluffy bottom of my hom bow, sinking my teeth through the layers of sweet yeast roll and into the hunks of Chinese barbecue pork. Hand to my mouth, I finished my tale. "And then, he starts going on and on about how hard it is for him, because he's bitten and not born, and it just makes me want to strangle him even more." Chewing, I shook my head, staring out into the pulsating crowd of people.

Lily, having finished her food a few minutes earlier, wiped her hands clean with a napkin. "How did it make you feel when Mama hurt him?"

"What?" I thought about it for a moment, and took another bite of bow, scowling. "I don't really know. It all happened so fast."

So fast that I had almost been unable to restrain myself from going for Mama's throat.

I swallowed too soon, the gooey mass of food sticking in my gullet and making me cough. I knew that Lily couldn't read minds, but the side-eye she shot at me as I struggled to get my food down made me paranoid.

Lily hummed, dropping her napkin into her lap. She rolled her shoulders back against the stone bench, folding her hands together. "So, somebody's out there killing werewolves. And they came after you."

I popped the last bite of bow into my mouth, shrugging. "I mean, it's nothing new, really. There's always someone out there killing werewolves. It's just usually some kook in a cabin somewhere who offs some low-level den member who's being reckless, picking off local hikers or something. Never den leaders." I crumpled my napkin into a ball. "We're too well protected for that."

"You seem pretty calm at the prospect of having a target on your back."

I paused mid-action, sucking my fingers clean of sauce and crumbs. I blinked. "I guess I haven't really thought about it. Been too angry."

"Jesus, Grace." Lily glanced around, lowering her voice and leaning in toward me. "Two werewolves are dead, and the person who did it has already come after you once! And they would've killed you...if Marcus hadn't been there to pull your ass out of the fire."

Hearing it phrased like that, I winced. "I would've figured something out, I'm sure."

Lily scoffed, shaking her head. "Sure, you would've." Shifting on the hard bench, she leaned back and fixed me with a stare. "You're wrong by the way. About Marcus."

"Hm?"

"You've always been wrong. He's dealing with something you've never had to experience. Being an outsider, being othered —"

"I've never experienced being an outsider?" I cut in, sputtering.

"Being seen as less than, just because of what you are?" Lily plowed forward, an edge of anger to her voice.

I passed the crumpled paper I was holding from hand to hand, squeezing it tight. "If he would just... I don't know —"

"What? Pull himself up by his bootstraps? It's not that simple, Grace, and you know that. Damn, it's like you're being dumb on purpose." Lily shook her head and swallowed. "Take it from me. Try to see things from his perspective. Put yourself in his place, and ask yourself what that kind of systematic oppression does to a person day after day, year after year. There's a reason he is the way he is."

We sat without speaking for a few minutes. It was a comfortable silence, a silence that needed no easing or explanation. We sat and watched as the parade of people passed before us, each of us lost in our own thoughts.

I leaned down, my elbows resting on my knees. "I...owe him an apology. Don't I?"

Lily nodded. "At the very least. Damn."

I groaned. "I hate apologizing."

"I know you do." Lily stretched her arms in both directions across the back of the bench. "But it sounds like you two are going to be rubbing shoulders for a while, and if you'd like to do that without killing each other, an apology isn't a bad place to start."

Chapter Eleven

Marcus

Standing in the middle of my hotel room, I was in the midst of unbuttoning my bloodstained white dress shirt when a single knock rang out from the other side of the door. Undoing the buttons at my cuffs, I crossed the room toward the door and peered through the peephole.

Grace stood in the hallway, arms hanging limply at her side, her gaze heavenward. I leaned back from the door, tongue probing the inside of my cheek. I could always pretend not to be in. But somehow that level of pettiness just took too much damn effort. Sighing, I reached down and unlocked the door.

The portal swung open with a shushing sound, sliding over the plush carpet of the room. I stood in the doorway, jaw clenched, an expectant expression on my face.

Grace took a step back and looked me over. She rubbed at her arm. "You look gorgeous."

I instinctually lifted my hand to the puffy white cotton gauze taped over my nose. Purplish green swathes of skin stretched under both of my eyes. Thanks to my werewolf constitution, in a few more hours, the bruises would go yellow then disappear. I dropped my other hand from the door handle, resting my weight on my back foot and looking down my nose at her. "I always thought bruises brought out my eyes."

Grace answered by jerking her head toward the room behind me. "Can I come in?"

I could have said no. I should have said no. So naturally, I stepped back, sweeping my arm inward. Grace slid past me and into the room, walking past the bathroom, and into the main living area.

The curtains were drawn back from the windows, sunlight illuminating the otherwise dim room. The place was sparse and clean — the only indications that the room was occupied at all were the open laptop computer on the desk, and the two large suitcases stacked next to the dresser.

Slipping her fidgeting hands into her pockets, Grace stopped in the middle of the room. "Where'd you get the gauze?"

"First aid kit, front desk." I moved around her and sat down on the end of the bed. "They wanted to call an ambulance, but I talked them out of it."

Grace nodded and began pacing, her attention fixed on her feet. "Did you have to rebreak it?"

I lifted a brow. "You volunteering?"

Grace stopped mid-step and shot me a dirty look. I smiled wryly, pleased to get a rise out of her, collapsing farther into the mattress until I was leaning back on one arm. "No. My boyish good looks will remain intact."

She resumed her pacing. "Good." She stopped again, wincing. She risked a glance in the mirror in front of her, and focused on me. I met her gaze in the mirror and she looked away first, crossing her arms under her bosom. "Hey, about what I said before..."

"Yes?"

She took in a breath through her nose, turned around, and pressed a hand to her chest. "I was... I was just...in the car, that was..."

Her mouth opened and closed, but no words came out. She cleared her throat. "I guess what I'm trying to say is... I was... Well, I was out of line. And taking my crap out on you. Which isn't, really, unusual..."

She pinched herself through her jeans and glanced up at me once more. Brows raised, I could feel the corners of my mouth twitching. Frustration seemingly reaching its peak, Grace slouched violently, her head lolling back on her neck. "Look, I'm really fucking sorry, okay?"

"Good God." I let out a huff of air, seesawing onto my feet. "That was painful to watch."

I disappeared into the bathroom and returned with two crystal glasses. Setting them on top of the mini-fridge, I bent over and opened the tiny appliance. After rummaging through the contents, I straightened, a snack-sized bottle of bourbon held aloft. "Drink?"

"No." Grace sighed, walking over and taking my place on the end of the bed, her hands falling between her knees. "Why doesn't apologizing ever make me feel any better?"

"Because you still screwed up, and saying you're sorry doesn't change that." I cracked open the screw-top, sipping at the bourbon. "If it does make you feel better, I accept your apology. It was a rough morning for both of us."

"It does. It does make me feel better," she said, watching me as I emptied the entire bottle of liquor into one of the thick glasses. She shrugged. "What now?"

After a moment of hesitation, I lowered myself onto the bed next to her, mimicking her slouched stance. "Well...think we can work together?"

Head hanging low between her shoulders, Grace took in a deep breath and let it out slow. "Honestly, Marcus, I don't know."

"Oh, come now." I nudged her shoulder with my own. "It'll be fun. Just like old times."

"That's what I'm worried about."

I took another drink to steady myself, being this close to her still difficult. I held my finger to my lips as I swallowed. "We'll take it one step at a time. I promise."

"And what's step number one?" Grace lifted her head, her tired eyes lighting up with surprise as she looked into my bruised face. Before she could stop herself, she raised her hand to my cheek, thumb ghosting over my bandaged cheekbone, fingertips resting against my jaw.

"Shit," she whispered. "Mama really did a number on you, didn't she?"

I froze for a moment, the touch and concern both so unexpected and so, so deeply wanted. Before I could overthink what either could mean, I leaned my face into her hand, the tip of my tongue darting out to wet my bottom lip. "Not as bad as last time." I closed my eyes, grimacing a little at the memory. "Last time I was in bed for a week while everything healed."

Grace shook her head. "Every time you come here you get hurt. No wonder you never came back."

My eyes fluttered open. I furrowed my brow as I reached up and wrapped my hand around her wrist. "I couldn't."

She stared back at me, her eyes wide, uncomprehending. I took a deep breath and brought her hand down, moving so our fingers became interlaced. "Grace, when the Feóndulf Council found out what happened between us, I was..." I swallowed and looked away. "Well, I had overstepped the boundaries of my duties, let's put it that way. They didn't let me leave Cardiff again for years. That's why I never came back." I brought our entwined hands up to my chest, looking up at her from under my brow, shaking my head. "Did you think —?"

Pulling her hand free, Grace stood, striding quickly toward the open windows, her voice flat and heavy as concrete slabs. "It doesn't really matter anymore, does it?"

"It does," I said, hurrying after her and recapturing her hand. "It does to me."

Grace turned around, lips parted to speak, but words went silent between us as we stood there, looking at each other with unvarnished earnestness and regret. All this time, she had thought I had abandoned her. All this time she thought that I had run away from her, from what we had. No wonder she...

Grace looked down at our hands, and her face flushed. I couldn't stop myself. I closed the distance between us with a step and guided her face up with a gentle push of my forehead against her own, breath sticking in my throat when she didn't resist, when she leaned in, when I felt her lips on the corner of my mouth.

The laptop on the desk beside us flashed to life and burst into song. We flew apart as if struck by lightning, with me cursing aloud as I rushed over to my computer, leaning down to see exactly what it was doing.

"Fuck," I said after a moment. I straightened, rubbing my chin with one hand as I gestured to the screen. "It's, ah, it's the Council. They're calling. I, I have to take this."

"Yeah, right, yeah." Grace pushed her hand back through her hair as she stumbled backward toward the connecting door that joined our two rooms. "I'll just…"

"You don't have to go," I said, spinning the desk chair around so I could collapse into it. "This should only take a minute."

"No, I'm going to…" Grace nodded and hurried through the still ajar portal, waving an awkward goodbye. "Yeah. It's fine."

Grace

Scuttling out of Marcus' room and into my own, I pushed the door halfway closed behind me, my hands on my face in an attempt to calm myself. Heading for the bathroom to splash some cold water on the back of my neck, I heard Marcus' voice take on an edge of surprise as he answered the video call.

"Mr. Hughes, sir!"

"Bowen," answered a male voice. There was a pause, then, with revulsion dripping from every word, the voice continued. "You look like hell, boy."

I froze. My nose wrinkled as my upper lip pulled up into a disgusted sneer. Before I could convince myself not to, I stepped back toward the connecting door and eased it open an inch.

The back of Marcus' head blocked most of the screen, but past his shoulder I found myself staring into a sharp, small face. Olive eyes pricked at my skin through the screen as the older man glared at Marcus, a scowl drawn tight across his lips, like an arrow drawn back on a bow string.

"Yes, sir," answered Marcus. He straightened in his chair, tugging at the bottom of his dress shirt. "Sorry, sir."

The man on the screen blinked. He drew in a deep breath before leaning back in his chair, which I noted was high-backed and plush. He surveyed Marcus with a look I knew well — if he'd been wearing glasses, he'd be looking over them at the younger man.

"The old bat did that to you, did she?" he said, not without sympathy.

Marcus moved as if he were going to turn down the volume on the computer, but seemed to think better of it. He nodded instead, his hands twisting in his lap. "Yes, sir."

I felt my eyes narrow, and my grip on the edge of the door tightened.

"We expected to hear from you after your meeting, get a full report." The man, Hughes, pursed his lips. "We were...surprised to receive word from the Nameless first."

"I'm sorry, sir. I'll be more prompt in the future."

"It would be appreciated," said Hughes. "But still, if you were attacked, it can't be helped."

"Thank you, sir."

"I understand that Mama wishes for you to continue your investigation into these killings from America. You'd be operating under her protection, and under the supervision of her granddaughter, Grace Holtz."

Marcus leaned forward. "More in cooperation with, than under the supervision of, sir."

Hughes seemed to consider this for a moment, his brow furrowing. At length he shook his head, his hand coming up to wave through the air. "Needless to say, the Council finds this suggestion utterly unacceptable. We sent you there in a show of good faith, to warn Mama and her people about what was coming. Now that impossible woman thinks she can usurp the situation to her own benefit."

"But, sir," said Marcus, "with respect, if Mama and her heir are the next targets, doesn't it make sense to stay close to them? Ms. Holtz has already been attacked once."

"And what did you do when you had the chance to capture the assassin?" Hughes brought his fist down onto his knee. "You let your past history with the Holtz pup cloud your judgment so severely that the murderer escaped from right under your nose! This is your chance to redeem yourself, Bowen—a chance not everyone on the Council thinks you deserve. I had to personally reassure several members that we could rely on you."

"I understand that, sir, but—"

"Do you?" The older gentleman leaned forward into his camera, his face becoming stretched and distorted by the lens. "You're bitten, Bowen. I don't expect you to fully appreciate the intricacies of den politics, but understand this. Keep thinking with your balls instead of your brains, and you risk losing them. We've done far worse for far less."

I felt an ache in my jaw, and realized that I'd been grinding my teeth for the past few minutes. My breath came out in short, quick bursts through my nose. Seeing Marcus debase himself in front of this pompous, vainglorious old wolf, knowing what I knew now about the years I had spent in abject misery in the house on Queen Anne, nursing my pain until it cooled and turned to hatred, turned into action — violence was never my first instinct, but I found myself struggling to keep the wolf in check.

Oblivious to the feelings he was arousing in me, Hughes continued to instruct his foot soldier. "For the time being, the Council will allow you to remain in Seattle and continue your investigation. But you are still answerable to us. If the Nameless wish to provide their aid in this matter, that's their business. Your first priority is the capture, or extermination, of the individual who murdered our den leaders — everything else is immaterial. Everything. Am I understood?"

Marcus rolled his shoulders back against his chair and lifted his chin. "Perfectly, sir."

The older man reached forward toward his computer. "We've arranged for you to have access to all your materials digitally for now. Evidence from the first two crime scenes, police reports, et cetera. Let me know if there's anything else you require, and I'll see what I can do." Hughes smiled, leaning forward. "Happy hunting, Bowen. Remember — I'm counting on you to do your duty this time."

The video flashed to black, and Marcus' own reflected face filled the screen. My breath caught in my throat at the sight of him. His shoulders were stooped, and his normally lively face was as still as stone, expressionless and hard. After a moment, his eyes flickered up and met mine.

"Heard all that, did you?"

I re-entered the room, stopping a few feet behind Marcus' chair. "Who the hell was that asshole?"

"Lawrence Hughes, he's the head of the Council." Marcus slid down in his seat and let out a long breath. "He takes some getting used to."

"He's a dickhead, that's what he is," I pronounced with conviction. My opinion made clear, I stepped toward Marcus, knitting my brows together. I lifted my hand toward his arm. "Hey, are you okay?"

Marcus stood and walked around me, avoiding my hand. "Yeah, I'm fine." With quick, mechanical movements, he untucked and unbuttoned his white dress shirt, discarding the bloodied item of clothing onto the floor. "Lunch?"

"Had it." I watched him, my head falling to one side. "You sure you're—"

"I'm sure." He didn't snap, but his tone left no room for further discussion. Marcus slid open the closet and slipped a black silk shirt off a hanger. He threw it over his undershirt as he spoke. "Hungry is all. I'm going out, get some food."

Turning on his heel, he strode to the computer and, after clicking and typing for a few moments, a series of windows popped open. He straightened and gestured toward the device, before finishing tucking in his fresh shirt. "Why don't you get yourself up to speed on the case, such as it is? All my notes, evidence analysis, it should be there." Without waiting for me to answer, he headed for the hotel room door, swiping his keys and jacket into his hands as he walked. "I'll be back in an hour."

"O-kay," I said, but I said it to a closing door. Once again, I was alone.

Chapter Twelve

Marcus

I stood in front of my car, keys in my hand, staring at the black vehicle but not really seeing it. After a moment, I glanced up at the façade of the hotel, searching for the windows of the room I had just left. I shoved the keys into my pocket and took a step backward, falling against the side of my rental car with a thud. I closed my eyes and felt the sun on my face. I took a deep breath, but shame still burned hot in my chest, like a poker that'd been left to heat in a fire.

Opening my eyes with a shake of my head, I started to walk down the street, my hands shoved deep in my pockets.

All these years, and nothing had changed. I still wasn't good enough.

I thought back to that first night Grace and I had been together in that very hotel...the only night fate had, thus far, allowed us.

I tossed and turned in the hotel bed, unable to sleep. My thin gold bracelet stuck to my forearm, catching at the sheets as I moved. The air in the room was close and heavy, like lying inside a cotton ball. Turning over onto my back, I forced myself to lie still, one arm thrown up over my head. I breathed in the thick air. Grace's scent surrounded and penetrated the room, the older werewolf sleeping beside me, curled beneath a single thin sheet, breathing heavily. I glanced over at her, and the magnitude of what we'd done settled on me like a weighted blanket. I struggled up off the bed, careful not to wake my companion, and walked to the open window. Even at this late hour, I could watch the occasional car slide by on the street below. I leaned my naked body against the sill and crossed my arms over my chest.

What was I doing?

This wasn't part of the plan. This didn't help me. This didn't help her. But…

I looked back at the sleeping Grace and felt the tug in my chest. I closed my eyes and rubbed my forehead.

Shit.

At times like this, I caught myself wishing I'd never been bitten. True, my options had been limited at the time, bleeding to death as I had been under the snow-covered trees of the Ardennes. Immortality had sounded particularly enticing when looking at my own entrails, no matter what the cost.

It had never occurred to me then, or since, that one day I would meet someone who meant more to me than all the years of life I could possibly live — that I would die, right then and there, if it meant keeping her safe. How could someone prepare for that kind of love?

Love like that did not exist in my world. My father had left when I was a child, running off to live with another woman. Seeing in me only the reflection of the man who had broken her heart, my mother cared for me the same way other people cared for farm animals – dutifully, but without attachment or adoration. When I was old enough to strike out on my own, I knew I would not be welcomed back.

I remembered with clarity the time when she had a diseased kidney removed. A pessimistic woman, she had a letter delivered to my apartment the day of the surgery. "To my son," *the letter started,* "in case the worst should happen, and I die on the operating table, I want you to know I have only one regret in life – giving birth to you."

I enlisted the next day.

I had never been more than a mediocre soldier. I had no love for the military and I was a disposable cog in a merciless machine, one man in a sea of millions. The Second World War came, and I was swept onto the continent and left there to die. After being bitten, I felt the first flush of love, or what I had thought was love. I belonged. I was part of a family that depended on me. I was useful in a way I had never been before. It didn't matter that there were certain parts of that family that resented my existence – every family had to have a black sheep. As long as I was included, as long as they felt something about me, it was better than nothing. But a tool was only valued when it worked the way it was supposed to – now, it turned out I couldn't even do that. I was dysfunctional – a diseased kidney in the body of the Feóndulf, in danger of being removed.

I opened my eyes and turned to drink in the sight of her sleeping form. I was only somewhat disappointed to find her sitting up on the edge of the mattress, sheets crumpled and pooled in her lap, staring at me in the dark.

"Did I wake you?" *I asked, my arms falling to my sides.*

Grace shook her head. "You thinking of jumping, or just admiring the view?"

A surprised laugh tripped from my lips. "The second, I promise."

Her head falling to one side, Grace extended a hand toward me. Without hesitation, I crossed the room, taking her hand and collapsing onto the mattress with her. She laid me down and, once I was reclined, she curled her body against my side and rested her head on top of my chest. I reached up and smoothed her wild hair out of my face, kissing the top of her head and closing my eyes as I tried to memorize the feel of her body. For this woman, I had risked what little happiness I had known. With her, I saw the possibility of love, not in spite of my faults, but because of them. I saw someone who might love me because of my fragility, my human foibles and my weaknesses.

Did I deserve that kind of love?

"I'm not what you need, Grace," I murmured.

Grace shifted against me, bringing her hand to rest flat against my abdomen. "What do you mean?"

"You need someone…" I closed my eyes, feeling the words like marbles in my mouth. "You need someone strong. Someone brave and…whole."

Grace hummed and I felt her head pivot to look up at me. "But I love you."

I smiled ruefully in the dark, drawing my hand through her hair once more. "Ah. More's the pity."

Grace moved her hand from my abdomen up to my shoulder. She squeezed me tight. "Don't sell yourself so short, Marcus."

"I know what I am, Grace," I said, shaking my head.

"You're the only person who ever looked at me, and told me I could be more than what other people wanted me to be."

I closed my eyes and breathed her deep into my lungs. "I love you, too."

Over thirty years later, I repeated the gesture, walking down the street in search of a meal that would fill the empty pit of my stomach. But I could only smell the city around me, and not her. I was as I'd been for a very long time — alone and hurt, with only my memories to keep me company.

* * * *

Grace

I did my best to focus on the autopsy findings and forensic reports that Marcus had left for me. Aidan and Colquhoun had been bloody coagulations of flesh and bone by the time they had finally been put out of their misery, with silver bullets to the heart. Beaten, branded and sliced... The medical examiner had theorized that they would've been unconscious for most of the horror that was visited upon them. But the medical examiner was not as intimately familiar with the werewolf constitution as me. They didn't know the amount of pain and damage our bodies were capable of withstanding.

I was sure the Colquhouns had been awake and aware of every agonizing moment. The woman who had taken me would've made sure of it.

The torture troubled me. Aidan's injuries, I could almost understand. If the woman who had kidnapped me was a creature of habit, doubtless she had been probing the younger Colquhoun for information about his father. But why torture Colquhoun? Just to get at a few musty personal diaries? Or was there something else? Something I wasn't seeing?

The hour passed quickly, and before I knew it, the sound of a keycard against a lock roused me from my contemplations. I sat up straight in the desk chair, stretching my stiff back. "Enjoy your lunch?" I asked without turning around.

"Americans — why is everything here served in inhuman proportions? I swear, I was given a French dip the length of my arm."

"We do it big in the States." I shifted in my seat to look at Marcus, tossing my hands out toward the screen. I had pulled up the crime scene photos in which Aidan Colquhoun and his father's dead bodies were on full, horrific display. "Thanks for sharing these. I'm going to have nightmares for weeks."

The door clicked shut behind Marcus as he undid the button on his suit jacket. He bared his teeth in a grimace, his arms akimbo. "Yes. Gruesome, isn't it?"

"When you said 'some time' was taken with Aidan and his father, I didn't know you meant anything like this..."

Marcus walked to the lounge chairs that sat beside the workstation and folded himself into one, sighing as he sat. "Someone was very unhappy with them."

"Or wanted something they didn't want to give." I looked over at him and answered his questioning glance with a smile. "Based on my own experience. The woman who took me wanted information. About Mama. I'm guessing Aidan was asked similar questions about his father."

"That might explain the location of Colquhoun's murder." Marcus gestured toward the laptop. "At his private residence. We were confused how an outsider gained access, but if Aidan gave her information about the layout of the house, grounds, security protocols — "

"And he would've. After all this, he would've." A shiver passed through me as I considered how close I had come to sharing Aidan's fate. Shaking the thought away, I scowled, turning my mind back to the questions at hand. "Still…a ballsy choice, yeah? I mean, why not wait until the old man was someplace more public and kill him then? Like they did with Aidan—he was taken from outside one of his favorite Dublin clubs. Why risk going on to Feóndulf turf? Was Colquhoun particularly vulnerable at home?"

"Of course not. That place was guarded like Buckingham Palace."

"Then why?"

"A scare tactic? Show the rest of us they can get to us wherever we are?" Marcus slid down in his chair, resting the side of his head against his fingertips. "Or maybe there was something the killer wanted or needed at Colquhoun's home. Perhaps it wasn't mere opportunity that led them to rifle through Colquhoun's private papers. Perhaps they were the goal all along."

"What was in these diaries anyway?"

"No idea," Marcus conceded. "It's not as if I'm allowed to read them."

"What? Why not?"

"Bitten, remember?" He avoided my gaze, forcing himself farther down in the plush chair. "Hell, even most of the born Feóndulf aren't high enough on the food chain to get that kind of access. The Council has got them locked up tight. The only reason I was able to read Colquhoun's letter to Mama was because I got to it first."

"Then there's that." I swiveled in my seat to face him. "What did that letter say?"

Marcus hesitated. I reached over, grabbing his forearm. "You read it, Marcus. What did it really say?"

"I did want to tell you about Colquhoun naming you as his heir, Grace." Marcus sighed. "I just didn't know what to say. It's not the sort of thing you drop on someone out of the blue."

"What the hell was he thinking?" I released him and pushed away from the desk. Standing, I threw my hands into the air. "Feóndulf don't even allow women on the Council. The idea of one leading the entire den — the Council must have gone out of their minds."

"They're…not happy. But there's not much they can do about it. Colquhoun's word was, very literally, the law."

I stood in front of the recumbent werewolf, my arms crossed over my chest. "What do you think I should do?"

"About the Feóndulf?" Marcus smiled ruefully, pushing his hand back through his hair as he straightened. "Grace, I know you well enough to know that you're going to do whatever you think is best, regardless of my opinion. So, why bother asking for it?"

I gave a snort of laughter before rolling my eyes. "Politeness, I suppose. Interest." Sobering, I shook my head. "I have no intention of becoming anyone's den leader, Marcus. I'll resign or abdicate, or whatever they want to call it, before I let that happen."

Marcus nodded. "I can't pretend to be surprised. And of course, I support you all the way. If it's not what you want, it's not what you want. All that being said…you'd have done a hell of a job, Grace."

The sincerity in his voice touched me more than I cared to let on. I turned away from him, my hands falling to my sides. "Let's just…table that part of the letter for now. What else did it say?"

"Honestly, it didn't make much sense. Not to me, anyway." Marcus stood, shoving his hand into his trouser pocket. "The old man was pretty torn up about

Aidan, that much was obvious. He went on about fathers burying their sons, and how it was against the natural order of things. How it was punishment for what he'd done, that God had finally seen fit to punish him and Mama both, and that soon Mama would know what it felt like to see all that she built destroyed. And that giving you the den was the only way to make amends for what happened."

"Punishment? What did he do?"

Marcus drew his brows to a point. "The lawless bastard was over a thousand years old. It'd be easier to figure out what sins he hadn't committed."

"It sounds like he was expecting to die. Why? Did he know someone was coming after him?" Frowning, I walked back to the laptop, leaning over and clicking through the various pictures and reports. "What about Aidan's death made him think he was next?"

I stopped on the picture of Colquhoun's mutilated body, and stared at it for longer than I cared to. The stout, muscular old man was splayed out in a plush leather chair behind a large wooden desk, hands and feet bound to the chair with chains. Blood colored everything in the picture in various shades of brown and red, seeping into the white and blue striped pajamas the man had been wearing. A large bullet wound was visible in the chest, the skin and cloth charred black. It was the charring that enabled the splotch of white to be visible at all in the photograph. It caught my eye like the glint of a knife, and I zoomed in on the speck until the picture pixelated beyond recognition.

"What's this?" I circled the blotch of color with my finger. "On his chest, there?"

"It's a daisy," said Marcus. "Curious, isn't it? We found one on Aidan, too. Same position, placed there after death, near as we can tell." He switched his gaze from the pixelated photograph to my face, brow furrowing. "Does it mean anything to you?"

"No." Grimacing, I straightened. "Something very strange is going on here. The person who took me wasn't a hunter. I'm sure of it. Something about all this isn't right."

"I agree," said Marcus. "But I can't go back to the Council with a 'something doesn't seem right' feeling. I need evidence."

"You're the detective. Where do you suggest we start?"

"Well, whoever this woman is, hopefully we've thrown her off your trail."

"You think?" I said. "Doesn't take a genius to predict that I might end up back in the city, after what happened. Scared right back into Mama's protective arms, as it were."

"True, but even if she knows that, Seattle is a big place. She'll have no idea where to start looking." Marcus rubbed his chin, his gaze distant. "She'll need an in. She'll have to find a werewolf to squeeze for information."

I grinned. "I love it when you talk cop."

Marcus shot me a glare, but couldn't smother a smile of his own. "If you were her, and you needed to track down a werewolf in a strange city where you knew no one, where would you start?"

I thought for a moment. "Get the lay of the land from some experts," I answered at length. "Get information from people who know the area, and know anything about my targets." My head tilted to one side and I looked past Marcus' shoulder. "Huh. I wonder..."

"What?"

I pursed my lips. "It's a long shot. They might not even be active anymore. But there was a group, years ago..." I crossed my arms over my chest. "A few local wolves got sloppy. Well, reckless, really. Mama...dealt with them, but the damage was done. This local collective of monster hunters got interested, and were poking around for a while."

"Do you think the Nameless still keep tabs on them?"

"Oh, definitely. Once you're on the Nameless' radar, you never really fall off. We're very vigilant like that. Or paranoid, depending on how you want to look at it." I started forward, walking through the open connecting door and into my own room. "Let me make a call."

I plucked my cell phone off the dresser where I had tossed it earlier and unlocked it, typing in the number from memory. My gaze flickered up to Marcus as he moved into the doorway, leaning up against the frame, but the sight of him watching me did nothing to ease the jittering of my nerves while I waited for the other phone to pick up. When it did, I turned away from him, lowering the volume of my voice without intentional thought.

"It's me." I nodded. "Yeah, I'm... I don't really want to get into it." I sighed, casting my eyes heavenward and tapping my foot. "Look, do you remember those kooks from a decade back who were trying to track werewolf sightings in the Seattle area?"

While the person on the other end of the line talked, I scrambled for a pad of paper and a pen. "Yeah, that's them. They still around?" I scribbled onto the hotel scratch pad, nodding. "And where do they meet up?" I underlined the place and time and smiled. "Great, thanks. I owe you one."

I hung up the phone and turned back to face Marcus. "We're in luck. They're having a get-together tonight."

Marcus rubbed his hands together, grinning. "I sense we're going to be crashing a party."

"Kind of." I tapped my phone against the pad of paper. "How do you feel about libraries?"

Chapter Thirteen

Marcus

As she described it, the Central Branch of the Seattle Public Library held a special place in Grace's heart. Although she had been a devoted patron of the first two iterations of the library building, she admitted to a certain fondness for the newest design. The jagged glass and steel structure had become her sanctuary as she had worked toward her finance degree in secret.

Standing on the bright yellow escalators, looking out over the wide reading rooms, I caught Grace smiling. She looked relieved, some of the tension that had been present in her since our meeting with Mama having left her body.

Behind her and one step below, I leaned forward. "How did these people secure space in a place like this?"

"Hey," said Grace, stepping off the moving staircase. "Libraries are for everybody. Nobody is unwelcome — that's one of the great things about them. Everyone can find their place here."

I lifted a brow, my hands swinging at my sides as we walked toward the stairwell that would take us the rest of the way to the sixth floor.

Grace held the door to the sixth-floor landing open for me and, after walking down a long, silent hallway, we stopped in front of the room marked 'PACCAR Inc., Meeting Room Six.' Grace double-checked the information scribbled on the piece of paper in her hand then, sighing, slid the creased scrap back into her pocket, nodding. "This seems to be the place. Gird your loins."

It was one of the smaller meeting rooms the Central Library had on offer, but it was full of people. I had to give the Cryptozoological Society of Seattle their credit — they could draw a crowd. When we entered the room, at least ten people were sitting in a circle of vinyl rolling chairs. There was a table at the top of the circle, and another table sitting flush against the back wall of the room. This back table had a white plastic tablecloth spread over it, and was partially filled with unopened boxes of donuts and two spouted coffee carriers.

The front of the room housed a projector screen. A bald Caucasian man in thick, black glasses who had been working on starting the mobile projector looked up and walked over to us, his face wrinkled in confusion.

"Hi there," said the gentleman, then understanding lit his wide brown eyes. He pointed toward the door. "Oh! The Romance Readers' Couples Book Club is actually down on Level Five."

Grace turned to look at me, the wide smile spread across my face seeming to throw her into further confusion. "Oh, uh, no—" She struggled for a moment. "Is...this is the meeting for the C.Z.S.S., isn't it?"

"Yes, yes, it is!" The man clasped his hands together in excitement. "How fantastic, new recruits!" He gestured toward the semicircle of chairs behind us, waving us further inside. "Come in, come in! You're just in time. We were just about to get started."

We crossed the room and sat in the two chairs closest to the projector screen, nodding and smiling to the already settled people around us. The room, buzzing with conversation, quieted as the bald man and a plump Asian woman walked toward the front of the circle. The man stopped at the laptop set up on the front table and, with a few clicks, brought up the official C.Z.S.S. logo onto the projector screen.

"Right," he called out, clapping his hands together.

The chatter ceased, and expectant eyes turned to the bald man. He gave a wave. "Hello and welcome to the one-hundred-and-ninety-third meeting of the Cryptozoological Society of Seattle. I am your local chapter president, Harvey Steward, and this is our vice president, Jessica Kwan." The plump woman smiled and waved as well.

Harvey picked up a small black remote from the tabletop. "Before we get started, let's go around the room and introduce ourselves, okay? Tell us your name and your favorite cryptid. You want to get us started?"

Grace plastered on her most charming smile when Harvey indicated her. "Sure." She pivoted toward the center of the circle, her hands clasped in her lap. "Hi, everyone. My name is Anne Hill, and I'm not a hundred percent sure that this counts as a cryptid..."

"Go ahead, go ahead," said Harvey, his hands flapping.

"But I'm really interested in werewolves."

I scanned the assembled faces before us. One or two people broke out into smiles, a few rolled their eyes, but there was one man on the far side of the circle who, at the mention of the word, straightened in his seat and swallowed, staring at Grace with interest.

For his part, Harvey smiled, bringing his hands together around the remote. "Fascinating! Yes, you know, many serious cryptozoologists are hesitant to use the word 'werewolf,' because it conjures up all kinds of ideas about witchcraft and devils and all matters of supernatural nonsense." He paused to laugh, and several members of the group joined him.

Grace looked appropriately bashful.

Harvey continued, nodding in encouragement. "But there are many, many accounts of humanoid creatures with canine features, too many to ignore. The Michigan Dogman, for example, or the Beast of Bray Road. There was even a time, oh it was a handful of decades back now, well before my time in the Society, when there was a rash of so-called werewolf sightings around Seattle itself! The C.Z.S.S. went into full investigative mode then, I can tell you that! And certainly, the lay person would take a look at any of these animals and call them 'werewolves,' almost absolutely. So yes, you can definitely be interested in 'werewolves'."

Harvey turned his attention to me, his brows lifting. "Next?"

I threw my arm around the back of Grace's chair and gave a lazy wave. "Chris Hill, hello all. I'm going to have to go with a classic, and say the Loch Ness Monster."

"Excellent choice," said Harvey, bouncing onto the balls of his feet. "Tonight's talk should be right up your alley then!" Adjusting his glasses, the bald man gestured to the two of us, a smile forming on his lips. "By any chance, are you two...?"

Grace took my hand in hers and squeezed it so hard I gave a strangled cough of pain. "Oh no!" she said with a cheerful grin. "This guy is just my little brother!"

"Oh yeah," said Jessica, nodding. "Now that you say that, I can totally see the resemblance. It's so sweet that you do stuff like this together!"

I waited until a few more members of the group had introduced themselves before extracting my hand from Grace's firm grip.

"Little brother?" I muttered under my breath.

"Very little," Grace responded, lips barely moving.

What followed was a half hour long lecture from Harvey about something called Caddy of Cadboro Bay, an alleged dinosaur or some kind of sea creature that was said to lurk in the waters around Victoria, British Columbia.

As Harvey droned on, I scanned the assembled crowd, taking in deep breaths through my nose. I didn't catch the floral chemical scent that Grace had described her kidnapper smelling of, but that didn't mean the woman wasn't here. I eyed the women in the group with particular interest, but everyone appeared engrossed by Harvey's talk.

At length, Harvey reached his final slide, a picture of an Inuit canoe with an image of Caddy emblazoned on the side. "...and so, you can see that in spite of all these proposed 'explanations' for Caddy—whether it be the enticingly plausible Zeuglodon or basking shark, or the patently ridiculous pipefish or sea lion—no one can fully yet explain the sightings that continue to occur. Until one of these specimens are captured alive, it will be impossible to determine for certain if we are dealing with some kind of ancient throwback, or a new species entirely." He crossed to the far wall and flipped on the lights, his smile broad. "Thank you."

There was a polite round of applause, then Harvey gestured to the table in the back of the room. "Now please, everyone, help yourself to some refreshments, and let's get to know each other even better!"

We got up from our seats, stretching and sharing a look that spoke to our mutual desire to get something useful out of this ordeal as soon as possible. We waited for the group to mingle and coalesce into pockets of conversation, pouring ourselves two cups of thick coffee, then approached Harvey, who squatted alone at the front of the room, dismantling his mobile projector.

"Great talk, Harvey," I said, raising my waxy paper cup to our host. "Really fascinating stuff."

Harvey straightened, brushing off his hands. "So glad you enjoyed it, Chris. I hope you two will become regulars."

"We'd like to," Grace said, nodding.

I took a sip of coffee. "We were curious what kind of crowd you normally get for these monthly meetings, mix of interests, that sort of thing."

"Well, we usually get a few fresh faces, like yours, every meeting." Harvey unplugged his computer from the projector, pursing his lips in thought. "But our tried-and-true members are always anxious to participate in—"

"Any other werewolf enthusiasts lately?" Grace interjected.

I cleared my throat and shot her a look over my coffee. She ignored me.

"Nothing to be enthusiastic about," a voice from behind us growled.

We turned to look at the grizzled older man whom I had noticed staring at Grace earlier in the evening. He had a hiking pack balanced on top of his feet and wiry gray hair sprouting from every direction underneath the orange beanie he wore, which was shoved tight around his oblong temple. Sharp gray eyes glared out of a tan face, the rest of his features hidden by a thick bushy beard. He took a large bite of a powdered donut as I looked him over, nodding slowly as he chewed, his gaze never wavering from Grace's face.

"Ah, Dan," said Harvey. "I was wondering when you'd—"

"They're everywhere, you know," Dan continued, talking around his mouthful of chewed pastry.

Grace shared a look with me as I put an arm around her shoulder. "Who?" she said.

"Werewolves." Dan took a large, slurping gulp of his coffee, tossing his head at our host. "Not like Harvey here would have you believe. They're not skulking through the undergrowth of some backwater, shitting in the woods like animals. They're right here, in this city. Among us, every minute of every day."

Harvey smirked and came around to stand next to me. "Dan here is one of our oldest and most...open-minded members." He leaned in, voice dropping to a whisper. "Mostly just comes in for coffee and something to eat."

I gave an exaggerated nod and winked, but Grace pressed on, her eyes wide. "What do you mean? Wouldn't people notice big wolves walking around downtown?"

Dan leaned forward. "They don't look like wolves all the time. That's the secret."

"Oh. Shapeshifters." I rolled my eyes. "Right."

"Man-eaters are what they are," said Dan with conviction. He popped the last bite of his donut into his mouth, and wiped his fingers on his outer layer of clothes. "And they've got their fingers in everything. Business, politics, the police. It's how they get away with it."

My stomach clenched. Outwardly, Grace maintained her air of innocent awe. "Get away with what?"

"Now, Dan." Harvey stepped up next to the older-looking man, hand ghosting over his shoulder, but ultimately failing to connect. "Anne and Chris don't want to—"

"They take people from the shelters. Say they're going to move them into temporary housing, or get them jobs outside the city. But they never come back. No one ever hears from them again."

I bit down on the inside of my mouth and scoffed. "What makes you think it's werewolves?"

"They took me!" Dan's eyes glazed over as he stared at the space just above my shoulder. "Took me out to Blake Island in the dead of night with about ten others. Hunted us through the woods, picked us off one by one." His gaze flitted down to Grace's face, the terror of the memory writ clear on his face. "I saw them with my own eyes. Huge beasts ripping through men like they were paper dolls. I only got away because I'm a good swimmer. Made it to the beach and swam out until I couldn't swim anymore. A passing sailboat picked me out of the water in the morning."

I took a sip of my coffee, nodding. "Lucky."

Dan fixed me with a glare. He opened his mouth to speak, but Harvey stepped in front of him, his arms raised. "Chris, Anne — let me introduce you to Jessica, okay?"

Grace

We allowed ourselves to be bustled away from Dan and back toward the larger group of C.Z.S.S. members. I kept an eye on the older gentleman, however, and when he tossed back the last of his coffee and headed for the door, I interrupted the flow of conversation.

"Sorry, where's the restroom up here?"

"It's just down the hall," answered Jessica, round face beaming. "Would you like — ?"

"I'm sure I can find it, thanks." Smiling, I strode out of the room, taking out my phone to shoot Marcus a quick text outlining what I was up to, in the hopes that he would follow when he could.

I trailed my quarry at a discreet distance, grateful for the open nature of the library's architecture, as it made him visible from every angle. I watched as Dan exited onto 5th Avenue and, sensing an opportunity, headed out after him.

Pushing the library doors open, I hurried out onto the street, looking this way and that for Dan. For a moment I thought he'd somehow given me the slip, then I spotted him, standing by the bus stop shelter. He had his camping pack hanging off one shoulder and swung in front of him. Muttering to himself, he seemed to be looking for something inside the deep, full bag.

"Dan?" I crab-walked toward the older man, my hands stuffed into my jeans' pockets. "Can I talk to you for a minute?"

Dan pulled and pulled and soon extracted a threadbare blue blanket from the confines of the pack. Without looking up, he shoved the blanket at me, his other hand still pawing through his belongings.

I hesitated, but wanting to form a rapport with the man, took the blanket with one hand, draping it over my left arm to keep it from scraping against the ground. "Dan," I said. "It's obvious that something happened to you. Why don't you talk to someone about it?"

Dan barked out a laugh and shook his head, still rummaging through his pack. "What, like the cops? I went to them. Told them what happened. They tried to hand me over to them again!" He took out an old handkerchief and placed it on top of the blanket, then paused his search to pull his knit cap more snuggly around his temples. "They really are everywhere."

I leaned toward him. "What about the rest of the C.Z.S.S.? Won't they help you?"

"You heard them in there." He dug a pair of socks out of his bag, unrolled them, and shoved them into his jacket pocket. "They don't believe. Well, most of them don't." He met my gaze at last. "You don't."

"Maybe I do." I turned to look behind when I heard the library doors open, hopeful that Marcus had managed to detangle himself from the C.Z.S.S. and join me. "Dan, has anyone else come to the meetings asking about werewolves lately?"

"Maybe. Why?"

"I was thinking, if there were more of us who believed, maybe there would be something we could — "

At that moment, Dan placed something into my open hand. It began to slide across my palm, and I instinctively closed my fist to catch it.

Pain shot up and down my arm, a searing, blinding pain that made my whole body convulse before I could identify what was causing it.

"Shit!"

I shook my arm free of Dan's things, opened my hand and threw the silver St. Christopher medal I'd been holding onto the ground. Grabbing at my hand where an angry red welt was already rising, I stared up at Dan. Face contorted in a mixture of rage and fear, the man struggled to close his backpack and scramble backward at the same time.

"I knew it!" He spat the words at me. "She said you'd come for me! You're one of them. A fucking dog!"

The door behind us opened again, and we both turned to see Marcus standing there, gaze jumping from me, doubled over, holding my hand, to Dan, panic written on every line of his face.

Swiping his medal off the ground, Dan took off in a run. Without needing to be told, Marcus started after him, legs pumping furiously, feet pounding against the pavement. I hesitated, still woozy from the pain, and in that moment, I lost sight of the two men as they rounded the corner.

Cursing, I cast about myself. Scattered around me like so much collateral damage were Dan's belongings, including the handkerchief he had pressed on me. I picked up the small piece of fabric with my good hand and shoved it in my pocket.

After reentering the library to run some cold water over my throbbing palm, I returned to the street, hopeful that Marcus would reappear, while at the same time unsure of what else to do but wait for him. After twenty agonizing minutes, he came back around the corner, disheveled and alone.

I jogged down 5th Avenue to meet him, my hands up in the air. "Well?"

We met in front of an old newspaper dispenser. Marcus, breathing heavily, shook his head and shrugged. "I'm a werewolf, not Superman." He gulped down a large mouthful of air, hands on his hips. "I lost him in the park."

"He definitely knows something. Someone warned him we'd be sniffing around," I said. "I can't be sure it was the same person who killed Colquhoun and took me, but—"

"It's a lead worth following up on, I agree." Marcus drew his hand over his face. "But I lost him."

Grimacing, I lifted my hand between us, showing Marcus the soiled handkerchief I had managed to scoop off the ground. "I think I have a way to find him."

Marcus regarded the rag with deepening horror. He took a step back. He looked at me then back to the handkerchief, the flush of blood draining from his cheeks. "Oh no. No, no, no." He jerked his head toward me and brought his arms across his chest. "You do it."

I advanced on him, the fabric outstretched before me. "You're the detective!"

"And you're supposed to be helping me, so help!" Marcus shrugged, his shoulders coming up to brush the bottom of his ears. "Besides, you're more used to filtering out the smells of the city. I'm liable to get lost."

I was shocked that he had managed to come up with a good point, and I would've told him so if it hadn't made me so damn irritated. Looking down at the dirty handkerchief, I sighed. I squared my shoulders, lifted the rag to my face and took in a deep breath through my nose, my mouth falling open, my nostrils flaring.

It was the smell of the inside of a plastic trash can sitting in a hundred-degree heat, a trash can that was holding the scraps of several day-old raw chicken, moldy avocado, several dozen bags of dog shit and one dead raccoon.

I threw the handkerchief onto the ground and veered away toward the curb, gagging. The coffee I'd consumed climbed up my throat, and I struggled to swallow it back down. Hands on my quivering knees, I spat into the street, eyes closed tight.

As the worst of the nausea passed, I became aware of Marcus' hand on my back. I looked up and over my shoulder, noting that his other hand was holding my hair up and away from my face.

I straightened, but did not move away from his touch. "Oh…I hate my life so much right now."

"I know," said Marcus, patting my shoulder. His brows drew together in a point and he stepped back, shoving his hands in his pockets. "Where to?"

I wiped my mouth clean with the back of my hand and shook myself. "Show me where you lost him."

We headed north on 5th and took a right on Seneca, then headed into Freeway Park, a park made more of geometric blocks of stone than trees or greenery. We wound through the maze-like interior for almost fifteen minutes, before I stopped to sniff the air. It was a strange thing to try to describe to humans, this seeing by smelling. I liked to think of it like those old cartoons. Some matronly character would put a fresh baked pie on a windowsill, and the tendrils of steam would waft across the frames until they found some poor hungry slob, tap them on the shoulder and beckon them back to the precious pie. It was like that, except instead of one single tendril of smell to follow, there were hundreds — thousands in big cities like Seattle — and following one was like trying to follow a single thread in an elaborate tapestry. It could be done, but it took concentration, practice and patience.

I closed my eyes and took in another breath of air, opening my mouth slightly.

Without stopping to see if Marcus was following, I turned on my heel and strode back out the way we had come. I walked us out of the 8th Avenue entrance of the park, then turned back onto Seneca. We passed hotels and cafes before turning again on 3rd Avenue. Almost fifteen minutes later, we came to Yesler Way and, after a few more steps, I stopped short in front of a tall brick building.

The building itself was nondescript in appearance. It could've been one of hundreds anywhere across the city. Its main entrance were two sets of double doors, which sat atop a short flight of stairs. A handful of young men were currently reclining on and around the stairs, and they began to watch me with interest when I moved toward them, sniffing.

"He went in here."

Catching up to me at last, Marcus grabbed me by the arm and pulled me back. "You sure?"

I glared and he released me, his hands held up in front of him. "Sorry, sorry. You're sure." He looked around the street, then started walking backward. "You wait here. Make sure he doesn't come back out and give us the slip. I'll go back and get the car."

I spent the next twenty minutes pacing the block the building sat on, ignoring the stares of the young men on the steps and those of other passersby.

A honk from the street drew my attention, and I turned. Marcus' rental car sailed down the street. The car rolled to a stop next to a parking meter a block down on the opposite side of the street. Jogging across the road, I reached the car in a matter of moments. I climbed into the passenger seat, slamming the door shut behind me.

Chapter Fourteen

Marcus

"So," Grace asked, settling into her seat on the passenger side of the car, "what now?"

I undid my seatbelt, reclining my chair so I could peer out through the back window and up at the dilapidated building at the same time. "Now, we wait."

"For how long?"

I shrugged, folding my hands on top of my chest. "Until something happens."

Frowning, Grace twisted toward me, foot coming up to rest on the lip of the seat. "Can't you get a warrant or something?"

I blinked in confusion and fixed her with an incredulous stare. "Based on what, exactly?"

"Call Mama." Grace drummed her fingers against the door handle. "She can make a warrant happen, no questions asked."

"Let's say I do that, and we get a warrant." I reached forward and grabbed the steering wheel, lifting my back off the seat. "The police go in and find...what? Dan in his flophouse?" I pursed my lips, nodding before settling in once more. "Very incriminating. I'm sure Mama will be glad she pulled strings."

"The cops can take him to the den house, and then we can ask him some real questions." Smug smile twisting her lips, Grace crossed her arms over her stomach. "Simple."

I let out a deep breath. "And just what do you think will happen to him after we're done with our questions?" I glared. "You think Mama will just let him go?"

Grace went silent. Her smile disappeared. She squirmed under my pointed stare and looked away.

I shook my head. "He's already escaped from the Nameless once. I don't think they'll let him do it again. I don't know about you, but I don't want that man's death on my conscience if I can help it."

"All right, all right," muttered Grace, sinking down in her seat. "Point taken. I don't need any more human blood on my hands."

My glare softened and I cleared my throat, hand coming up to scratch at my stubble. "How long has it been for you, anyway?"

"How long has what been?" Grace didn't bother to mask the irritation in her voice as she watched the entrance to the building in the rearview mirror, head falling against the seat rest behind her.

"Since you participated in the sacrament?"

Closing her eyes, Grace swallowed hard. "I haven't hunted a human since..." She opened her eyes, blinking. "Well, since we parted ways."

"Oh?"

She rolled her eyes. "Don't get a big head about it. It had more to do with Lily than it did with all your moralizing. It's hard to be friends with a human, and then go out and eat one."

"But 'my moralizing,' as you call it, did it have a little something to do with it?" I pressed with a pleased, half-smile on my lips.

"You only talked about it every time we went out together. You were like a broken record."

I leaned my arm against the driver's side door and felt my smile widen. "Interesting. Half of the time when we talked, I wasn't sure you were even listening to me."

At that, Grace gave a loud guffaw, throwing a glare in my direction that would have cut leather. "Don't lie—you knew I was hanging on every word." She lifted her crossed arms higher until they were hugging her chest. "That's why you liked taking me out so much. It fed your ego."

"It did," I admitted evenly. "After all, what man doesn't want to be seen with a beautiful woman on his arm?"

I watched in unabashed fascination as the familiar blush rose in Grace's face. She turned toward the passenger-side window in an attempt to hide her reaction, but I could see how much my compliment had thrown her. "Why do you do that?" she demanded.

"Do what?" I sat up in my seat, pretending not to notice her agitation, my neck craning to take in the streets around us. "We used to meet somewhere around here, didn't we?"

"Central Saloon, down on 1st Avenue," answered Grace a tad too quickly. "It's still there, you know."

"Well, we need to go again when this is all over," I said, smiling. "Have another drink."

Grace rubbed her arms, her lips twisted into something caught between a frown and a smile. "Yeah…that's probably not a very good idea."

"It never was." I ran my hands down my legs and shook my head. "Didn't stop us though, did it?"

"Maybe it should have."

I whipped my head up, my face falling. "You don't mean that." There was a plea in my words that I couldn't hide. "Do you?"

Smile fading, Grace shook her head with some reluctance. "No." She returned her attention to the building behind us. "No, I guess I really don't."

As the sun disappeared behind Seattle's skyscrapers, we fell into a contemplative silence. While we waited in the dark, my mind wandered to the past, to our last meeting at the Central Saloon, when Grace, with her usual bluntness, had asked me point blank if I was in love with her.

I had been honest. There was no other way for me to be.

I had said yes. Who wouldn't have fallen in love with her?

I wondered, as the city came to life around me, what I would say to her if she asked me the same question right now.

The truth, I supposed. I was nothing if not an honest man.

"That's him."

I started in my seat. I looked over at Grace, whose attention was fixed, as mine should have been, on the front of a building, where a beat-up yellow taxi had pulled up to the curb. Hurrying down the building's front steps, Dan cast furtive glances down the street in either direction before throwing himself into the backseat of the cab.

"Yeah," I answered, clearing my throat.

"What now?" asked Grace, straightening in her seat, her feet coming down to lie flat against the floor.

"Now," I said, reaching across and fastening my seatbelt, "we follow him."

I started up the car, but waited until the cab had almost disappeared down the dark street before pulling out to follow it.

"Where do you think he's going?"

I tilted my head to one side, readjusting my grip on the steering wheel. "With any luck? He's going to lead us right to the person we're looking for."

It was verging on midnight when we arrived at the waterfront. By that time, even the cargo boats that had pulled in late were quiet and deserted, their sailors unleashed on the city of Seattle like locusts on a wheatfield. Ship horns could be heard in the distant black.

The taxi stopped at the edge of the waterfront district, and Dan hopped out. In the time it took him to rustle through his clothing for the fare, I slid neatly into a street parking spot, and the two of us left the comfort of our vehicle to follow our prey on foot.

Like most places in a city like Seattle, the waterfront was never really deserted. Warehouses, thrown up haphazardly during economic boom times, still stood close to the boardwalk, their narrow alleys giving cover to deeds that shouldn't see the light of day. I was aware, as I walked, of movement all around me, but just out of sight, not unlike standing in the middle of a forest. The creatures of the night were awake and hunting, and I hoped that we would slip their voracious notice. Our footsteps kept time with the lapping of refuse-dotted water against the piers as we followed Dan, turning corner after corner through a labyrinthine series of side streets and alleyways. We hung back when he turned down one final, skinny lane that was less like an alleyway, and more like a bit of overlooked space between buildings. The space was dark except for a single flickering yellow bulb hanging naked off of one of the buildings.

As we watched, Dan strode to the end of the road, fumbling a ring of keys out of his pants pocket as he went. He reached a rusted metal door and, after twisting a key into the lock, scurried inside.

"Let's go," whispered Grace, stepping out from the corner behind which we had been crouching.

"Grace!"

Grace turned around, still jogging, and shrugged at me, still standing by the alley's entrance, a scowl on my face. Rolling my eyes, I started forward, running to catch up with her.

I placed a restraining hand on Grace's arm as she reached for the metal door's round handle. "Grace, hold on."

Grace looked up at me, her forehead wrinkling. "What for?"

"Remember earlier, when you said we should call in a favor from Mama?" I said. "Now is when we should call in that favor."

"What? What are you talking about?"

I gestured to the door in front of us, my brows shooting high over my eyes. "We have no idea who, or what, is behind that door. The Nameless could have a

SWAT team here in a few hours, their own security team in maybe less than that."

"Are you kidding? You want to wait?" Grace threw her hands up in the air. "You said it yourself—Dan could be leading us right to the person responsible for all this. You want to give them a chance to get away?"

I hugged myself, letting out a loud huff of air. "Have you considered that we might be walking into a trap?"

"Well, how do we know unless we spring it?" She grinned and tapped me in the chest with the back of her hand. "Come on, we can handle this. You're a cop, I'm... Well, I'm a loan officer, but a loan officer with several decades of fight training under her belt."

I gave a firm shake of my head. "No. It's too dangerous." I released myself, digging my cell phone out of my jacket pocket. "I'm calling Mama."

As soon as my cell phone was out in the open, Grace plucked it from my relaxed fingers and held it behind her back.

I stared at her, wide-eyed. "Now, that's just childish."

Grace shrugged, slipped the stolen phone into her other jeans pocket, then tried the door. She frowned. "It's locked," she said, looking back at me.

I responded to her expectant stare with an exasperated shrug. "You think I know how to pick locks?"

"Don't you?"

"As a matter of fact, I do. But the assumption is insulting." I shoved my hands into my pockets. "Besides, I'm not going to do it."

"Fine." Grace narrowed her eyes and took a step back from the door. "I'll break it down."

"Someone inside might hear that," I said.

Grace shrugged. "It's not ideal, I agree."

The two of us stared at each other for a few tense moments. I broke first, pulling my hands out of my pockets and letting out my held breath in a rush. "For the love of..." I muttered. I got a pen out of my jacket and unscrewed it, separating the ink cartridge from the body. "You are so damn stubborn, Grace..."

Grace smiled. "With you around, I have to be."

She stepped back from the doorway to allow me the space I needed. She watched in silence as I knelt to work at the keyhole, my jaw clenched in concentration.

With a grinding click, the door shuddered into an unlocked position, relaxing in its frame. I placed my hand on the doorknob and stood. "Last chance to change your mind and come up with a less reckless plan, Grace."

"Stop stalling, Marcus," said Grace.

Shrugging, I twisted the knob and pushed the door open, shifting back into a defensive stance as the slab of metal swung inward.

Chapter Fifteen

Grace

As soon as Marcus opened the door, a solid wall of animal stench struck me like an open-handed slap across the face. I turned my head away and stumbled back, instinctually trying to escape the assaulting odor.

Marcus reached up and put a steadying hand on my shoulder. "You all right?" His own eyes were watering, and he shook his head from side to side.

I lifted my arm and nestled my nose into the crook of my elbow. "Yeah."

"You know, we don't have to go in there."

I scowled and dropped my arm. I rolled my shoulders back. "I'm okay. Let's go."

Marcus swallowed hard and sighed. "Okay. Just, let me take the lead. All right?"

I nodded, tears leaking from the corner of my eyes.

Squaring his shoulders, Marcus walked through the door and into the dim warehouse. I followed, kicking the door shut behind me. My eyes adjusted quickly to the dim light of filthy overhead fluorescents, and I surveyed our surroundings with suspicion as much as interest. The walls of the hallway were covered in graffiti, none of it fresh or legible, all of it an overlapping, unfathomable mishmash of lines and faded colors. Rusted pipes and large ductwork crisscrossed the space above our heads. The air was hot, heavy, laden with liquid, like the inside of an orchid-breeding greenhouse. I didn't so much breathe it in as bite off chunks of it and swallow it down. It slithered down my throat like warm gelatin. I gagged and coughed, as did Marcus in front of me, the sounds of humming, rattling metal and rushing water masking our more organic noises.

Together, we moved through the tight, maze-like series of hallways. The ceilings grew tall, lost in shadow above us. Whenever we came to a turning or intersection of paths, Marcus would pause, take a delicate sniff of the air then proceed forward, his shoes somehow silent against the concrete floor.

After five minutes of creeping deeper into the seemingly abandoned building's interior, we turned a corner and found ourselves staring at a rotting wooden door at the far end of the hallway. To our right, a little further along the corridor, was a second door. Appearing to be made of metal, painted black, this one stood ever so slightly ajar, open just enough to be tempting.

I started toward the side door, but Marcus placed an arm across my chest, holding me back. I shot him an annoyed glare, but relented. I had agreed to let him take the lead, after all.

Marcus crept forward, hands flexing at his sides. A few inches away from the door, he took in a sniff of air and his face contorted.

"What is it?" I whispered.

"Blood." Marcus placed one hand flat against the door, using the other to gesture behind him. "Stay here."

Before I could object, Marcus disappeared into the dark room. I watched the crack in the door for his reappearance, trying to calm the fluttering mix of anxiety and excitement in my stomach. The atmosphere was oppressive, bearing down on me like the weight of several feet of water.

From the other side of the door came a sudden flash of light and a burst of sound.

I rushed the door, and forced my way into the room. The overwhelming animal smell became mingled with the smell of feces and blood. But the blood was not human, familiar as it was. The sound, startlingly loud from out in the hall, was earsplitting inside the room itself. The overhead floodlights were almost blinding after the murkiness of the hallways, but I could still make out every detail of the hellish chamber in which I now stood.

The cages were stacked four high and lined both sides of the cramped room. From what I could see, each pen had a floor of cheap untreated wood, cut to fit the size of the metal rectangles that held each animal. Aside from this, the cages were empty of anything but the dogs themselves, which varied in size from thirty pounds to well over a hundred. Each of the over thirty canines had a unique voice, but at the moment Marcus had entered the room and switched on the lights, they had all started barking, whining and growling at the same time, the room filled to bursting with their cries.

At the end of the row of cages stood a closed red door. A rusted metal chain was wrapped around and through the pull-handle and through a hole next to the door itself. Through the cracks at the top and bottom of the door, I could see the flicker of dim, sporadic lights against an otherwise black space.

I took another step farther in between the kennels, my gaze intent on the bottom of the door where the moving lights were clearest. The dog on my left threw himself against his cage door, and I jumped back. The steel mesh flexed and jangled under the onslaught, but the door remained latched shut. The dog, some kind of dobermann-rottweiler mix, bounced back into the recesses of his pen, snarling and growling. I met his deep brown eyes, and he licked his barred teeth, but it was too late. Underneath the bluster, the threats, the declaration of hunger, the boasting of superiority, I heard the strain of pain and fear in his voice.

I heard the plain, animalistic plea to not be hurt anymore.

Skin crawling, I walked backward until I stumbled into Marcus' frame. I jumped and spun around, my breathing heavy.

If Marcus registered me running into him, he didn't show it. He too was staring around the room in open horror, his mouth a twisted grimace, his entire frame tensed, the corners of his eyes wrinkled into a wince. At last, he looked down at me and, shaking himself, said, "Only way through is forward."

His voice barely registered over the ruckus. "What do you think? Door number one" — he nodded to the door at the far end of the kennels — "or door number two?" He jerked his head back toward the hallway, indicating the wooden door we had seen sitting at the end of its grimy length.

I regarded the chained red door and the flickering lights. The hairs on the back of my neck bristled. "Hallway," I heard myself say, even as my feet stayed glued to the floor.

"Good choice," murmured Marcus.

He placed a hand on my biceps and tugged. I allowed myself to be led from the hideous room, my eyes glazed as we snuck down the hallway to the door at the far end. As we neared this darkened end of the corridor, I became aware of the sound of muffled voices drawing closer, of the boom of a faraway bass, and, most incongruous of all, muted laughter and shouting.

We paused in front of the closed door, Marcus' hand coming down to rest on the doorknob as if he were cupping the bulb of a tulip. Then, with a quick, sharp twist of his wrist, he turned the knob and eased the rickety portal open on its half-rotted hinges. He stepped through swiftly, with me on his heels. In fact, I realized I had followed too close when I bumped into the back of him, standing stock still.

"Oh, sorry," I stuttered without thinking.

"Uh..." Marcus dropped his hands to his sides. "Is this what you were expecting?"

I moved around him, blinking in the bright, multi-colored lights. I found myself looking out into a brimming crowd of people. The whole space echoed with loud music, laughter and shouts.

"Huh," I answered. I scanned the crowd, my gaze stopping on a group of three serious-looking men in black tracksuits and ski masks, each carrying a large firearm slung in their arms. They stared back at me with an intensity I didn't like.

"Uh-oh." I plastered on a smile, threaded my arm through Marcus' and forced him out into the crowd. "We better look like we belong here."

Keeping a steady but relaxed pace, we mingled with the crowd. I tried my best to adopt a bored, neutral expression, while at the same time keeping a tally on the number of weapons in the room and the location of the exits.

"Well," I said, "looks like we found where the party is."

We passed by a pair of amorous young men who, although they stood several feet into the room, were acting out their romantic fantasies as if they were the only people alive. My eyes tracked them as I walked past, looking away only when the taller of the pair dropped to his knees to take the shorter one into his mouth. My cheeks flushed. "Yep, definitely a party."

Marcus furrowed his brow as we threaded our way through and around small groupings of people. "Yeah, but is this the kind of place our Dan would frequent?"

"I agree, he didn't seem like the partying type." I scanned the room. "But when we find him, maybe we can ask him."

Marcus slipped his hand around my waist and tugged me to one side, pointing. "Looks like most of the fun is happening over there."

I allowed myself to be led toward what looked like the largest grouping of people in the space. I fell behind Marcus as he maneuvered through the crowd, holding onto his arm. But soon we were forced to separate as the crowd became thicker. For a few moments, I lost track of him entirely. I kept moving forward, however, my heart sinking the more I saw what I was moving toward.

Concrete street barriers were set up end-to-end to form a large circle from which there was no obvious exit or entrance. Rebar had been driven through the tops of the barriers, then welded together at right angles to form a rough, unyielding fence. Some enterprising women had climbed up onto their partners' shoulders and were banging against the rebar with thick glass bottles as they shouted and screamed — but even then, the top of the fence sat a good six inches above their heads. Barbed wire hung in loops from the top of the rebar, steel stars catching the light.

Out of habit, I took a sniff of the air. I screwed my eyes shut as my mind reeled with sensory overload. There were the smells of the city, but concentrated and magnified, as if someone had bottled up Seattle then sprayed it right up my nose. But there were two crucial additions to the usual city stench…the smell of canines and blood.

I craned my head this way and that, but it wasn't until the crowd shifted that I caught sight of the two dogs in the center of the arena. One was a German shepherd, almost entirely black from nose to tail, the other a tan pit bull. The dogs circled each other, spittle dripping from their already bloodied jaws. Their tongues flashed out of their mouths, flickering over rows of bared teeth, jagged and white like perfect porcelain knives.

The pit bull kept low to the ground, while the German shepherd bounced and paced from one side of the arena to the other, dancing toward his opponent then darting away at the last second. Both dogs were barking and growling, but their voices were lost among the roar of the crowd, which hung over and pushed against the concrete barriers that formed the ring itself. The mob's shouts grew louder and cruder the longer the dogs hesitated to attack.

Without warning, the pit bull threw itself at the shepherd. The shepherd jerked away, but the bulkier, more muscular dog scrambled and clawed at its exposed shoulder and side, gouging red grooves into the fur-covered flesh. The shepherd responded by rolling onto the ground, snapping its longer neck around to fix his teeth onto the nape of the pit bull, biting down with the full force of his powerful jaws. The pit bull struggled to tear away, nipping at the underbelly of the shepherd, but even injured, the shepherd was the more agile, avoiding fatal bites and scratches by twisting and pulling his body this way and that until he was back up on his feet. The shepherd attempted to pull and shake the pit bull into a more vulnerable position, but succeeded only in loosening his own grip enough to allow the pit bull the room it needed to wriggle away. Neck muscles torn and exposed, the pit bull's head hung twisted at an awkward angle as he circled the shepherd, who likewise limped clockwise around the ring, snarling and bleeding.

I wanted to look away, but couldn't, sickened and mesmerized by the violence taking place in front of me. The crowd around me was in constant motion, forcing me forward and backward like powerful waves against a rocky shore. I tried to plant my feet, but the dynamic nature of the group didn't allow for stillness, for mere observation. I would participate in this bloodletting whether I wanted to or not.

Pushed to the front, wedged between a stout muscular man with a handlebar mustache and a pair of what looked to be identical twins in matching corsets and skirts, I watched as the pit bull rushed the shepherd again, his useless neck slowing him down this time with disastrous consequences. The shepherd held his ground until the last second, then jumping to one side, aimed a bite at the underside of the pit bull's throat.

The shepherd's teeth ripped into the soft flesh, tearing it apart like hungry hands ripping into a fresh loaf of bread. The crowd bayed ravenously as the pit bull tried in vain to free himself from the death grip, succeeding only in making his wound more lethal as he pulled away. Blood spurted in every direction, some of it even hitting the delirious spectators closest to the action, but most of it falling and pooling onto the concrete.

With a thud, the pit bull fell dead.

Buffeted this way and that by the cheering crowd, I stared at the fallen warrior, fighting the urge to crawl over the barrier and go to him. The German shepherd paced the ring, chewing on his hard-won meat, blood matting his dark black fur. He did not go near the body of his opponent, but seemed instead to be looking for an escape, for a weakness in the wall, a reward for his kill that went far beyond food.

What he got instead was a wire lasso around his neck, choking the air and the fight out of him. He tried to snap and struggle, but his captors were well-practiced and aided by the lasso on the end of a six-foot metal pole. One man in a black ski mask and black sweatsuit worked the pole while other identically-dressed men corralled the crowd and made an exit for the dog and their compatriot. The dog's nails dragged along the concrete, but it was no use. He was going back to a tiny kennel in that dark room from which Marcus and I had fled. Would they even tend to his wounds? Or would they let them fester?

I pushed my way past the twins to my left, trying to follow the egress of the victor, when a hand gripped my wrist and pulled me back. I turned around with a snarl, but my face softened when I saw it was Marcus, his brow furrowed in concern.

"Grace!" He shouted to be heard over the hubbub. He jerked his head behind us, back the way we had come. "Come on!"

With a final look toward the disappearing dog, I allowed myself to be pulled through the large press of bodies, muttering "excuse mes" and "sorrys" whenever I bumped past someone. Soon the pack thinned, and I could see where Marcus was leading me.

Marcus

Crisscrossing the ceiling of the huge warehouse were a number of catwalks, accessible via rickety metal stairs that lined the walls. I pushed my way around a couple of junkies, passed out at the bottom of the nearest set of stairs, and began to climb.

My shoes stuck to the grime-coated metal beneath me, and I did my best not to touch the railing as we headed up into the rafters. Some festive soul had strewn toilet paper from catwalk to catwalk, and the empty tubes littered the grating. The catwalks hummed with conversation and laughter, a popular perch for those who wished to escape the crush and heat of the party below.

We worked our way to the front of the catwalk, jockeying for position with a few other spectators. From here, we had a clear view of the chaos beneath. There had to be a hundred or more people spread across the warehouse floor, with the majority of the crowd clumped around the main arena. A few enterprising individuals had driven pickup trucks and vans in through the now-closed loading bay doors, and were selling various drugs and drinks off the backs of their vehicles. The crowd was a mix of styles and classes that only Seattle could offer. Scantily dressed prostitutes mingled with bespectacled tech types, who were swallowing pills bought off colorfully clad ravers and mohawked punks. Everyone was showing off their tattoos in the humid space. Flesh was, after all, the main entertainment of the night. I caught the sounds of a dozen different languages, the smell of heated heroin and smoky marijuana, but everything was underscored by the taste of blood on the air itself—thick and wet— like an uninvited tongue probing my mouth.

I tried to avoid looking down into the arena, but from our current vantage point, it was impossible. My eyes were drawn to the patches of drying rust brown that stained the concrete, so fresh the light still reflected off the pools of blood. I watched as two skinny men in wife-beaters dragged the dead pit bull from the middle of the ring, the crowd jeering and throwing pieces of trash at them as they worked. Numb, I watched as the torn skin around the open throat flapped and fluttered, slick sinews exposed to the open air as the men jerked the body forward. I wanted to look away, to not see, to not think about what it tasted like to rip out the windpipe of an animal, but I was frozen to the spot, my hands gripping the railing of the catwalk.

I wasn't sure at first why Grace put her hand on top of my own. But the sensation of flesh pressing against mine brought me back to myself in time to feel the older werewolf step close behind me.

"There's Dan," she shouted into the shell of my ear. She pointed down into the crowd that surrounded the ring.

I leaned into her, trying to follow her line of sight. My gaze flitted from unfamiliar face to unfamiliar face until I zeroed in on Dan, who stood close to the ring's inner edge. His backpack was gone, but he retained his dull grayish-green raincoat and faded knit cap. He was in the midst of a close, heated conversation with an emaciated young woman, whose straight, long blonde hair hung like a curtain in front of her face. She wore a sequin-covered party dress, which reflected the blindingly bright overhead lights of the warehouse like a disco ball. Her four-inch heels had her towering over Dan, talking down to him like he was a child.

"I see them," I shouted back at Grace. "Do you think she's the one who—"

"I don't know," said Grace. "It could be."

We watched as Dan and the mystery woman argued, hands flying into the air, mouths moving quickly. I sniffed the air and regretted it, the smell of blood and freshly torn flesh rushing to fill my senses. Wincing, I pinched the bridge of my nose. "It could just be his girlfriend, or someone he owes money to…"

The woman below held up a hand to Dan. The man stopped talking, his face drawn. The blonde closed her eyes and, turning away from Dan, took in a deep, open-mouthed breath. She twisted her head this way and that, breathing in and out with a deliberateness that we both recognized, but I could not believe.

I recoiled from the railing. "Shit. You don't think... Can she smell us?"

Grace also took a step back, but more slowly, shaking her head from side to side as she grimaced. "In this crowd? With everything going on in here? There's no way."

The woman opened her eyes and looked up at the catwalks. She scanned each one carefully, breathing so deeply I could see her chest rising and falling, even from a distance. After a moment or two of searching, her eyes stopped on Grace.

"Oh...shit."

The woman smiled. She lifted a ring-laden hand, and gave a lazy wave.

"It's her." I pulled at Grace's arm as I stepped back toward the stairs. "We need to go. Now."

She scoffed, her upper lip coming away from her teeth in a sneer. "Run away? Why?" She tossed her hand out in the direction of the blonde woman. "There's two of us, and one of her. Let's take her out."

As she spoke, the blonde's hand fell to the side of her face, her fingertips pressing against her ear. Her lips moved, although her gaze never left Grace. From the edges of the room came a flurry of movement, as every visible black-track-suited soldier moved from their positions, some walking, others jogging, but all headed toward the catwalk.

Nodding, Grace rushed ahead of me, scrambling down the stairs at a strident pace. "Right. A tactical retreat. Good call."

Chapter Sixteen

Grace

I dove headfirst into the crowd, with Marcus following close behind me. Keeping my head down, I wove around the bodies of other partygoers, trying not to force a path that would be easily spotted by our hunters. I hoped Marcus would follow my lead.

Emerging from a tight knot of people, I paused to glance over my shoulder, searching for him. Marcus burst from the crowd a few feet to my left, and I returned my attention to where I was going. I stuttered to a halt in front of a tracksuit soldier who hadn't been there a moment ago, his brows drawn low over glaring eyes as he fumbled with the safety on his semi-automatic.

With hesitation, I swung my foot up into the man's crotch as hard as I could. He crumpled with a strangled gurgle of expelled air and pain. As he descended to the floor, I grabbed the gun from him then, checking that the safety had indeed been switched off, fired a short burst of bullets up into the air.

The panic was immediate and intense. Screams and shouts filled the space as people began stampeding through and over one another to reach the exits. The tracksuit soldiers tried in vain to push against the crush of bodies and reach Marcus and me, but they were battered back by the force of fleeing people.

Taking advantage of the chaos, we ran for the door through which we had entered. I forced it open with my shoulder and ushered Marcus through before following him up the dingy hallway.

We ran past the still-open black metal kennel door, the thudding of our feet against the floor riling the dogs inside. Soon, a cacophony of rattling cages and howls accompanied our escape.

The barking and yowling faded as we ran, but the sounds echoed in my ears. I shook my head, trying to keep my focus on the twists and turns of the hallway in front of us. I tried to convince myself that the most important thing right now was getting out alive, but guilt settled like a brick at the bottom of my stomach, weighing me down until I struggled to put one foot in front of the other.

My guts churning, I skidded to a stop, one hand clenched at my side. Marcus glanced back at me, slowing his step.

I shook my head again. "I can't do this."

"What?" Marcus stared at me, confused. Then his confusion cleared and was replaced by worn annoyance. He pinched the bridge of his nose, his other hand gripping his hip. "Grace...we can't do anything about the dogs right now. Come on, let's —"

"I can't just leave them." My eyes began to water. I turned, starting back down the passageway that would lead me to the kennel.

Marcus hissed my name and started after me, grabbing my arm. "Look, right now I can't guarantee that we will get out of here in one piece, let alone any of those mutts." He sighed sharply. "Besides, it's not like we can fit them in the car or anything. You want to just leave them on the streets?"

"Better the streets than this! Marcus, I can't, I just can't — just — "

His hand slid down to grab mine. "Grace," he repeated, his voice calm and consoling.

I met his gaze and felt myself still. His eyes searched my face for a moment. Without knowing why, I squeezed his hand, my lips parting.

Jaw tightening, Marcus jerked his head back toward the kennel, dropping my hand. He took the semi-automatic from me in one swift movement and started back in that direction. "Come on then."

I smiled grimly and jogged after him. We reached the corner of the hallway, pausing to glance around before continuing forward. The kennel door was across the way, and the door to the warehouse was about a hundred feet farther down the hall. When no one appeared, Marcus, his weapon drawn, rounded the corner.

As soon as he was out in the open, the door at the end of the hall burst inwards. Five men, all in black tracksuits with balaclavas pulled over their faces, poured through the entrance. The barrels of their guns reflected the fluorescent light, the steel standing out against their dark clothes. They stopped, staring in shock at the target that had just stepped into their field of vision.

Before they could recover from the surprise of seeing their quarry before them, Marcus lifted his gun and fired, hitting the lead mercenary square in the chest. I took advantage of the confusion to scurry across the hall to the still partially open kennel door.

Standing in the doorframe, I reached for the light switch. A bullet ricocheted off the steel frame just behind me.

"Shit!" I ducked low and threw myself into the darkened room.

"Come on, Grace!" shouted Marcus, more shots beginning to ring out around us. He shoved the door fully open and knelt on the threshold, taking cover behind the frame. He lifted the semi-automatic and squeezed off several bursts down the hallway, his teeth grinding.

I threw myself at the nearest cage I could see in the dim light, an eye-level cell close to the room's front door. I gripped the padlock and tugged, the bolt snapping like brittle bone in my hand. Flinging open the door, I looked inside the five-by-five cube for the first time. At the back of the cage, a dark mass huddled, quivering. It tried to make itself smaller as I extended my hand, curling in on itself as if it were an ouroboros and could swallow itself whole.

I took a deep breath, doing my best to ignore the sound of shots going off mere feet from me. I kept my voice quiet, my gaze steady. "Here we go, love." I rested my hand flat against the plywood floor of the cage. "No one is going to hurt you anymore."

The shape in the kennel let out a whine.

I smiled.

The sustained clink of metal on metal echoed from my right. Turning, I watched as the chain securing the second door, the red door at the other end of the kennel, disappeared up through the drilled hole where a lock should've been. With a thunderous crack, the red door was shouldered open.

The wolf within me could have taken the man that emerged, but there was no full moon to help me now. Even with my standard enhanced speed and strength, I stood no chance against the behemoth that pounded his way out of the doorway. Well over six feet tall, he was a wall of solid muscle from his neck to his calves. He grinned down at me with all ten of his browning, rotten teeth. His steps reverberated through the room, rattling the metal cage doors.

It wasn't until he cocked back the second hammer that I even noticed the sawed-off shotgun in his massive hands.

My mind raced, my body acting on instinct as I threw myself toward the ground. Were the shotgun cartridges packed with conventional steel ball pellets? Or were they rock salt or silver? Would I be killed outright? Would Marcus?

I hit the floor, the force of the fall causing the air to leave my lungs, and my eyes snapped shut.

The next thing I heard was a scream.

I wrenched my eyes open and looked up. The cage door above me swung to and fro, still shaking from the momentum of the dog as it jumped out and onto the shotgun-wielding man. The animal's jaws punctured cloth, skin and muscle with all the ease of a fork pushing into a moist piece of cake. Screaming, the man reared back as he tried in vain to escape the dog's attack. His fingers contracted, and the shotgun's twin barrels blazed, emptying their load into the ceiling.

The gigantic man hit the floor, writhing as blood spurted from his wound, the spray coating the kennels, and driving the dogs into a frenzy. The freed dog, a dappled pit bull, tore its way up from the man's groin, moving its jaws to his face and throat. The man's screams died away into soggy, guttural coughs.

Pushing myself up on scraped hands and bruised knees, I whistled as loud as I could. The dog, blood and flesh stuck to its short fur, turned and trotted over to me. Grabbing onto the scruff of its neck for support, I heaved myself up onto my feet and, one hand outstretched for balance, I began to move back toward the door that led out to the hallway.

Marcus slammed the door shut, leaning against it as he flipped the deadlock in place. He jerked away as a hail of bullets pinged off the other side.

"We're not getting out that way," said Marcus, rushing past me and heading into the other room that had been hidden behind the red door.

I ran after him, the dog keeping pace at my side. I slammed the red door shut behind us. This left the three of us squashed up against a row of TV monitors on which various parts of the warehouse could be viewed in grainy black and white. The monitors were controlled through a central computer, and everything sat on top of a rickety, plywood desk, under which was a broken computer chair.

There was no way out, except back the way we had entered.

Marcus checked the magazine of the semi-automatic. I looked over his shoulder. He was down to four rounds. He looked back at me and shook his head.

Concentrated gunfire and the braying of panicked animals surrounded us. Marcus pushed me behind him, facing the door and scowling. "Do you still think not calling in the Nameless was a good idea?"

I swallowed down a gasp of air, unwilling to accept that this was going to be the room in which I died.

A metallic glint on the floor beneath the desk caught my eye. My heart seized. "Wait a minute, wait a minute!" I shoved Marcus away from me. "Move that chair!"

Without stopping to ask why, Marcus did as he was told, brow furrowing as I dropped down and crawled beneath the desk. Fingers spidering along the floor, I soon gripped the latch of some kind of access hatch that had long ago rusted shut.

The hatch came open with a rip and groan of old metal. I hung my head inside the square opening and popped back up, my face covered in cobwebs. "Electrician's tunnel!"

"Go!" commanded Marcus, his gaze sweeping back up toward the door.

I slithered down into the dark tunnel, dropping the last few inches to the floor with a rubber thud. I whistled, and the dog scrambled after me, tumbling into my arms with a yelp. I stepped back, just in time to miss being flattened by the jumping Marcus, who closed the hatch neatly behind him as he fell.

The tunnel was claustrophobically thin, crowded with bundles of cables and high voltage boxes. We were in total darkness, only able to navigate the space thanks to our superior night vision.

Marcus swept the area, his gun at the ready. He jerked his head forward. "Let's keep moving. It's not going to take them long to figure out where we went."

I bent over, placing the dog down on its four feet. "Which way?"

But Marcus was already moving before the question had left my lips. "And you call yourself a wolf?" He broke into a jog. "Car's this way."

Chapter Seventeen

Marcus

An hour later, Grace leaned into the doorbell to Lily's apartment, rain dripping into her eyes. It had been five minutes with no response, but she was persistent, and of that I was glad. Half because I didn't know where else to go, and half because I was too damn tired to move any farther.

The speaker above the buzzer crackled to life at last, and a sleep-laced voice demanded, "Hello!"

"Lily, would you let us in, please?" Grace slid her finger against the speaker button. "It's Grace."

Lily's voice came bouncing through the speaker, thin and distorted. "Gracie?" There was a pause then a terse, "Hang on."

The outdoor light above us flickered into life. Grace stepped back from the door, wrapping her arms around herself to stave off the worst of the cold, the rain coming off her in steady streams.

I listened as the sounds of bare feet thudding against old wooden stairs reached us in the back alley outside the butcher's shop, the footsteps keeping time with the thunderous pounding of the rain.

Lily undid the chain and deadbolt and swung the door open, holding her robe shut tight around her neck.

"Gracie?" Lily released the edges of the robe, revealing her dark blue pajamas beneath. The confusion in her eyes melted away, replaced with deep concern. "It's two in the morning and pouring rain, what are you—?"

The pit bull, which had been sitting behind Grace, took this opportunity to trot up to Lily and snuffle at her hand. Lily looked down at it, her brow creasing. "Hello."

Grace shook the rainwater off her face and out of her eyes. "I need a place to keep him."

I pushed my tousled mop of wet, loose hair out of my eyes, and leaned back to glance at the back of the dog. "Her."

"Her," corrected Grace. "And we could use a place to dry off, regroup."

Lily eyed her friend, warily. "Gracie, what in the world—"

Grace shuffled closer to the doorway, attempting to find some shelter under the short awning. "Lily, please? I'll explain everything inside."

With a sigh, Lily stepped away from the door and gestured for us to come inside. Grace started forward, the pit bull at her side. I slid past Lily with a quiet 'Thank you,' giving my head and jacket a quick shake before starting up the staircase.

The dim light in the stairwell flickered as we ascended. Lily moved up the stairs so she was walking next to me. "You both should know better than to disturb a woman my age at this hour of the night," she said, one hand gripping the banister as she climbed. "Interrupting my beauty sleep."

I offered her my arm and smiled. "You mean you can look even more lovely than you do right now?"

"Hm." Lily wrapped her arm through mine and looked me over. She smacked her lips together. "Mm. I can see why Gracie likes you."

Grace whipped her head around, a look of betrayal in her brown eyes. "Hey!"

"You know the way!" Lily flapped her free hand at her, frowning. "Ring out your clothes in the tub, and I'll put them in the dryer. You do want dry clothes, don't you? Werewolves can still catch colds?"

"Strangely enough, yes," I answered, water dripping from my hair into my eyes.

"Nobody's perfect," said Lily, shaking her head.

The front door to the apartment opened, and we all peeled off in different directions. Lily walked to her linen closet and gathered up a few large towels. She beckoned to me, indicating the spare bedroom down the hall. "Marcus, you come with me. Grace, you know where to go."

Grace squished her way into the bathroom, slamming the door behind her. With a last worried glance at the closed bathroom door, I followed Lily into the spare bedroom, stripping off my suit jacket and folding it over my arm as I went. The room was small, but cozy, with a full-sized bed tucked into one corner and a large, old-fashioned chest of drawers next to a walk-in closet.

Lily put two of the fluffy towels down on the bed, sighing loudly. "All right. Get yourself out of those wet clothes and dry off. There should be something to fit you between the dresser and the closet, so just help yourself."

I toed my shoes off and nodded. "What should I do with—?"

"Just toss them out in the hall. I'll put them in the dryer," said Lily, already heading for the door. "I'll be in the kitchen, drying off this damn dog. And where you all managed to find a dog in the middle of the night, I can't wait to hear..."

Smiling ruefully, I did as instructed. I stripped and toweled myself off, before changing into an oversized University of Washington T-shirt, the large husky head seeming more than apropos. When I wandered out into the kitchen, Lily gestured to a stack of clothes and asked me to bring them to Grace in the bathroom. Seeing as she was straddling a pit bull at the time, I didn't see why I should argue.

I knocked on Lily's bathroom door and waited until I heard Grace's familiar, "Yeah?" before entering the small room, my bare feet padding across the tile, my attention fixed on the bundle of clothes balanced in my arms.

"From our hostess," I started, indicating the clothes. "She's drying off the dog as we—" I took one look at Grace. An embarrassingly quick flush raced up my neck and into my cheeks at the sight of her naked body. I snapped my head back in the direction of the door, spinning around, my gaze directed toward the ceiling. "Oh, I'm so sorry."

Grace gave a snort of disdain, pausing the tousling of her hair to fix me with a disbelieving grin. "You've seen me naked, Marcus."

"Context is everything," I said, backing up into the room. "As is consent." I thrust the handful of fabric back toward her abdomen. "Here. From Lily's bottomless closet."

She took the sweatshirt and sweatpants with a nod. "She has a lot of family who visit without much notice. They leave things here, so they don't have to bring them next time."

I slipped my hands into my own pair of borrowed track pants and started for the door. "Very sensible. I'll leave you to it."

Grace reached forward and tugged at my shoulder. "Marcus—"

But I refused to turn around, swatting her hand away as I screwed my eyes shut. "I'd rather have a conversation with dressed-Grace, as opposed to naked-Grace, if at all possible."

"Look"—grimacing, Grace threw on the faded blue sweater and pink sweatpants as quickly as she could—"I'm just trying to say thank you."

I turned at last, my mouth gaping open. "Whatever for?"

"For backing me up in there." Grace tossed her hand toward the door. "Helping me with the dog." She drew her hands back through her tangled mess of hair. "It was really dumb."

My mouth closed into a smile. "Yeah, yeah, it was." I extended my hand toward her shoulder, but thought better of touching her, settling instead for shaking my fist at her instead. "But it was also very...you."

There was silence. Grace's brow furrowed. "Um. Thanks?"

"That didn't come out the way I meant it to," I said. "I just meant...decisions like that? Being concerned

183

about the little things, when your own life is at stake? You're a good person. That's why I fell in love with you."

Grace's cheeks went pink and she opened her mouth to respond, doubtless to joke, to jab, to otherwise deflect, but I didn't let her, neatly changing the topic of conversation instead.

"We should get back out there." I swept my arm toward the door, stepping back so Grace could squeeze past me. "Lily deserves her explanation, and we wouldn't want her to rush in here, thinking that she has to defend your honor."

Grace snorted out a laugh. "Lily wouldn't do that." She started for the door and her smile shrank. "Probably."

Chapter Eighteen

Grace

Thirty minutes later, I had finished narrating our adventurous evening to our sleep-deprived host. Marcus made himself comfortable in the recliner in the living room, thanking Lily effusively when she handed him a cup of coffee spiked with whiskey. I sat at the kitchen table, my own mug of coffee warming my hands, while Lily paced the kitchen, listening intently.

She paused, staring down at the dog who was currently muzzle-deep in a bowl of shredded roast chicken, beef broth, peas, green beans and some scraps of overcooked steak.

"Well, this one must not have been fighting too long."

My heart lifted a little at the thought. "You think?"

"Starved near half to death, but doesn't have many scars or marks on her." Lily reached down and patted the hound's hips as it worked its way through the bowl. "Seems to still trust people anyway."

Marcus swallowed a huge gulp of his fortified coffee, stretching his legs out in front of the radiator. "We're not exactly people."

"Right." Sighing, Lily lowered herself into the chair across from me, her hands falling into her lap. "So...where do you go from here? What's the plan?"

I rolled my shoulders back against my chair, tipping my head to one side. "Well, we now know what that psychotic freak who kidnapped me looks like. We know she's a wolf, and we know she's been tapping Dan for information."

Lily leaned forward. "And you know she's been planning this for a long time."

Silence followed this declaration. Marcus and I stared at Lily, who shrugged. "Dog-fighting rings like that don't just pop up overnight. And the way you described those goons moving and responding to her? They were trained, and had plenty of practice working together as a team. That only makes sense if she's been here awhile. Wouldn't be surprised if she had some powerful backing, either."

"Backing? From where?" I said. "One of the other dens?"

Marcus scoffed.

I rolled my eyes in response. "What? It wouldn't be the first time one of them came after us." I put my mug down and leaned back in my chair. "On the other hand, she did take out Colquhoun and his son first. Who would be ballsy enough to take on two dens at once?"

"That's not balls, that's suicide," said Marcus, sitting up in his recliner.

"True," said Lily, her voice tense and tired. "But maybe they hired an outsider to do it."

"Hold on," I said, a thought occurring to me. "How did an outsider, how did anybody know how to find me in Klamath Falls?" I looked at my friend, one brow raised. "Lily, you didn't—?"

Lily held up her hands, straightening in her chair. "The only person I told was your boyfriend."

The words tumbled out of my mouth as a reflex. "He is not my boy—" I swallowed the last syllable and shook my head. "You know what, that's not important right now. Marcus, did you tell anybody where I was?"

"No, of course not." Marcus paused, his mug halfway to his lips. "Well, I mean, I did report back to the Feóndulf that I'd found you."

My eyes began to widen. I nodded and shared a glance with Lily. "So, the Council knew."

"Yes, but..." Marcus stood, scowling. "Now just a minute! Let's not forget that it was my den's leader and heir that were murdered first. Why would the Council want that to happen?"

"Depends," answered Lily. "With those two werewolves dead, who would be next in line to lead the Feóndulf?"

He gestured into the kitchen. "Grace."

I waved this response away. "Let's pretend Colquhoun didn't write that letter. Who would be next in line then?"

Marcus paced from the living room into the kitchen, placing his mug on the table in front of me as he spoke. "Well, the Council would decide, ultimately. But I suppose, the most likely person..." His brows knitted together. His voice dropped to a hush. "Lawrence Hughes. He's head of the Council, he's next in line."

Then, as if giving himself a slap, Marcus shook himself and began pacing once more, volume rising with his agitation. "But this is ridiculous, Hughes would never do this!"

"Why not?" I pressed, leaning forward.

"Because...because this isn't the bloody fifteenth century, is it?" He turned on his heel and fixed the floor with a glare, his hands slicing the air in front of him. "Werewolves do not kill other werewolves. And if they do, they certainly do not hire outsiders to have them assassinated. It's — it's profane!"

"It makes sense," mused Lily aloud, as if she hadn't heard Marcus' outburst. "This Hughes guy wants more power, finds some psycho wolf to point at Colquhoun and his son, and when it turns out the man named you as head of the den, he sends his pet killer after you."

"I don't know." I shook my head. "That's the one thing that isn't explained by Hughes' involvement. Why did Colquhoun write that letter? How did he know he was next? Why warn Mama?"

"Right, I'm putting a stop to this now," said Marcus, shaking his head and drawing a hand down his chin. "I'm telling you, there is no way Lawrence Hughes or the Feóndulf Council are involved in this."

"How else can you explain how this woman found me?"

He threw his hands into the air. "Me! I'm the only person who knew where you were, right? Lily told me. Maybe this woman followed me from Cardiff, to here, to Klamath Falls. That's a possibility, right?"

I considered this. The pit bull trotted over from her now empty bowl and leaned against my legs. I scratched her under her chin without thinking. "If that's what happened, then Lily, we've got to get you someplace safe."

Lily jumped at the sound of her name. "What? What are you talking about?"

I grimaced and ticked off the points on my fingers. "This woman knows we're onto her, she knows I'm back in Seattle and she knows you know how to find me. You're in danger."

Lily's brows fell in a hard line over her dark brown eyes. "I work in a butcher shop. I've been carving up meat since I was nine." She took a sip of her black coffee. "I'd like to see somebody try and threaten me."

"I wouldn't." I turned back to Marcus, ignoring the sputtering of the human woman. "Where can we take her?"

"Take me—you're not taking me anywhere!" said Lily.

Marcus shrugged. "The den house would be the safest place. Plenty of security there."

Lily gave a derisive snort. "Plenty of werewolves there, you mean. I'll be as safe as a chicken in a foxhole."

Marcus gave what I assumed was meant to be a reassuring smile. "We won't bite. Now, go pack your things."

The older woman crossed her arms over her chest and stared Marcus down, the line of her jaw tight and firm. "I'm not going anywhere. This is my home."

"Lily, please," I said. I reached out and grabbed hold of Lily's arm, squeezing gently. "I couldn't live with myself if something happened to you."

Lily's muscles relaxed under my hand, but the woman's expression remained resolute. "What about the dog?"

"Mama won't like it, but she'll just have to go with you."

With a sharp huff, Lily stood and walked across the kitchen into the living room. "You still need to name it, you know."

"What's wrong with Dog?" I exclaimed, only half-joking.

"I'm serious." Lily stopped at the mouth of the hallway that led to the bedrooms. She glared over her shoulder. "You saved the damn dog, you've got to take some responsibility for her now. She needs a real name."

I watched my friend disappear down the hall and, frowning, muttered, "I'll give it some thought."

Marcus stood from his chair, cast a furtive glance toward the hallway then whispered, "Grace, are you sure this is a good idea?"

Sighing, I moved my hand over the dog's smooth fur. I looked into her adoring eyes and shook my head. "No. Not at all. But we don't have a lot of options right now."

"We may be giving Mama something — someone — she can hold over you later," said Marcus, pulling at the waist of his sweatpants.

I had my mouth open to answer, but snapped it shut when Lily poked her head back around the corner. "How much should I pack?" asked the older woman.

I plastered what I hoped was an easy smile onto my face. "Just enough for a few days. We'll have this all wrapped up by then." I looked up into Marcus' face, widening my eyes pointedly. "Right?"

Marcus nodded and followed suit, smiling back at the butcher. "Sure, yeah, of course."

Frowning, Lily withdrew once more. Marcus moved over to where I was still sitting, his hands outstretched. "What exactly is our next move here, Grace?"

"Once we get Lily stashed away at the den house, we'll take a security team and head back to the waterfront," I said, standing. The dog followed suit, ears perking up.

Marcus shook his head. "The warehouse will be cleaned out by the time we get down there."

"Let's hope they leave something behind in their rush." My face brightened. I looked from the dog to Marcus, smiling my first real smile since leaving the warehouse. "How about Sadie?"

Chapter Nineteen

Marcus

No one spoke on the drive to Queen Anne. The only sounds in the car were Sadie's panting. She sat next to Lily in the back seat, her nose pressed to the window, tail patting against the cushion. At the stoplights, Grace would twist around in her seat to glance back at Lily, but the older woman was always looking out of the window, her chin resting in her palm, a deep frown on her face — she was not in the mood for casual conversation.

With sunrise more than an hour off, and the rain still coming down in sheets, the city slunk by in the dark, deserted at four in the morning except for the odd street cleaner or transient.

When we crested the hill on Queen Anne, the sudden flashing of red, blue and white lights cut through the monotone world like an explosion. Grace threw up a hand to shield her eyes and peered through her fingers out of the windshield, blinking away sudden tears. I jerked the wheel sharply to the left, pulling around the chaos with a breathed expletive.

"What the hell—?" muttered Lily, sitting up in her seat and gripping Grace's headrest with one hand.

As we drove past our destination, the scene resolved and became clearer. The tall gate that protected the den house was thrown open, and parked in the driveway was what looked like a fleet of cop cars, ambulances and unmarked but decidedly governmental vans spilling out into the street. A pair of uniformed police officers were setting up a cordon of rope and caution tape around the entrance, while other individuals in body armor moved in and out of the front door of the house. Groups of people in pajamas and robes were clustered around the driveway, and a sheet-covered body was being loaded into one of the ambulances.

"Shit," said Grace. Her fingers dug into the handle of the door. She whipped around to face me, her face drawn and pale. "Marcus..."

"I know." I nodded, swallowing hard.

I pulled the car up to the curb across the street. Before I had put the car into park, Grace had her door open. She hopped out, hitting the pavement at a jog, trusting us to follow her. Hair flying behind her, she headed straight for the main gate, her arms pumping.

One of the uniformed officers saw her coming and stopped what he was doing, one hand falling to his belt. He strode forward to intercept her, his other hand outstretched, shaking his head as he said, "Ma'am, you have to get back, you can't—"

"I live here, this is my house," said Grace, cutting him off. "I'm Grace Holtz."

His eyes widened, but he kept his arm stretched out in front of himself, forcing her to stop or run straight into him. "Oh. I see." He glanced around at the hubbub, then turned to one side, hand falling to the radio on his shoulder. "Just…one moment, ma'am."

Hands clenched into fists at her sides, Grace waited. As she stood there, Sadie trotted up next to her, followed closely by Lily and me. Grace was about to turn and speak to me, when the cop returned his attention to her, giving her a nod.

"You're good."

Grace pushed past him, and Lily and I had little choice but to follow. I glanced at the sheet-covered body inside the ambulance, but I couldn't tell anything beyond the obvious — that whoever was under there wasn't moving.

Grace took the front steps two at a time and strode through the open door. The golden three-tiered chandelier caught and reflected the colored light that poured in from the outside. I had expected more cops inside, but I should have known better. I spotted a few men and women in cheap, wrinkled suits, badges on their lapels or belts, but overwhelmingly the entryway bustled with the Nameless' own security forces — female werewolves in black tactical gear, some with weapons slung over their backs or clipped to their hips.

What unnerved me more than anything else was the silence. From the chaos outside, I had expected the inside of the house to be in uproar, but the hushed whispers that floated through the cavernous house disturbed me even more. As my heart fell to my stomach, my gaze flickered around the entryway.

In front of the half-circle reception desk knelt a large, muscular woman. Her blonde hair trailed down her back in a thick Dutch braid. She was whispering to another young woman. whose blonde hair stood frazzled out from her head. She was still collapsed on the floor, leaning against the desk and sobbing. With a start, I recognized Sylvia. At the same instant, Sylvia looked up and over the muscular woman's shoulder and her bloodshot eyes locked onto Grace, widening. Grace rushed forward, her tennis shoes slapping against the marble.

"Sylvia!" Grace shouted to her. "What is —"

"This is all your fault!" Sylvia's shout rang out clear and loud in the hushed room. Grace skidded to a halt before her, and watched as the blonde struggled to her feet, gripping onto the lip of the desk to pull herself up. Her green eyes, raw and red, burned with hatred, even as tears eked their way from the corners. "You stupid bitch!"

Sylvia lunged toward her on unsteady feet, hands outstretched, acrylic nails flashing.

Grace stumbled back, ducking into a defensive posture. But the receptionist was being restrained by the blonde security specialist, who lifted her into the air by the waist as she continued to kick, swipe and scream.

"If you hadn't left! If you hadn't come back!"

The security specialist's face was blank as she jerked her head. Two other women, similarly kitted out, ran forward and grabbed hold of Sylvia by either arm. With her feet never touching the ground, they pulled her away into one of the drawing rooms, but not before she gave out one last shout of, "This is all your fault!"

We all stared after Sylvia, our mouths hanging open. A low 'ahem' drew our attention, and we looked up into the brown eyes of the head of Nameless Security.

The blonde lowered her strong chin, one hand falling to rest on the butt of her handgun. "Ma'am." The woman addressed Grace, pressing her free hand to her chest. "I don't know if you remember me, my name is —"

"Of course I remember you, Kassandra." Grace swallowed hard, and I shifted uncomfortably on my feet. It had been Kassandra who had discovered me sneaking into the house all those years ago. She had handed me over to Mama. She had been the one who had restrained Grace, forced her to watch me beaten bloody. The woman's face — and scent — wasn't one either of us was likely to forget.

Grace straightened, shaking her hair out of her face, her expression growing stern. "What is going on? Where's Mama?"

Something flickered in Kassandra's eyes, a moment of panic. But it was gone before I could be sure I'd seen it, and the woman just nodded again. "I can take you to her." The werewolf sniffed, and her gaze fell over Grace's shoulder. Her tan face went blank, but the disapproval in her tone was evident as she asked, "What is he doing here?"

Grace followed her line of sight. She turned to face me, where I was standing behind her with Lily and Sadie just behind me. Grace licked her lips and sighed. "He's with me."

Kassandra gave a nod then asked, "And the human?"

"Lily Donovan," explained Grace, her patience wearing thin. "She's the den butcher."

"I know who she is. What is she doing here?" Kassandra released a huff of air as she took in the sight of the panting pit bull sitting docile at Lily's side. "And why'd she bring her pet?"

"It's not mine," said Lily, patting the top of Sadie's head all the same.

"I need her somewhere safe," said Grace, her hands falling to her hips. "We think that the person who killed the Feóndulfs, and tried to kill me, may come after her next."

Kassandra twisted and pursed her lips. She shook her head, sending her braid bouncing behind her. "She can't stay here. Nobody can. This location is compromised." She mimicked Grace's stance. "But we can keep her at one of the safe houses. There's one in Northgate that should be secure."

"Northgate?" exclaimed Lily, distaste dripping from the word.

Grace walked back to her friend, her arm outstretched. "It's just for a couple of days, Lily."

Lily frowned and gestured around us, leaning forward. "I don't like this, Gracie."

Grace gripped her upper arm and put on a grim smile. "Everything is going to be fine." She pulled the stout woman into a hug. "I'll call you as soon as I'm done here. Make sure you're settled in okay." She broke away and nodded down to the pit bull. "Her name's Sadie, by the way."

Lily nodded, swallowing. "Sadie." She drew in a deep breath and let it out. "All right. You watch your back, Grace." She looked around Grace and nodded to me. "You too, Marcus."

The butcher was led away through the front door by a small contingent of security. Grace's eyes followed her longingly.

I cleared my throat and stepped forward, one hand fiddling with my bracelet.

"Can I be of any use?" I asked Kassandra. "I'm a detective, if that—"

"I know who you are, and I know what you are," Kassandra stepped on my words with the force of a bully flattening a sandcastle. Her eyes burned, but the rest of her face remained dispassionate. "And if it were up to me, you'd be out on your ass where you belong. But it's not up to me." She turned to Grace, treating me to the coldest shoulder I had ever known. "Ma'am?"

Grace nodded, scowling. "I'd like him to stay. Especially since you still haven't told me what the hell is going on."

The large werewolf stepped to one side and gestured toward the main staircase, inclining her head. "Follow me."

Sharing a glance with me, Grace trailed after the large woman. My senses alert, I did my best to stick close. I could hear crying from the living room and kitchens. I felt eyes, heavy and assessing, following our progress up the stairs. The faint whiff of sweat and blood suffused the air.

Kassandra faced forward as she spoke, her words clipped and precise. "After your meeting with Mama, we increased the security presence in and around the property. Thirty minutes ago, one of our perimeter patrols missed their check-in and we went into lockdown. My people found the patrol down at the back of the property and—"

"What do you mean, 'down'?" I demanded, the sinking feeling in my stomach solidifying into a hard, lead ball.

"Dead. All three of them." There was a hitch in Kassandra's step, and the blonde woman's gaze fell to the ground, her voice quieting. "Good werewolves. Trained, experienced women." Then she shook herself, and we continued toward the bedrooms at the back of the house. "Silver bullets. The intruder must have used a silencer, because we didn't pick anything up over comms. Cleaned up after themselves too—no casings. We'll see what we can find out from the slugs, but I'm not hopeful."

My forehead furrowed, I shook my head. "Someone must have heard something. Why wasn't there someone posted here? Security inside the house?"

"Mama's orders," explained Kassandra, sparing me a glance. "She wouldn't allow surveillance in her private rooms, and although we did have someone patrolling this floor, they weren't static. As to why she didn't cry out—I don't know."

The three of us came to a stop in front of the door to Mama's bedroom. Kassandra turned to face us. "We think she was attacked while asleep. Maybe dosed with something, wolfsbane, like you were, ma'am. If she wasn't, she should have screamed." Kassandra's dark brown eyes flicked up to meet Grace's and the sadness I saw there sobered me more than a slap across the face. "She would've screamed. It's...it's not good in there, ma'am."

"Grace," I said, my voice low. "You don't have to—"

Grace reached back, grabbing my hand without looking at me, her gaze locked on the door. "Yes. I do."

I squeezed her hand once before releasing her. Grace took in a deep breath, closed her eyes and opened the bedroom door.

Grace

Describing the scent of blood to a non-werewolf was like trying to describe the color yellow to someone who had been born blind. The concept could be made clear to them — the idea of the thing, the feelings it evoked — but it was all academic. It lacked lived experience, complexity and depth.

The scent of blood flooded my senses for the second time in the span of a day. It was a mixture of fresh and dried, of heart's blood and viscera, and it told a story to me…a story of rage, fear and pain.

I smelled my grandmother's scent under it all, even though it was fading fast. The scent that had surrounded me as a child, that had led me through my first change… She had loved me, even if she had never understood me.

I opened my eyes.

Sliced open from groin to collarbone, Mama lay exposed on her bed, her intestines spilling out onto the sheet beside her, shiny in the moonlight. One eye was a mangled, bloody mass in her socket. Her lips had collapsed back against broken teeth. Her ribcage was broken in several places, torn open at the heart, through which a thin silver spike had been driven.

I stood, frozen. I took in the sight of the ruined body without a flicker of emotion. My head turned to the open window, where the woman who did this had doubtless gained entry.

I looked down to the windowsill and swallowed hard. I crossed the room slowly, my shaking hand outstretched toward the small piece of paper, and the single white daisy that lay on top of it. Stuffing the flower into the pocket of my track pants, I unfolded the sheet of paper, doing my best to avoid touching the brown smears that lined the edges.

Grace —
So nice to see you again.
Sorry to have missed you.
We'll catch up next time.

Crumpling the paper in my fist, I spun on my heel, rushing toward the opposite corner of the room. Falling to my knees, my whole body heaved as I retched, head bashing against the wall, my eyes shut tight.

Did I do this?
Did I provoke the killer into action?
Is Mama dead because of my recklessness?
I should never have come back.

I became aware, after what felt like forever, of an arm thrown around my shoulders and a hand holding back the hair from my face. I allowed myself to lean into Marcus' body as much as I could, but threw up twice more, nothing but saliva and bile at this point. As I struggled to breathe, Kassandra's low, feminine voice probed at my throbbing brain.

"...how should we proceed?"

Coughing, I reached back and grabbed onto Marcus' arm, pushing one foot under myself. "What? What did you say?" I heard the shaking in my voice, felt the tears streaming down my face, the salty taste of them mingling with the acidic tang of bile on my lips. I wiped my arm across my chin, and looked up at Kassandra.

The wolf shifted her weight from foot to foot, her hands tightening on her utility belt. She swallowed, her low voice gentle. "I said, it's up to you how we should proceed, ma'am, but I'd recommend —"

"What do you mean, it's up to me?"

Kassandra blinked. She took a step back, her heel dipping into a pool of fresh blood. Her brown eyes darted between me and Marcus. "Mama's dead. With her gone, you... You're our den leader now, ma'am."

With a lurch, my body convulsed as I threw up again.

I was only vaguely aware of what happened in the next handful of minutes. Marcus and Kassandra held a hushed, but heated conversation above my head. The older wolf left, returning a half-minute later with a thick knit blanket, which Marcus draped around my quivering body.

"Come on, Grace."

I looked over at him with bleary, tear-filled eyes. Marcus pulled at my shoulders. "Let's get you somewhere you can sit down. Come on."

I gave a weak nod and, after a few false starts, managed to get my feet under myself and force my body upright. "Sunroom," I muttered, shuffling toward the door.

Leaving him no choice but to follow, I stumbled to the sunroom. Marcus flicked on the lights as we entered, but I groaned in pain, and he turned them off again, leaving the room in shadow, save for the few gray rays of light struggling through the clouds.

I collapsed into Mama's wicker chair in front of the bay windows. I doubled over, tears flowing freely down my face. Head hung low, I clasped my hands together in front of my knees as if praying, squeezing them so tightly that my skin went white.

Marcus knelt in front of me. His hands cupped my own, rubbing them with a tenderness I knew I did not deserve.

Taking in a shaky breath, I lifted my head. Marcus' blue eyes regarded me with open concern. I quickly looked past him to the view outside, unable to bear the sight of his empathy.

"What do you need, Grace?" Marcus tightened his grip on my hands. He closed his eyes and swallowed. "Just tell me what you need."

I watched the water in the bay begin to glow with sunlight. I took in a deep breath, the chilled air of the room washing against my raw throat like a salve.

"I don't know," I said at last, releasing the held breath. I collapsed back in the chair, pulling my hands free of Marcus'. Closing my eyes, I pressed my palms against the sockets, so hard that the black of my eyelids became starred with white. "This is like a nightmare. I keep trying to wake up, but I can't."

My bottom lip began to quiver. I pulled it between my teeth and bit down. The pain focused me for a moment, and I sat up straighter.

I looked into Marcus' eyes. "I just want to go back to Klamath Falls," I said. "I just want to go back to my boring job, and my boring life, and be…be boring. I don't care if, if this person — if she finds me and kills me." I shook my head, my hand curling into a fist as I pushed it into my chest. "I don't want any of this. I never did. Oh God, I just want to be normal."

"Do you?"

Marcus squirmed beneath my disbelieving stare, his lips firming into a line. "Grace, if you want to go back to Klamath Falls, if that's what you really want, I will fight our way out of here, put you in a car and take you there myself. You'll never have to see me or another wolf as long as you live." The dark-haired man drew a hand down his jaw. "But you have to know... You'll never be normal."

I couldn't hold back the whimper that escaped my clenched teeth. I curled in on myself, trying to hide the tears that were falling off my cheeks and down my chin. "Because of what I am? Who I am?"

"No, that's not—" Marcus let out a long breath through his nose and dropped down onto one knee, his hands reaching out to grip the arms of the wicker chair. "Grace, you could have been born a human, like me, and you'd still never have been normal. You could have been born into any number of dens, been any one of a hundred anonymous werewolf foot soldiers, and you'd still never have been normal. It's you, Grace." Without a hint of hesitation, he reached out and gripped my knee, squeezing gently. "You are extraordinary. Not because of who your mother was, or what blood you have running through your veins—because of the thoughts in your head, and the colors of your soul. You were never going to be normal, because Grace Celeste Holtz is not a normal person—she's like a firework or a flower that blooms once in a lifetime." Marcus' voice grew quiet. "Grace, if only you could see yourself the way I see you, you'd know why I fell in love with you all those years ago. And why I'm so certain that you're going to find the right thing to do now."

I turned my face up to look into Marcus' shining eyes. I took in a deep breath, then, with a suddenness that I was sure was disconcerting in the extreme, my eyes narrowed into slits and my forehead wrinkled. "Wait, what did you say?"

Marcus stared at me for a moment, his eyes widening. He licked his lips, the corners of his mouth curling up into a sardonic smile. "Uh, which part? I said quite a lot." Then, when I did not immediately respond, his smile widened into a grimace and he scoffed. "Hey, hold on, were—were you really not listening?"

"You said…" I rocketed up from my grandmother's chair and began patting myself down. "Flower. Flowers. Flowers!"

Scrambling out of my way, Marcus turned to watch as I stepped forward toward the bay windows. I tore into the pockets of my track pants and with a triumphant "Ha!", I withdrew the wilting, withered flower that had been resting near Mama's deathbed.

I brandished the crushed daisy like a dagger, jabbing it under Marcus' nose. "There was a flower just like this left with Colquhoun and Aidan. Why? Why leave flowers?"

Marcus rose from where he was kneeling, shaking his head. "Paying your respects to the dead type of thing, I suppose?"

"Respect?" I sneered, squeezing the stem of the plant flat between my fingers. I spun away and began pacing in front of the large windows, my gaze fixated on the crumpled petals. "She doesn't have any respect for us. No, this is a message. Colquhoun read it. He read it loud and clear when he saw this flower on Aidan—it's the only thing that makes sense, that's how he knew."

"Knew what?"

"That someone was coming for him!" I shouted, throwing my fists heavenward. I strode toward Marcus and stopped in front of him, my breathing labored. "It's the only thing—it explains it! Everything he wrote in that note to Mama! To write that note in the first place, he must have known that whoever killed his son wasn't going to stop there. And the only thing out of place with Aidan was this." With a single nod, I shoved the flower back into my pocket and walked around Marcus, heading for the door. "We've got to figure out what this meant to him."

"And how are we going to do that?" pressed Marcus, hurrying to catch up with me.

"The records, his diaries—maybe he wrote about it. We need to look at those damn records." I tightened my jaw and squared my shoulders. "And I know just how to get them."

Chapter Twenty

Marcus

Getting back to The Maxwell proved to be more of an ordeal than either of us had anticipated. Kassandra was waiting for us outside the sunroom, and immediately tried to take charge of the situation, starting to cobble together a convoy of cars and security personnel to accompany us to the hotel.

"I don't need it," Grace said for the fifth time in as many minutes, her irritation reaching a fever pitch. "I'm heading back to an upscale hotel, not a war zone, and I'm not the fucking queen of Sheba."

"This person has already kidnapped you in transit once, ma'am." Kassandra clenched her jaw. "It's not going to happen again on my watch."

"I need one car." Grace extended her pointer finger. "One — got it? If you really want to come along and sit outside the hotel all night, I guess I can't stop you, but I don't need a damn entourage!"

In the end, I managed to broker a compromise, and we found ourselves sitting in the back seat of an armor-plated sedan. Kassandra took point from the front passenger seat, while a second security officer sat behind the wheel.

When we arrived at the hotel, Kassandra and the other security officer, a slight woman with a head full of braids named Naomi, preceded us up the side stairs and into the hallway where our rooms were located. Grace reached toward the door lock with her keycard, only to have Naomi pluck the plastic from her fingertips and step in front of her.

"Ma'am," said Naomi, her free hand firm against Grace's shoulder. "We need to sweep your rooms."

Grace scoffed, her hands on her hips, a scowl pulling her lips taut. "Don't be stupid, we don't have time—"

"Please," I said from behind, cutting her off. "Do what you need to do."

I waited until the two security officers had entered the space before stepping up next to Grace, a scowl cutting across my own face. "For God's sake, Grace, let them do their job. They're just trying to keep you safe."

Grace leaned against the door jamb, crossing her arms over her chest. "Fine. But we don't have time for this."

"Listen, whatever it is you're thinking, I'm sure it can wait." I tilted my head to one side and sighed. "You need a few hours of sleep, at least."

Grace shook her head hard. "No—I can't risk him hearing about Mama before I tell him. I need to see his reaction."

I furrowed my brow. "Who?"

"Lawrence Hughes." Grace's brows fell into a hard line. "I think it's well past time for an introduction."

When the rooms were declared safe, a small, heated discussion took place around continued surveillance. Grace was staunchly against it, but she was the only one who thought it unnecessary. I insisted that Kassandra, at the least, remain nearby, in the lobby or parked across the street. Grace relented when it became clear that doing so was the one way she was going to get to do what she wanted.

Kassandra and Naomi left to take up their stations. As soon as the door latched, Grace made for the connecting door to my room, pulling it open and striding toward my laptop. She ignored my protestations as I trailed her from her rooms, my exasperation clear in my voice.

"I already told you, Grace, the Council won't let us look at the Feóndulf records. There's no way."

Grace plopped down into the swivel chair in front of the computer, waving away my concerns like so much secondhand smoke. "I'll handle it. Call him."

When I made no move to comply with her command, she rolled her eyes in exasperation, her hand closing into a fist. "Damn it, call Hughes!"

I leaned over Grace and began pulling up the required program, shaking my head. "Okay, okay! I'll bite. Why am I calling Hughes?"

"Just call. You'll see," said Grace, shaking her hair away from her face and tugging on the hem of her sweatshirt.

We waited as the video call struggled to connect over the hotel Wi-Fi. I stared at Grace's reflected image on the screen as I wondered what exactly it was she planned to say.

With a flash, a small, sharp face filled the screen. Olive eyes pricked at us like needles, and I felt, for the briefest of moments, protective of Grace, wishing to save her from their assessing gaze.

She threw on her most dazzling smile, inclining her head toward the camera. "Good morning, Lawrence. I'm not sure if you know who I—"

"Evening, actually, Miss Holtz." That explained the lush black dressing gown, the mussed nature of the man's silver-gray hair and the tired annoyance that wrinkled the edges of his eyes as he drew a smile taut across his lips. "Time difference and all that." His face fell back into something akin to practiced boredom as he turned his attention to me. "Bowen, how goes the investigation?"

Before I could answer, Grace cut in, her head falling to one side. "That's what I wanted to talk to you about, Lawrence."

Hughes blinked. He drew in a deep breath, then threw a glance back at Grace. "Oh?"

"Has Mama been in touch with you in the last two days?"

"Not since her initial communiqué regarding her receipt of Colquhoun's final message." The man's eyes darted toward me and narrowed. "Why? Should she have been?"

"Just curious." Grace swallowed, tossing her hair over her shoulder. "She's dead, you see, so I can't ask her."

Lawrence blinked. He leaned forward in his chair. His shoulders, thin and angular, had gone tense under his robe as he repeated the words she had spoken. "She's...dead?"

"Looks like Colquhoun was right to warn us, doesn't it?" Grace crossed her legs, sighing. "Not that it's done a lot of good."

The older man recoiled from the screen, teeth gritting as he sputtered, "Dead? Murdered?" He settled a glare on me. "Bowen, you idiot, you were meant to—"

"Marcus was busy doing his job when all this happened," interrupted Grace coolly. "Which, I shouldn't have to remind you, was to track down whomever is behind these attacks on us—not to protect my grandmother."

Lawrence tore his gaze away from me. He focused on Grace after a beat of silence, his fingers digging into the arms of his chair. "Us?"

"Your den and mine." Grace forced a small, smug smile onto her face. "Well, I guess they're both mine, now, aren't they?" She shook herself. "Anyway, I just thought you'd want to know. That, and one other thing—the den archives."

Hughes lifted a brow. Grace continued, steepling her fingers in front of her chest. "Your histories, the oldest ones you've got written down? If you're anything like the Nameless, you must have texts that go quite a ways back."

Hughes simply nodded.

"I want to see them," said Grace.

"Absolutely out of the question."

"Let's say your three—no five, oldest codices." Grace continued as if she hadn't heard the other wolf, her eyes heavenward. "And Colquhoun's oldest private diaries. You have them digitized, I assume?"

Hughes grimaced. "Of course we do, but—"

"Great! You can get them to Marcus however you like. FTP them, set him up with some credentials, send him a flash drive. I don't care how you do it, but do it fast, okay?"

"Miss Holtz—"

211

"Please," said Grace, flattening her hand against her collarbone. "You can call me Grace."

"Miss Holtz." Color had risen into Hughes' ashen cheeks, blotches of red against his pale skin. I watched as his hand curled into a fist before disappearing from view under the lid of his desk. "You are not a Feóndulf. You are an outsider. And a woman. And Marcus Bowen is bitten, not born. Under no circumstances will either of you be allowed to see any of the den records, for any reason."

Grace's smile widened. "Try this reason on for size, Lawrence. I'm your fucking den leader now." I had to say, I relished the way the older werewolf flinched at the expletive. Grace narrowed her eyes. "You? You answer to me. Woman or not, Nameless or not, Colquhoun put me in charge of you."

Hughes clenched his jaw so tightly that I could see the lines of muscle beneath his skin. He swallowed and forced his mouth open to hiss, "Young lady, I had the honor of serving Colquhoun for over one hundred years, as head of the Feóndulf Council, and if you think—"

"Well," said Grace, tucking a piece of hair behind her ear, "now you'll have the honor of serving me. Congratulations." Her smile disappeared. She lifted a finger. "Don't try to bullshit me, Lawrence. Colquhoun's word was law. Your entire den is built on that fact. And he picked me. Me. Your little boys' club is over." She clicked her tongue off the roof of her mouth. "You had a good run. But I'll have those records now, please." She met Hughes' gaze, her head falling to one side. "Or do I need to fly over there and rip your throat out with my teeth?"

The corners of Hughes' mouth twitched. He collapsed back into his armchair, gaze falling to his desktop. "You'll have them within the next twenty-four hours."

"Make it twelve."

He crossed his legs and waved away her request, frowning. "If you need them that quickly, I'll just bring them myself."

Grace, her hand extended toward the keyboard to end the call, froze. "Excuse me?"

Still not meeting her eyes, Hughes smiled tightly. "I'll be on a flight first thing in the morning for Seattle. Myself, and a few other members of the Council. There are certain legal formalities to get out of the way, information on which you must be brought up to speed and so on—if you're to fulfill your duties as leader of this den." He straightened, adopting an air of concern that did not suit him. "I trust that's not a problem?"

"Looking forward to it, Lawrence," Grace shot back. She wiggled her fingers at the camera. "Buh-bye."

A few keystrokes, and the call was disconnected. Grace deflated back into the office chair, sliding down until she stared limply up at the ceiling.

"Well, shit," she pronounced at length.

I stepped into her field of vision, hovering over her. "You know, for someone who doesn't want to be a den leader, you did that very well."

"I had Mama to watch for two hundred years. You pick up a thing or two." She forced herself upright. "Didn't count on them coming over here, though. What is Hughes up to?"

"What makes you think he's up to anything?"

Grace snorted, staring down at the carpet beneath her feet. "You don't get to where he is in life by playing things straight."

"How cynical you've become in your old age," I observed with affection, leaning against the back of the chair.

"I've always been like this," lied Grace. "Besides, he just happened to have a flight booked for the day after Mama turns up dead?"

I straightened up, shrugging. "Coincidence."

Grace glared at me. "I thought detectives weren't allowed to believe in coincidence."

Rolling my eyes, I moved toward her, my hands outstretched. "We're also not supposed to make up crazy theories and throw baseless accusations around without a full night's sleep first." I grabbed hold of both her wrists and started walking her toward the still-open connecting door. "Come on. Bed."

"I don't need to sleep," she protested weakly, allowing herself to be led through to her room all the same. "Werewolf's constitution."

I flicked off the large overhead light as we entered, leaving the room bathed in the far more forgiving light of the bedside lamp. I pulled Grace all the way to the foot of the bed, where I positioned her in front of it, before forcing her to sit. "Werewolf's constitution or no, you need at least a few hours of shut eye."

Grace clicked her tongue off the back of her teeth, shaking my hands off her wrists. "No, Marcus, there's too much to do. With Mama gone, there are arrangements to be made, people to talk to, a whole den to reassure—" With an expression that would have been comical under different circumstances, Grace rocketed to her feet, nearly stepping on my toes as she exclaimed, "Shit, Lily! I told her I'd call her. Oh God, she's going to freak about all this..."

But I refused to move out of the way, pushing her back down onto the bed. "Let me talk to her," I said. "She likes me."

She drew her hand down her chin, but nodded her acquiescence. I turned away from her with some reluctance, rummaging through her belongings to find her cell, which had somehow ended up tossed into her duffel bag. I placed the phone in my pocket and headed for the open connecting door. Then, with a suddenness that surprised me, Grace said, "I didn't always hate her, you know."

I froze. I closed my eyes for a moment, willing my aching heart back under control. Turning, I watched her carefully. She sat on the edge of the hotel bed, unmoving, lost in the thought, her face a perfect picture of misery that moved me to tears. She looked up at me, her beautiful brown eyes red-rimmed from crying. "Mama, I mean. I didn't always... She was my..."

"I know," I said, my voice soft. I sighed heavily. "I'm so sorry, Grace." I looked up to the ceiling, willing my tears away, but one drop escaped down the side of my face. I swiped at it desperately, shaking my head and gesturing through the open door toward my own bed. "Listen, if you need me, I'll be right in the other room."

Grace stood, her arm outstretched toward me. "Wait, Marcus—"

I turned around on the threshold of the connecting door, raising my brows high in question, one hand resting in my trouser pocket.

Grace swallowed, rubbing her forehead as she gathered her words. She walked toward me, shaking her head and avoiding my gaze. "I...I haven't said thank you."

I grinned in confusion. "No need, Grace. it's just a phone call."

"Not for that. Though, yes, thank you for that," she said, hand falling to her side. She took a deep breath, stopping in front of me and looking me full in the face. "I mean I haven't said thank you for... Well, everything. Especially what you said to me earlier at the den house." Nodding, Grace let out a short huff of forced laughter. "I, uh, I think I needed to hear that."

I shifted my weight from foot to foot, pushing a hand through my tousled hair. "Oh. That." I attempted to plaster on a casual smile, but it was threadbare at best. "Yes, well, I—" The smirk faltered as I looked into her eyes. I sighed, dispensing with pretense and growing suddenly serious. "Grace, hell, it's what friends are supposed to do. And I'd very much like to be your friend."

"Marcus," said Grace, a waver in her voice. "Even after everything... During everything... Look, even when I hated you the most, I never, never stopped thinking of you as a friend. As my best friend."

"I would have understood if you had." My head drooped, my gaze focused intently on the floor under my bare feet. "You had every reason to hate me, Grace." I reached up and leaned against the frame of the door, letting go of a deep breath and closing my eyes. "Do you remember, the day before...before Mama sent me away? You called me here, at this hotel. You were certain Mama was beginning to suspect something. And you asked me to run with you."

It was a phone call I had obsessed over for the better part of thirty years. A memory I had replayed in the darkest hours of the night, when sleep eluded me, and the emptiness of my life gnawed at my gut.

Grace nodded. "I remember."

"And I said no." My hand curled into a fist. "I was so terrified of being on my own, without the Feóndulf behind me. I couldn't imagine surviving in the world denless." Lifting my head, I opened my eyes, focusing my attention just over Grace's left shoulder. "You called me a coward. And you were right. I was." My gaze flickered to meet hers then flitted away, jittery as a hummingbird. I licked my lips and shook my head. "We should've left together, Grace. Right then." I pushed off the doorframe and curled in on myself, shoving my free hand into my pocket. "I don't have many regrets in life, but saying no to you — that's one of them."

Chapter Twenty-One

Grace

Heart aching, I reached forward and slid my fingers under his chin, lifting Marcus' face up to look into mine. His eyes were open, his naked stare reflected my own pain and longing and, as if on instinct, I leaned forward and pressed my lips to his, kissing him softly.

The sensation of his lips against mine rippled through me like a shot of whiskey, warming and intoxicating, setting my blood dancing while at the same time making me shiver. When he reciprocated the gesture, when he reached out to hold my cheek with trembling fingers and shifted against my lips without withdrawing, the tight coil of control in my chest unraveled. I took a step forward, my body flush against his, and lifted my hands to grip at Marcus' shoulders with a possessiveness I barely recognized.

Marcus mimicked my stance, but instead of pulling me closer, he took a step back, breaking the kiss with a small gasp. My eyes flickered open.

While he shook his head, Marcus' eyes remained closed as he whispered, "Grace, we shouldn't—"

"Marcus." His eyes opened wide at the sound of his name. I gave a weak smile and lifted my hand to his face, trailing my thumb across his lower lip. "Don't be so stupid as to make the same mistake twice."

He blinked at me once, then twice. The corners of his mouth shot down into a frown and his hands dropped from my shoulders to my hips. He pulled me against his body while quietly whispering, "Ah, sod it, then," before kissing me hard.

I answered in kind, my hands skittering unmoored across first his jaw, then his shoulders, then his sides, then his chest. I deepened the kiss with a flick of my tongue at his bottom lip, a teasing, tentative request that Marcus answered with unabashed eagerness, opening his mouth to my explorations.

Slowly at first, then in a progressively frantic tumble, I pulled Marcus back into my room toward the bed. I kicked off my shoes as I went, running the tip of my tongue along the top of his palate. He tried desperately to keep pace with me, capturing my lower lip between his teeth and biting down, not too hard, but just hard enough. Still, there was hesitation in his movements. No longer content with the skin available to my hands, I began easing his shirt up and over his body. Marcus tried to register a verbal protest, but it was lost in the crush of our mouths. It wasn't until I relinquished his lips and began lavishing attention on his neck that he was able to say anything at all.

As soon as his mouth was free of mine, he breathed my name imploringly, caressing my back and shoulders through my thin sweatshirt. "Grace..."

"Don't worry," I answered, my words muffled as I pressed my lips against his carotid artery, my wandering hands pushing up under the hem of his T-shirt, fingers dancing over the newly exposed flesh at his side. "I'll take care of you."

A weak chuckle was Marcus' only response for a moment. "I...I think that's my line..." he managed before groaning in pleasure, head falling back as his eyes flickered shut, words lost to him as I slid my tongue up and down the column of his throat.

Pausing for a moment, I stepped back to remove his shirt entirely and regain my bearings. I stared at him, drinking in the sight of him. He was fit, as he had to be to stay in the police force, but lean and lithe, his white skin dotted here and there with constellations of freckles. His arms were muscular, his chest smooth and right then I wanted to devour him. Glancing behind him, I was pleased to find that we had made it to the end of the large king bed. Draping my arms over his shoulders, I leaned in toward him. Marcus closed his eyes, lips parted in expectation of another kiss, and I grinned at the gasp I elicited from him when he felt the very tip of my tongue flick at his earlobe.

"You didn't think I'd forgotten about this, did you?" I whispered into his perfect ear.

"You're a wicked woman," groaned Marcus. He drew in a sharp breath, his body shuddering. "Gra—" My name was lost in another uncontrollable moan as I took the top of his ear between my front teeth, nibbling my way around it. He lifted his hands to my shoulders and squeezed me tight. I ran my tongue down, probing just inside the fold as I went. His forehead came down to rest in the crook of my shoulder.

For the next five minutes, I licked, bit, sucked and blew at the skin of his ears, and none of Marcus' strangled cries, cusses, shivers or pleas could get me to stop. He must have said my name a hundred times—

my ears rang with the sound of it. He snaked his hands up under my sweatshirt, strong fingers digging into my muscles, but he soon gave up on the upper half of my body and instead moved to the lower, cupping the round curves of my backside so hard I began to ache with the pleasure of it.

Pressed against him as I was, I marveled at how hard I had managed to get him in so short a time. He was throbbing against me, his moans gaining an extra edge of desperation the few times I rocked my hips against him.

"I want you," I growled against his ear, the words sounding like a curse in the dim room.

Marcus nodded emphatically as he panted against my cheek, his hands coming up to press against the column of my throat. "I'm yours," he said, shuddering. He pulled away from me for a moment, leaving a trail of kisses across my forehead before his lips fell next to the shell of my ear. "Oh, Grace, I'm yours, just *please* touch me..."

"Where?"

He jerked back from me, blinking in disbelief. "Are you serious?"

I continued to smile at him, enjoying myself immensely as I repeated, "Tell me where..." even as I slipped my fingertips beneath the elastic band of his boxers, rubbing my thumbs in circles in the hollows of his hips.

Keening softly, Marcus reached down between us and groped for my wrists, his eyes flickering shut. "Oh, darling, you're so *close* – "

With a forcefulness just shy of painful, I grabbed hold of both of Marcus' wrists and yanked them behind him. The jerking motion arched him backward over the edge of the bed, but he was just able to keep his feet by widening his stance, allowing one of my legs to slip neatly between his own.

He had forgotten that I was older and stronger than him, and if what I was feeling on my thigh was any indication, this brief, timely reminder was making him even harder. I leaned into his face, grinding my leg against his clothed member as I hissed, "Say it, or I'm not touching shit."

"My cock, all right," he shouted, eyes still screwed shut, teeth gritted. "Please, *please*, for the love of God, touch my cock!"

With a pleased groan, I grinned. In a swift motion, I kicked one of his feet out from under him and pulled back on his pinned arms. The younger wolf fell onto the corner of the mattress with a grunt, landing hard on his backside, his sharp blue eyes flickering open as I released him and said, "I'll do better than that."

I mounted him with ease, sliding onto his lap, scissoring my thighs around his hips. He sat up to meet me and we collided in a kiss that ached with the longing of years wasted, and burned with the heat of a passion that had never diminished.

I pushed him flat against the mattress and, when I'd had my fill of his mouth, I pulled away from his lips and began ravaging his neck and shoulders. I carelessly bit and sucked hard at the exposed skin of his throat, leaving a haphazard collage of broken skin and bruises in my wake. I slid off his lap and onto the floor, moving onto my knees in between his legs to get at his chest and abdomen, my teeth continuing to cut into him with tantalizing irregularity, making him jump and groan every time I tasted him, the red mark always smoothed over with my warm, silky tongue a moment later.

By the time I reached his hips, my tongue lapping at the hollows with excruciating slowness, I could tell from the way his muscles jumped under my tongue, and the sharp gasps he was unable to suppress that his body belonged to me. Pulling my lips away from his skin, I slid his sweatpants and boxers down to his ankles with one clean jerk.

He gave a start at being so unceremoniously stripped naked, and pushed himself up onto his elbows, panting and shaking his head as he demanded, "What are you — ?"

"Touch me" — I said, gathering my hair to one side — "and I'll leave." Frowning, I met his panicked, wide eyes, placing my hands on the inside of his upper thighs. "I'll head back to my room, and get that good night's sleep you were so concerned about. Understand?"

Adam's apple bobbing, Marcus swallowed hard, nodding but saying nothing.

I grinned. "Good."

When I wrapped my lips around the very tip of him, I heard him barely swallow down a loud shout of frustration. Marcus' hands hovered over the back of my head, but they fell away and twisted the hotel comforter into tight clumps as I took his cock into my mouth without using my hands, sucking and licking at his sensitive head before sliding the rest of him inside.

The taste of him was as intoxicating as a shot of good whiskey, and I soon lost myself in the rhythm of my lovemaking, in the way his taut skin felt against my tongue and the pressure of his heavy member in my jaws.

My gaze flickered up when the younger man struggled back up onto his elbows, his fingers digging into the mattress in an attempt to aid his ascension.

I had never seen him looking so delicious. His thick, dark hair glistened with sweat. His bangs were falling into his eyes, pupils were blown wide and dark with pleasure, the focus of which were me, and me alone. He leaned to one side, seemingly unable to support himself. I watched the muscles of his chest and abdomen jump and clench as I sucked and licked at his cock, entranced by my ability to affect him at such a minute level.

"Grace," he said, gasping for air. "Grace, please…"

Encouraged that I was on the right track, I pressed my fingers into the muscles of his thighs and dragged my fingertips down, causing the man beneath me to writhe and reach out a hand toward me in desperation.

"Grace, Grace, stop…"

I hummed in displeasure at the word and pushed him farther into my warm mouth, not stopping until I felt his head against the back of my throat. The hand that Marcus had outstretched toward me flinched and clenched in midair as he closed his eyes, moaning and grinding into me even as he begged, "*Stop*."

I twirled my tongue around his shaft and pulled him out of my mouth. Marcus came undone entirely, collapsing back against the mattress, his shaking hands coming up to cover his face. "Grace, I swear to God, if you don't stop, I'll finish right now, I won't, I *can't* – "

Exactly what I wanted to hear. I reached up and grabbed his hips in my hands, holding him in place while I took him in my mouth and sucked hard over and over again, leaving him a mewling mess.

Before long, the wolf came with a shout, every muscle in Marcus' body tightening, save for his tongue and jaw that let loose with a nonsensical list of the foulest words I had ever heard, and not all of them in English.

I gave one last pleasurable hum over him before drawing back and swallowing, cleaning him leisurely with my tongue before collapsing back onto my haunches. Marcus lay spent on the mattress, his limbs sprawled in every direction. The only thing that let me know he had survived this first encounter was the frantic heaving of his chest as he drew in and pushed out deep gasps of air. I smirked, drawing a finger down the corner of my mouth, and pressing my fingertips into the flesh of his inner thighs. "Language, Mr. Bowen," I chastised. I rested my head on his hip, my own heavy breathing making the skin there damp. For a few long minutes, there was no response from my partner, and I almost began to worry that I had done some serious damage to him. Then the body on which I was reclining took in a deep breath and let it out slowly.

"How?" demanded a voice from above me.

I looked up, smirking. "Which part?"

Sweat beaded on his forehead, Marcus was looking down at me, his chest still rising and falling at a steady pace. He fixed me with a glare, but it lacked bite. "No. How... how do you still have all your clothes on?"

"Oh." I stood on shaky legs and, without further prompting, removed my sweatshirt, unhooked my bra and stepped out of my sweatpants and underwear, leaving them all in a messy pile beside me.

I had been naked in far more public places, but as Marcus stared at me with undisguised lust, a flush began to creep up the side of my neck. I attempted to disguise my sudden self-consciousness with theater, forcing a hard smirk across my lips as I spread my arms wide. "Better?"

Marcus gave a large nod, sitting up on the end of the bed. "Much." He reached a tentative hand toward me. "May I...touch you?"

My smile softened into something more natural, and I moved closer to him. He settled his hands lightly on the back of my thighs, and I rested my forearms on his shoulders. "Please."

Marcus

Grace took in a sharp breath when I rose to my feet, my arms still wrapped around the back of her thighs, lifting her up. She clasped the arms she had rested around my neck tight and wrapped her legs around my waist, locking them at the ankles.

Grinning, I kissed one side of her neck, then the other, before backing up onto the mattress, climbing up on my knees, still holding her aloft. Spinning, I deposited her atop the bed, pressing her back into the expensive comforter, her head falling onto the mountain of pillows. I kissed her open-mouthed, languidly licking at the corner of her lips, bringing my hands up to massage her petite breasts and pluck at her hard nipples. I collapsed over her, the warmth of her body against my own so intimately erotic that it made me want to scream. Grace curled into me, burying her face in the crook of my shoulder as I peppered kisses down to the hollow of her throat. One hand roved away from her chest to grip the back of her thigh. I pulled her leg up so her knee was level with my hip.

When I began to tease the folds of her warm center with the tips of my fingers, she was already soaking wet with arousal. She bit into my shoulder to muffle a loud groan, and I responded in kind, slipping a single digit just inside her.

"Don't tease me, you bastard," she demanded, nails digging into my scalp.

"Oh ho, she can give it, but she can't take it?" I taunted, working her nipple between my teeth and sucking hard.

"Eat me," shot back Grace.

I pulled away from her with a growl. "Love to."

That was all the preamble I gave before I slid myself down between Grace's legs, spreading them wide with my hands and licking at her greedily. Grace's back arched off the mattress and she immediately grabbed the back of my head with her hands, digging her fingers into my hair and holding me in place. Not that she needed to... I was very single-minded when it came to this particular act of lovemaking.

I curled my tongue inside her entrance once, twice, three times before moving up to lick and suck at her swollen clit. Her body shook with pleasure as I slid the three longest fingers of my free hand inside her, beginning to pump the digits in and out in a slow, steady rhythm while I focused my mouth on her most sensitive spot. After a few minutes of this, I hummed, deep and guttural against her body, releasing her for just a moment, my mouth replaced by my thumb as I kissed her inner thigh.

"Thirty years," I said, a chuckle in my rough voice, "and you still taste just how I remember."

Thirty years. To think that I could have had this for the last thirty years...

With a groan, Grace redirected my mouth to where she needed it most, and I complied with vigor. Time expanded and contracted, then ceased to have any meaning at all as I worked at pleasuring her. Just when Grace seemed to have grown used to the pace of my ministrations, I would change one aspect of my technique—speeding up the pace of my fingers inside her, or slowing down, licking at her instead of sucking, abandoning her clit entirely to kiss at her thighs and hips.

As much as either of us might have wanted it to last forever, even Grace had her limits.

"Marcus, don't stop," said Grace, her breathing ragged, her legs beginning to shake. She released me and reached up to grab the corners of the pillows on which she was reclining, trying desperately to keep control of herself and not to twist away from me. "Oh, don't *stop*."

"Never," I promised, curling my fingers up so they rubbed against her. My breath was hot against her clit, and I could tell the irregular flicking of my tongue over her center was driving her to distraction. "Oh, darling, you're so beautiful. Come on, come for me, please..."

I asked so prettily, she was loath to deny me my simple request.

She came with an abandonment of propriety that I found hopelessly erotic, one hand coming down to bury itself in my hair as she shook and shivered. While she moaned into the overstuffed pillows, her fingertips flexing through my hair, I kissed and sucked at her center and inner thighs.

At length, Grace looked down at me, giving my hair a tug. I answered with a hum, glancing up, but not ceasing my tasting of her.

"Come here," said Grace, her voice rough with pleasure.

Grinning, I complied, drawing myself up over her with pointed slowness, pressing the entire length of my naked body against her, before kissing her languidly.

Wrapping her arms around my neck and shoulders, Grace pulled me close, threading her legs through mine, intertwining us completely. Then, as if it were the easiest thing in the world, Grace tumbled our coupled bodies across the bed until I was under her once more.

"We're not done," she whispered, teeth pulling at my bottom lip.

"Thank Christ." I breathed out the words in a sigh.

Grace reached between us and took my stiff cock roughly in hand, making me groan aloud. "I want you inside me."

"Thought you'd never ask," I joked, my head pushing back into the pillows as she stroked me.

Grace lifted herself upright, her legs straddling my hips. "Oh, I'm not asking." She grinned down at me, her hands splayed across my heaving chest. I shivered at her words, and, without further preamble, she slid my cock inside herself, filling herself with me in one fluid motion. Her eyes flickered shut, but they opened again when I gripped her hips tightly, as if holding on for dear life.

Our eyes met, and the magnitude of what we were doing, of this thing between us, came crashing down around my heart all over again. The midday sun snuck through the closed curtains and settled over her glistening body with a dim glow. She shone like the moon herself. Her head fell forward and she kissed me softly, reverently.

It was her. It was always going to be her.

"Marcus," she said, drawing away, her voice faltering. "I...I still love—"

"I know, Grace." I gripped her hips tightly, but kept still, my eyes wide and fixed on hers. "I know."

A groan tore itself from her chest. She closed her eyes and began to move her hips in a steady rhythm, pushing me in and out of her, slowly at first, but soon with increasing recklessness. She gripped and massaged her breasts with her hands, pulling at her hard nipples.

I matched her thrust for thrust, my breath growing rougher and heavier with every passing minute. My cock throbbed inside her, and the answering tightening of her, the sensation was too delicious for words. I was so lost in the movements of our lovemaking, that I didn't even notice when I started muttering Welsh curses under my breath.

"*Ffyc...ffyc mi...mae hynny'n teimlo mor dda...*" Sweat beaded in my hair, and I shook it away. "Grace," I breathed, my gaze never leaving her as she rode me. "I'm yours. I'm yours forever." I dug my fingertips into her hips and my eyes flickered shut as I growled, squirming deeper into the mattress. "Oh Christ, you feel amazing, you feel so good." My thrusts grew deeper and more irregular. I shook my head, rolling my lips under my teeth. "Grace, I can't, I *can't*, I'm going to — to — "

She reached forward and grabbed the headboard with both hands, throwing her head back. "Touch me," she commanded. "I want to be there with you. Touch me."

I pressed and rubbed the pad of my thumb in small tight circles against her clit, sending shockwaves through her already bliss-filled body. With flattering swiftness, I brought her to a heady peak, her fingernails biting and tearing into the fabric headboard as she came, tightening around me as her every muscle shook.

My back arching off the mattress, I thrust inside her at a punishing pace before I gave a shout and spilled myself inside her.

Unable to hold herself upright any longer, Grace collapsed on top of me, her face landing in the pillows on which my head rested.

"...fuck," she mumbled into the cushion. I rubbed her back, my breath warm and sticky against the side of her face. "What, again?"

"No." She shook her head and gave my bare chest a light slap. "I mean, yes, but give me a minute." I shifted beneath her, my hand coming up to cradle the back of her head. "Are you serious?"

Grace lifted herself just enough to nibble at my earlobe, prompting an exhausted chuckle from me. "You're going to kill me, woman. I'm a werewolf — not Superman."

"So..." Grace slid her hands up and down my torso. "...you don't want to join me in the shower then?"

I was silent for a few long moments. I sighed and cupped her ass in both hands. "On the other hand...what a way to die."

Grace laughed and rolled away from me, sitting up on the edge of the bed. Looking back at me over her shoulder, she shook her head. "Don't shuffle off this mortal coil just yet," she said. "I'm going to need your help with these so-called gentlemen from your Council."

The sudden shift in topic unsettled and confused my blood-starved brain. My brows furrowed. "Oh?"

"I want to greet them in style." Grace shook out her hair with one hand, her eyes unnaturally bright in the dark room. "Show them just what they can expect from me as the new head of their precious den."

I pushed myself up on my elbows, frowning. "Sounds dangerous."

Grace shrugged and smiled. "Just politics."

"Like I said." I reached for her, sighing heavily as I caressed her wrist and arm. "What do you need me to do?"

Chapter Twenty-Two

Grace

As one of Seattle's finest restaurants, The Rochester boasted spectacular views of the sprawl of Seattle, the distant, snowy mountains and the sparkling waters of the Puget Sound. The Rochester wasn't typically open for lunch, but I had pulled some strings—slightly disgusted that I still remembered which ones needed pulling—and had secured a private dining room and the necessary kitchen staff.

I had left the details of travel to Marcus, content that he would see that Hughes and the other Council members arrived at The Rochester at the appointed time, flights and SeaTac traffic allowing. I considered having a car sent for them, but I did not want to appear over-gracious. Better to let their own man deal with such niceties, than to give the impression that I was courting their favor.

The space was gorgeous, done up in tasteful wood and glass accents, which caught and amplified every bit of sunlight coming through the floor-to-ceiling windows. The table was round and made of polished cherry wood. I slid my hand along it as I walked to the seat closest to the windows, the skirt of my elegant black dress kissing my ankles as I moved. I settled in.

I had ordered all the food and drinks in advance. Everything had been plated and poured. All that was missing were the guests. I had ordered dishes of Cornish game hen for Hughes and the other Council members, but rare-cooked, twelve-ounce steaks for Marcus and myself. Inhaling the steam rising off the meat in front of me, I forced the muscles in my shoulders to relax.

"Think this'll work?" I looked up at the man standing beside me, and furrowed my brow. I shook out my skirt, arranging it so that the slit in the side exposed my freshly shaved left leg. "You're not going to stand there the whole time, are you?"

"No. Maybe. I haven't made up my mind yet." Marcus shifted from foot to foot, his gaze darting around the room, his hand gripping the back of my chair. "And do I think what will work? As far as I can tell, your plan is to intentionally piss them off, which from my own experience, you have a real talent for."

"We talked about this last night. I'm going to shake the tree and see what falls out." I reached across the table and topped off my full glass of champagne. I sipped at the expensive bubbly, my gaze again darting up to the tense frame of my companion. I shook out my shoulders. "Seriously, you can't stand there the whole time. You'll make me nervous."

"You should be."

Mouth open, a sharp retort on my tongue, I swallowed my words when the main doors swung open on their well-oiled hinges. The host ushered in our anticipated guests, who entered the room in a neat wedge shape that the tactician in me admired.

Lawrence Hughes took point, leading the pack of expensive suits and oiled hair as if he were born to it, which, I considered, he probably had been. He wasn't an imposing man, physically speaking, but his bearing was aristocratic to the core. He didn't spare the host a glance as he handed over his raincoat and umbrella, his gaze roaming lazily around the room. His expression remained a calculated blank, even when his attention settled on me and Marcus.

The three other men, a mixture of ages and general appearances, followed Hughes inside. Their expressions, however, ranged from a curious quirk of a thick brow, to a twisting scowl on lips, to a reddening of pallid cheeks.

I did my best to lounge wantonly in the plush chair, one hand swirling the champagne around my glass. I waited until the host left, closing the door behind himself as he went, before addressing the assembly.

"Lawrence." I smiled broadly, but did not rise to offer my hand or any other greeting. "How was your flight?"

"As enjoyable as could be expected, Miss Holtz." Hughes moved his briefcase from one hand to the other, gesturing to the men who surrounded him. "Allow me to introduce Mr. Thomas Gray, Mr. Jonathan Fitzpatrick and Mr. Hubert Stallingsworth."

I nodded to each man in turn, pretending not to notice their appraising stares and air of general disapproval. "Nice to meet you," I said. I gestured up to the black-haired Welshman standing at my right without looking at him. "You all know Marcus, I assume?"

"Yes." Stallingsworth stared at Marcus as if he were a particularly tasteless piece of art. The older man stroked at his sweeping mustache. "Though I must say, his presence here is entirely inappropriate."

"I have to agree," piped in Gray, a thick Scottish brogue coating his words as he stepped forward to stand next to Stallingsworth. "He is not a member of the Council, and to have a former human privy to these proceedings —"

"Oh, take that stick out of your ass and have a seat." My smile tightened, but my tone remained light and playful. "Marcus isn't going anywhere."

Gray's mouth contorted into a scowl, and his face began to redden, contrasting with his buzzed blond hair. Hughes placed a restraining hand on the stout man's elbow before turning to me, his tone measured. "I'm sorry, Miss Holtz. I'm not sure how things are done in the Nameless, but to have someone bitten involved at this level of den politics — it's unthinkable."

"Think it." I allowed my smile to wither. "It's not up for negotiation."

A soft cough from beside me broke my concentration, and I looked up into Marcus' face, my brow furrowed in annoyance. Marcus took his seat beside me, and leaned toward me, his body angled so the Feóndulfs could only see the back of his head.

"Grace," whispered Marcus, his breath warm against my cheek. "I appreciate what you're trying to do, but it's really not worth it."

"You are not leaving me alone with these guys, Marcus." I slipped the words into the shell of his ear with a hiss, then resumed my welcoming posture with a sigh, saying in a far louder voice, "I really don't think you all came almost five thousand miles to stand around and argue protocol with me, did you?"

Not one of the men standing in front of me answered. They stared at each other, at the space above my head, at Marcus, and, in Hughes' case, directly into my eyes.

I rolled my lips under my teeth and reached for my glass of champagne. "Look, the wine is getting warm, and the food is getting cold. If it's not to your liking, order whatever you please — it's on me."

Adam's apple bobbing as he swallowed, Hughes was the first to move, stepping toward the closest chair and sitting in it stiffly. Stallingsworth and Gray shared a look before parting ways and sitting on opposite sides of Hughes, leaving the chair beside Marcus unoccupied. Fitzpatrick, a young, brown-haired man with thick, black glasses, frowned, gave a light sniff of disdain and took the spot with great reluctance.

I looked from face to face, smiling with all my teeth. I spread my arms wide. "There," I drawled. "That wasn't so hard, was it?" In one sudden, fluid motion, I rose to my feet, taking up my flute of champagne. I held up the bubbling alcohol to catch the sunlight. "A toast. To the future — may it be bright."

Glasses were lifted, polite sips were taken but no one repeated my words.

Resuming my seat, I dug into my food with relish, forcing the others to at least pick at theirs and give the appearance of partaking in the expensive meal. No one spoke, the silence textured by the sound of cutlery scraping, chairs creaking and soft sips of champagne.

After swallowing a tiny morsel of his golden, roasted hen, Hughes reached down and opened the briefcase one-handed, slipping a small black hard drive out of an inner pocket. He placed it in the center of the table, resting his fingertips lightly atop it. "This should be everything you requested," he said, his attention fixed on me. "Although what you hope to glean from all this ancient history, I really can't fathom."

"Nothing happens in a vacuum, Lawrence." I reached forward and grabbed hold of the small drive with one hand. "Everything's connected. The killer went through Colquhoun's personal papers, right? That means they were looking for something. Maybe"—I wiggled the drive in the air before placing it beside my plate—"there's something in here."

Gray squirmed in his seat, his food untouched. "The future is of more concern to us, Miss Holtz."

"I told you, call me Grace." I spread my arms wide, tilting my head to one side. "I'd like to be on as good of terms with the Feóndulf Council as I am with the Nameless."

Fitzpatrick straightened, swallowing down a mouthful of game hen. "So...you intend to head both dens?"

I popped a torn-off hunk of bread into my mouth, nodding. "Of course. It's what Colquhoun wanted, don't you think?"

The four men shared a series of glances that bounced between them like ricocheting bullets, sharp and pointed. Hughes cleared his throat, cutting into his meat with measured precision. "We wouldn't presume to speculate on what Colquhoun did or did not—"

"Well, I do," I said, resting an elbow on the pristine tabletop. "He wanted me in charge, and he knew the Nameless would have to answer to me one day, too. Maybe not this soon, but, fate, right?" I began cutting my steak into manageable pieces. "Our two dens haven't been on speaking terms since the schism of 1562—well over five hundred years. That's long enough, don't you think?" Placing my knife down against my plate with a clatter, I adopted a pensive expression. "Of course, there will have to be some changes."

Stallingsworth toyed with the end of his mustache, a smile that was more like a grimace stretched across his lips. "Changes?"

"Your attitude toward women is absolutely ridiculous." I reached for the pepper and sprinkled some over my meat. "It's not the eighteen-hundreds anymore—not that you all act like it." I gestured with the tine-end of my fork as I relinquished the pepper shaker. "Let's get some women on the Council for starters. That should send the right message."

"Unfortunately"—Gray gave a rough, mirthless laugh, his knife plunging into his helpless hen—"all Council positions are currently filled."

I frowned and shook my head, my attention never moving from Hughes' face. "I'm sure I can encourage some of your good old boys to retire." I jerked my chin toward his plate. "How's your chicken?"

He blinked slowly. Pushing his plate away with one hand, he drew his napkin over his lips with the other before answering. "Dry."

"Oh, that's a shame. You should send it back." I speared another cube of meat and popped it in my mouth, nodding as I chewed. "Try the steak. They'll cook it so rare that you'll expect it to sit up off the plate and moo at you."

"Charming," Fitzpatrick mumbled into his champagne flute.

"Speaking of meat," I said around my mouthful, pausing to swallow another masticated bite. "The sacrament. Time for that to go, don't you think?"

Stallingsworth, his face ashen, allowed his utensils to clatter onto his plate as he exclaimed, "You can't be serious!"

I fixed him with a lazy stare, wiping my lips dry and tossing the silk napkin down into my lap. "I am. When I joke, I smile a lot more." I wrinkled my nose. "It's outdated and barbaric. We don't need it."

"The sacrament of the flesh is our birthright!" Fitzpatrick sputtered indignantly, his hands beginning to flail in front of him. "It's — it's what separates us from common humans! If we gave that up, we might as well just be... Well...animals."

"Animals," I answered, taking a sip of champagne, "don't kill for sport."

"This is your doing, isn't it, Bowen?" Fitzpatrick turned his outrage toward the younger werewolf beside him, his face a mask of disgust as his volume rocketed. "It has the rank smell of the bitten all over it!" Sneering, he tossed his head toward me, but his gaze stayed fixed on Marcus. "Just because you're bedding this slut, you think — "

Fitzpatrick's glasses skittered across the floor, Marcus' fist buried in the side of the man's face before he could finish his sentence. Leaping to his feet, Marcus gripped the slight man by the lapels of his jacket, and heaved him out of his chair. Fitzpatrick's kicking legs knocked at the table, which teetered, but did not upend entirely. Everyone's champagne went tumbling, one glass shattering against the edge of the cherry wood. But what really did the damage to the dishes was when Marcus slammed the older werewolf down onto the table, throwing another punch into his teeth for good measure. I attempted to remain nonplussed when one white nugget of bone bounced across the table in my direction.

Marcus, both hands once more twisted in the jacket and shirt of the man under him, leaned into Fitzpatrick's face. "Think very carefully about the next words out of your mouth." I could hear the wolf in his words, and the hairs on my arms rose in response. "Or I'll have your tongue, along with your teeth."

Fitzpatrick struggled to speak through a mouthful of blood. The words came out thick and sticky. "Sorry." He coughed, his hands tight around Marcus' wrists. "I'm sorry."

"Are you just going to sit there?" Hughes hissed.

Blinking, I looked away from Marcus. Hughes and the other two male werewolves had started from their seats when the violence started, and were now standing at the edges of the table, staring in disbelief. Hughes' hands were clenched at his side, his teeth bared, his gaze boring into me like a drill.

I leaned back in my plush chair, crossing my legs and smiling. "Things are going to change. You can either get on board, or get out of my way. But make up your mind fast, because patience is one thing Mama was never able to teach me." My smile disappeared. I reached beside me for the bottle of champagne, shaking my head. "Now get out."

Stallingsworth and Gray hurried around the table to collect their injured companion, who appeared quite dazed after Marcus' going-over, barely able to stand on his own. I wondered briefly what the wait staff would make of the battered man when he exited the restaurant, but I felt confident that the exorbitant fee I had paid would cover all manner of awkwardness. Hughes was the last to leave. With every muscle in his body tensed, he swiped his briefcase up off the floor and backed away toward the door, his eyes never leaving my face. "The Council won't stand for this."

Emptying the last of the champagne into my glass, I shook my head and forced a smirk onto my face. "I don't think you have a choice, Lawrence." I lifted my other hand and wiggled my fingers. "Buh-bye now."

The older man took in a deep breath, his chest puffing out. His attention moved from my face to my throat, and I could almost see the wheels in his head turning. I could feel his teeth against my skin.

But Hughes controlled his more violent instincts, and instead stepped through the private dining room's thick oak door. It slammed shut behind him.

I waited until the sounds of receding footsteps died away before allowing my carefully constructed mask to slip. My shoulders fell, and I let out a deep breath through my nose, setting my full glass of champagne on the table. Gaze hardening, I looked up at Marcus, prepared to take him to task for his recklessness, but the sight of him breathing heavily, his suit a rumpled mess, his hands still in fists at his sides... The sharp words died on my tongue.

Glancing away, I cleared my throat, forcing my thoughts to the present. "That wasn't necessary," I said, crossing my arms high over my chest.

Marcus, his gaze still fixed on the closed door at the other end of the room, reached down to the table. He picked up one of the discarded silk napkins and wiped the blood off his knuckles. "Nobody talks about you that way in front of me and walks away without bleeding."

Desire pooled hot and sticky in the bottom of my belly, like freshly melted candle wax. It took every ounce of my self-control not to look at him, not to reach for him and pull him into a long, deep kiss. I wanted to taste him, to lick the blood of our mutual enemy off his skin, to feel him inside me again.

Instead, I sighed, gesturing toward the scattered crockery and spilled champagne. "Now I've got to pay for all this."

I felt his eyes on me, and I couldn't help but look up at him. His plump lips were quirked in a crooked smile, as if he could read my thoughts.

Marcus

I opened my mouth to speak, but closed it after a moment. I dropped the napkin onto the table and stepped in front of Grace. With slow, measured movements, I got down first onto one knee then the other, reaching forward to twist her chair out from under the table so that she was facing me.

"I promise," I said, gliding my hands from the edge of the chair, up and onto her thighs, "I'll find a way to make it up to you."

She smiled down at me, a determined, hungry look in her brown eyes. Her breathing slowed and shallowed. I pressed my thumbs in firm, slow circles against her flesh, moving the hand on her left leg upward with single-minded determination.

My gaze never left hers, even as my hand slid up over her thigh and under her dress. "I do enjoy watching you give orders and put people in their place."

Grace's smirk widened, one corner of her lips skyrocketing up toward her ear. She relaxed under my touch, legs opening to surround me as she leaned in toward me. "How much do you enjoy it?"

I pressed the pad of my thumb against her sex, rubbing her clit through her thin underwear in the same firm, slow circles as before. I brought my lips to hers in a featherlight kiss before drawing away, whispering, "Shall I show you?"

I watched, pleased, as the last of her common sense dissolved with her resolve. Grace nodded, rolling her lips under her teeth. "I think you better," she said.

Insistent but gentle, I stroked and fondled her sex, pressing my fingers against her, but keeping the silk fabric between my hand and her center.

Grace leaned back in her chair, working hard to keep her breath steady even as her body began to respond to my attentions. Her eyes flickered shut and the back of her head rolled against the high, wooden chair.

"When did you become such a fucking tease?" she asked, her brow furrowing.

"I've had thirty years to think about all the things I want to do to you," I answered, drinking in the sight of her surrendering to my touch. I shook my head, smiling. "I'm not going to let you rush me."

Grace let out a shaky breath, shifting in her seat in an attempt to increase the friction. I let out a low chuckle. "When did you become so bloody impatient?"

Her underwear was soon soaked through. I moved the fabric to one side and slipped two fingers inside her.

"Oh, fuck," moaned Grace, biting into her fist in a vain attempt to muffle the sound. She writhed in her seat, pushing herself up and down on my hand. "Marcus, what if someone —"

"I'll hear them coming from a mile away." I curled my fingers inside her, my free hand caressing her inner thigh in slow, long strokes. "Let me give this to you, Grace. Please."

Grace swallowed hard, her eyes rolling back in her head as she breathed out a laugh. "How can I say no, when you ask so nicely?"

I fucked her with steady, measured strokes, refusing to change my pace. Without warning, I slid a third finger into her, stretching her in the best way. Just as suddenly, I dipped my face down to her, sucking at her pussy.

Grace jerked at the sensation, yelping in pleasure, her eyes shooting open. "What are you —!"

I shook my head, breathing heavily against her heat. "I can't —" My tongue darted out to flick at her clit and I groaned aloud. "You taste divine, Grace, I need to…"

"Shit," whispered Grace. I glanced up at her. She was looking down at me, her eyes wide, her face flushed. "Marcus, if you could see yourself…" She buried her hands into my hair and ground herself into my face, giving herself over to the moment.

"Marcus!" Grace's back arched away from the chair, her hands pulling at my curls. "Don't, don't you dare stop, fuck fuck *fuck* —"

Her string of expletives turned into a wordless groan as she shuddered through her orgasm, her entire body shaking. I didn't stop fucking her until she was entirely spent, looking down at me with bleary eyes, her breathing labored, but slowing at last.

I waited for her to release me before sitting back on my heels. I looked up at her, licking my fingers clean. She squirmed in her seat, chuckling and reaching for me with trembling arms. "Jesus, Marcus, the things you do to me…"

"You deserve every bit of it," I said with conviction. I started to lean in toward her thigh when I arrested the movement, whipping my head around toward the closed door. "Someone's com —"

The door to the private dining room burst inward, Kassandra leading a triangle formation of two other security specialists into the room, their guns drawn and at the ready. At the sudden, explosive entrance, I scrambled onto my feet, adjusting my clothes as best as I could, although I forgot about the rumpled mess of my hair. Grace tugged her skirt back over herself, cursing, all too aware that the scent of what had just occurred in the room would be easy for a fellow wolf to sniff out.

"Ma'am, is everything—?" Watching the determination in Kassandra's face contort into confusion, then dissolve into rosy-cheeked embarrassment was a unique experience for me. The large woman turned to the side, shoving her sidearm back into its holster, her head craning up on her neck as she stared pointedly up at the ceiling, tripping over her words. "Oh. I. Oh. Uh. Sorry." She gestured out into the restaurant proper, shaking her head. "I just—we saw—I thought there'd been an incident." There was a muffled snort of laughter from Naomi, and Kassandra swallowed hard, crab-stepping toward the door. "We can wait outside."

"No, no, it's okay," said Grace, rising to her feet, albeit with a bit more of a wobble than she probably would have liked. She cleared her throat and smiled. "We're done here. We got what we needed."

"Glad to hear it, ma'am," said Naomi, brows dancing playfully above her brown eyes.

I smiled at Naomi, even as Grace shot a glare in her direction and started for the door. I was about to follow, when she stopped and turned back to me, a thoughtful expression on her face. "Marcus, where exactly are the Feóndulfs staying while they're in town?"

"The Four Seasons," I answered automatically, attempting and failing to bring order to the chaos that was my hair.

"Do you know how long?" she pressed.

I lifted a brow, my hands falling to my sides. "They asked me to book them rooms for a full week. Why?"

"A week. Hm. That's interesting." Twisting her lips in a thoughtful grimace, Grace nodded, taking up the hard drive and tapping the edge of it against the chaotic tabletop. "Let's go."

Kassandra put a hand to her ear, muttered something to the team outside and led the way out into the restaurant proper. Grace readjusted her skirt and started after her, patting me on the chest with the drive as she walked past. "You and I have got some reading to do."

"Be still my heart," I answered, falling in step beside her.

"I'm sure we can find some way to make it exciting," she said, casting a coy glance at me.

I smiled at her and nodded to the drive in her hand, rubbing my chin. "I just hope there's something useful there. If there isn't, I'm not quite sure what line of inquiry we should follow next."

"A séance, maybe?" quipped Grace. She sighed as we exited the restaurant, ignoring the glaring wait staff. "Colquhoun knew something — so did Mama. We just have to hope that what they knew didn't die with them."

Chapter Twenty-Three

Grace

Arriving back at the hotel just after midday, I attempted once more to dismiss my security entourage, but without success. Kassandra insisted on remaining close by in case anything should happen, and on keeping Naomi with her for backup. I relented. I supposed I should be grateful that they seemed content to wait in a car on the street, instead of outside the door. Changing out of my formal attire, I settled down onto my mattress in a T-shirt and some underwear, my laptop resting at the foot of the bed. I plugged the drive into my computer, groaning as the files populated my screen. This was going to take a while.

"I hope you didn't have any plans for the night," I called out to Marcus, who I assumed was still in his room. When I looked up to the open connecting door, however, I was surprised to find him standing there, leaning against the doorframe, staring at me.

"I thought you said we had work to do," said Marcus, his face grim.

I straightened, concern growing in my chest. "We do."

"How am I supposed to focus on anything when you're all..." He gestured to me with one hand, breaking out into a wolfish grin.

I returned his smile, but shook my head. "Play time later, Marcus." Forcing myself to focus on my laptop, I lifted a brow pointedly. "There's still a murderer on the loose, remember?"

He sighed, loosening the knot of his tie and nodding. "Right. Sorry." Disappearing through the door, he returned a moment later, half undressed and with his laptop tucked under one arm. He entered my room this time and headed for the desk. "How do you want to handle this?"

I heaved a sigh, running my hand through my hair. "Why don't I send you the older stuff, and I'll read through the more recent documents?"

"Divide and conquer," said Marcus, nodding as he powered up his laptop. "Sounds like a plan."

The afternoon passed into evening in a pleasant silence, the two of us combing through the documents. When it had begun to darken outside, Marcus swiveled around in his chair, scratching at his chest and speaking aloud for the first time in hours. "How did the Nameless start? As a den, I mean."

I didn't look up from my laptop, my eyes continuing to scan the document in front of me. "We broke apart from the Feóndulf in the fifteen-hundreds. Some kind of inter-den dispute about how women were treated."

He gave a hum of curiosity and stood. Reaching for the ceiling, he lifted himself up onto his tiptoes, stretching. "I'd always heard it was about religion." He rolled back down onto his heels, his hands at his back. "Good old Protestantism versus Catholicism, that sort of thing. Still..." He reached back for his laptop and unplugged it from its charger, crossing the room and joining me on the bed. "Maybe...we're both wrong?" I peered over the top of my computer at him, my eyes narrowing. "What do you mean?"

"Have you ever heard of the Pâquerettes?"

"Sounds like a type of cookie," I answered, craning my head so I could look at his screen.

"It's a family name. Jean and Adeline Pâquerette. There's a family tree here." He gestured to the scan, a crumbling piece of parchment that looked as if it belonged inside an illuminated manuscript. When I'd been given ample time to examine the image, Marcus pulled up several other windows on the screen, all with the name, 'Pâquerette' highlighted. "Go back far enough, and the Pâquerette name shows up again and again in these diaries. It's almost as if..."

A thought occurred to me. I twisted to face my companion, my hand cupping my chin. "I don't suppose...were Colquhoun and his family always in charge of the Feóndulf?"

Marcus nodded. "Of course. They founded the den."

I twisted my lips into a grimace. I hummed in contemplation, returning my attention to the documents in front of me. "Keep talking."

"All I'm saying is, something isn't right. The name Pâquerette is simultaneously ubiquitous in these early documents, yet missing from the most important ones—deeds, contracts, diaries." Marcus pushed the laptop toward me, encouraging me to look through the records myself. "They are everywhere and nowhere, all at once. As if someone has tried, unsuccessfully, to minimize their impact on Feóndulf history."

I examined the documents, especially the ones Marcus had indicated. I huffed at length, rubbing at my eyes in irritation. "There are pieces of information missing."

Marcus sat back, his hands pressing into the mattress. "What makes you say that?"

"It's not obvious," I answered, throwing my hand out toward the computer screen. "But once you start looking, you can see. There are gaps in dates, documents that jump from one place to another, people who are referenced in diary entries, and then never come up again, like these Pâquerettes..."

I pushed my face down into the mattress, punching the pillow on which my own laptop rested with my fist. "Fuck," I muttered. "Someone's tampered with these. Deliberately." Rolling off the bed, I landed on my feet, swiping my jeans off the floor as I strode toward the bathroom. "Damn it, why did I expect Lawrence Hughes to—"

"Hold on, you don't know that it was Hughes," said Marcus, bouncing up onto his feet.

"Who else, Marcus?" I turned in front of the bathroom door to face him. I struggled into my jeans, agitation making my normally adept fingers fumble. "Who else would have the access? Who else would have the balls?"

The dark-haired man scoffed. "But...why? Why would he—"

I shook my head and moved past him, heading for my jacket, thrown over the top of the hotel dresser. "Because there's something in those records he didn't want us to find. Pieces he didn't want us to put together."

Shrugging the light hoodie over my shoulders, I caught sight of Marcus in the ornate mirror. He stood with his hands akimbo, scowling, his eyes downcast as he shook his head. I read disbelief in his stance, in his expression, and I slapped my hands against my thighs in aggravation. "Come on, Marcus—he's in this thing up to his neck!"

"No." The certainty with which Marcus delivered the two-letter word rankled. "No, it's not—"

"Goddamn it, Marcus!" The words exploded out of me in a shout as I spun around on my heels and shook my fists at him.

Marcus' face paled at my unchecked anger. He blinked at me, wide-eyed and silent. I struggled to get myself back under control, swallowing down my frustration and rage. I forced my hands to my sides and took in a deep breath, shaking my head as I closed the distance between us with a few quick strides.

"Why?" I begged. "Why do you insist on standing up for these people? All they've ever done is treat you like shit." I cupped Marcus' cheek and shook my head. "They kept you from me. For years. They're monsters."

Marcus lifted his hand to cover mine, leaning into my caress, his eyes fluttering shut. "Grace...they're my family." He swallowed hard, his Adam's apple bobbing. He held my hand in both of his, pulling it down to his chest. "I've given my whole life to them, they wouldn't... They wouldn't do this, Grace, I'm telling you."

I closed my eyes. As I nodded, the tip of my tongue flicked out to wet my lips. "Okay." My eyes flew open. "Okay. Let's go find out."

I stepped back from Marcus, pulling myself free of his grip, and dug my cell out of the pocket of my jacket. A few swipes over the screen were all it took to key in the number I needed. The call was picked up immediately, the voice on the other end clipped and professional.

"Kassandra." I did my best to keep any hint of anger or worry out of my voice, turning away from Marcus and tucking my hair behind her ear. "We're going downtown." I listened to the woman on the other end of the line, and shook my head. "No, I don't need an escort. No, we'll be fine. No, I don't—" Throwing up my hand, I rolled my eyes. "Fine. Fine. But we're heading out now."

"You're going to confront him."

I didn't turn, but stepped around Marcus without looking back at him, heading for the door. "Seems the best way to get the answers we need." It was only when my hand was on the doorknob that I trusted myself to face him, one brow quirked upward in question. "You coming along?"

"You don't have to ask." He strode into his hotel room, his face unreadable. "I'll be down in a minute. Don't leave without me."

* * * *

Marcus

With the lights of the Seattle Great Wheel glittering in the middle distance, Grace and I approached the front entrance of the Four Seasons. Either end of the soaring building stretched out toward the Sound, while the center sank in on itself like a collapsed soufflé. The immaculate lobby dripped with elegance, muted lights pouring their golden glow over dark, rich woods and polished floors. As we neared the front desk, I turned to face Grace, my voice low.

"Let me do the talking, all right?"

A nod was Grace's answer, and she receded a few steps to allow me to take the lead.

The receptionist at the desk looked up as we approached, folding his hands in front of his computer keyboard and smiling up at us, his oval eyes sparkling. "Good evening. Can I help you?"

I stopped a few inches away from the counter, one hand falling into my trouser pocket. "Yes, hello. My name is Marcus Bowen. I'm here to see one of your guests, Mr. Lawrence Hughes? He didn't give me his room number — do you think you could call him?"

The young man nodded, and reached for the desk phone. He punched in a few quick numbers then, in a hushed murmur, relayed the message down the line. Listening intently, he nodded once, then again and hung up the phone without another word. His smile hadn't dimmed the entire time. "Mr. Hughes is in Suite 1081," he said. He leaned across the desk and pointed farther into the building. "You'll want to take the middle elevator, and then follow the signs."

I thanked the receptionist and started toward the elevator, Grace following behind. I scanned the lobby for any sign of the other Feóndulf Council members. There was a lounge at one far end, a silver bar just visible from where we turned for the elevators. I made a mental note that they might be wiling away the evening hours there.

Once we were in the elevator, I looked at Grace, my fingers worrying my lip. "What exactly is the plan here, Grace?"

Grace was careful to keep her face forward, her expression neutral. "We're going to ask him why the files he gave me have pieces missing."

"And if he has no idea what we're talking about?"

She rolled her shoulders back, shaking her hair out of her face. "We'll ask him about the Pâquerettes. He's old as sin. He must have some idea why they're important. If they're important."

"And if you don't like his answer?"

Grace pulled her tongue away from the top of her mouth with a click. "What are you trying to get at, Marcus?"

I placed my hand on her arm. "You're looking for someone to blame. For Mama."

This, at last, got her to look at me, a pained glare in her eyes. I shook my head, but didn't look away. "I'm a policeman, Grace. I've seen grief before."

Grace's face went pale. She put her hand over mine and squeezed. "I'm fine."

"You're not," I answered firmly. "And that's okay."

The elevator doors slid open, the tenth floor beckoning. Releasing her, I waved my arm through the open portal. "I know you don't like Hughes, but this may not be the place to lay the blame. Just…try to bear that in mind."

Grace swallowed hard, but did not respond, settling instead for sweeping out of the elevator and into the hotel hallway. The muted gray carpet and dim lights made the narrow space even more claustrophobic. I felt unaccountably relieved when we arrived in front of Suite 1018, which sat nestled at the far end.

"Now, remember," I cautioned, readjusting the cuffs of my dress shirt. "You said you'd let me do the talking."

"Let's get this over with," snapped Grace, irritation plain in her tone.

I rapped my knuckles against the door. It swung inward half an inch into darkness.

The two of us shared a wide-eyed glance. We listened for any sign that the knock would be answered, but all was silent on the other side of the hotel door.

"That's...not a good sign..." I muttered.

Pushing past me, Grace had one foot inside the suite before I tugged her back by the shoulder, hissing, "What are you doing?"

She shook me off and threw her hands up into the air, matching my tone. "We're not going to get any answers by waiting out here, damn it."

I gritted my teeth for a moment before rolling my eyes and letting out a belabored sigh. Just as we had done in the warehouse, I stepped in front of her and entered the room first. Grace hurried after me.

The muted lights of the city, of the Great Wheel itself, pulsed through the drawn curtains, but most of the rooms remained plunged into deep, impenetrable darkness. Impenetrable to human eyes, at least. The furniture of the entryway stood out in my vision as clear as if the lights had been blazing, although the occasional flash of electric illumination from outside momentarily blinded me.

Directly in front of us was a small alcove, through which sat an office-type space, complete with desk and chairs. To the left, a small hallway extended, leading to the rest of the suite. With a look back at Grace, I started down the hall. "Mr. Hughes?" I called out, unbuttoning my suit jacket as I headed deeper into the space. I perked up my ears.

Someone had turned the air conditioning up to full. High end as the hotel might have been, the noise of pressurized, refrigerated oxygen rattling through the vents was still loud enough to drown out any other obvious sounds, even to my attuned senses.

We passed by the dining room, where a single cup of espresso, still steaming, sat abandoned. The hairs on my arms and neck stood at attention.

"Lawrence..." Grace tried again, her footfalls deadened by the plush carpet of the rooms. She moved away from me to the end of the hall, where another door sat closed. I could just hear her voice, could hear her call out as she entered the bedroom. "It's Grace Holtz. I just want to talk."

I moved farther into the living room, but everything looked pristine, untouched and empty. I spied Hughes' briefcase sitting on the floor, and I took in a deep breath through my nose and spun slowly in place. I narrowed my eyes.

I heard Grace continuing to taunt from the other room. "I can smell you, you old bas—"

The sound of shattering wood split the air as a chair connected across my back, my body slamming against the floor with a bang. As my head bounced off the edge of the coffee table, my vision went black.

Chapter Twenty-Four

Grace

I sprinted out of the empty bedroom, running full speed into the living room and into a swinging chair leg.

The thick wooden leg connected with the side of my head, sending me spinning off to one side like a pinball off a paddle. I ricocheted off a floating wall, the air leaving my body as a second blow cracked across the back of my ribs.

Blood dripped into my eyes, stinging and hot, the smell of it activating something feral inside me. As I scrambled against the plush carpet, my fingernails lengthened into sharp, lethal claws, and freshly sprouted fangs pricked at my cheeks. I snarled in pain. I could feel the form of my attacker standing above me. The air moved as they swung the chair leg back down toward me, and I braced myself for the impact.

Being beaten like this wouldn't kill me, but it damn well hurt.

Intervening at the last possible moment, Marcus tackled my attacker low around the hips, sending both men tumbling end-over-end across the living room floor. I smeared blood clear of my eyes to make out the form of Hughes, half-transformed, snarling and wrestling with my partner. As I stared, Hughes buried his teeth in the younger werewolf's arm.

"Marcus!" The shout tore itself from my chest. I forced my feet under my body and rocketed up unsteadily, still dizzy, but determined to help my friend before it was too late.

Too late came too soon. I watched, helpless, as the pair tumbled to the floor and Hughes managed to come out on top. He set to clawing at Marcus' exposed chest, scoring deep into the flesh and pulling a howl from the man that chilled my blood.

Picking up the discarded chair leg, I charged at Hughes. I brought down the bloody wooden rod with enough force to crack it in half across his shoulder blades, forcing him to turn his fury back on me and away from Marcus. But this time, I was ready for his attack. When he tried to stand to lunge at me, instead of stepping back and retreating, I leaned in and took hold of his clothes, using the momentum to spin him around before he could gain his footing. While he was disoriented and attempting to regain his balance, I retracted my claws long enough to punch him hard in the gut once, twice, three times, reveling in the feel of soft tissue bruising under my onslaught.

Hughes bit into my shoulder, tearing at the flesh with his newly-sprouted canines. I buried the pain as deep as I could and used the adrenaline pumping through me to keep standing. Growling, I pushed him back, slowly at first, but gaining momentum until I had us flying across the room.

I slammed him against the edge of the living room wall. The bookshelves cracked under the force of my attack, then I bashed the hardest part of my skull into his face. The satisfying crack of bone against bone shivered through me. Hughes gave a garbled grunt of pain, and went momentarily limp. I seized the opportunity, pinning him to the wall with my forearm pressed hard into his clavicle, sweeping my other hand low to lunge at his fleshy, vulnerable middle.

Breathing heavily, I froze, my claws pricking into his belly, but not gutting him just yet. "Move" — I growled, my spittle landing on Hughes' cheek — "and you'll get to see what your entrails look like." I twisted my head around to look at the prone figure bleeding on the floor. "Marcus."

The body remained still. The chest did not rise and fall with breath, but oozed with blood.

Panic clouded my mind, muddling my sharp senses. "Marcus!"

His hand twitched, his claws flexing. A quiet groan, deep and rough rumbled out from him as he curled in on himself.

Forgetting myself in my relief, I closed my eyes, swallowing hard. The sound of a choked laugh reminded me of where I was and what I was doing.

"Still alive, is he?" sneered Hughes, wriggling under my restraining arm. He smirked, Marcus' blood shiny on his teeth. "Pity. Useless bastard."

With a quick flick of my wrist, I sliced into the side of Hughes' left leg, my claws curving back behind his knee.

The older werewolf buckled, all of his weight resting on his now one good leg. "Christ!"

I lowered my hand to my side, the wolf within me reveling in the feel of blood dripping down my claws and onto the floor. "Do anything other than answer my questions, and I'll cut the other one." I leaned my full weight onto his collarbone, pressing down hard enough to make him wheeze. "Who is she?"

Hughes looked away from my penetrating gaze and licked blood off his lips. "Who?"

I shot my knee up into his groin. Hughes jerked and let loose a string of creative curses, but was kept from clutching his hurt by my restraining arm. I leaned in, putting my lips close to his ear, my claws scoring the wall next to his head. "Don't play dumb with me, you asshole. The blonde woman, the werewolf you sent to kill me, the one who killed your den leader and his son. Who? The fuck? Is she?"

I could smell the fear rolling off him now, thick and potent, like too much cologne on a teenage boy. He shook his head as much as he could manage. "She...she'll kill me."

I smiled then. Digging both my claws into his shoulders, I heaved him into the air, spinning around and throwing him down onto the small table behind us, hard enough to make the fine wood crack down the middle.

Releasing him, I walked around the table, so I was standing by his head. "Right now, I think you should be a little more worried about what I'll do."

Hughes coughed up blood, a fine mist of sharp red liquid dispersing into the air. He shook his head vehemently, his eyes closed. "She's no one. A denless, a freak."

I picked him up again and threw him like a bag of dirty laundry, sending him tumbling end-over-end over the nearby couch. As he fell into the living room, he crashed into the round glass coffee table, shattering it completely, the shards slicing what was left of his fine suit to ribbons.

"You're lying." I stalked toward Hughes, who struggled to push himself up onto his shaking arms. "If she's no one, then why did you doctor those files?" Before he could raise himself up under his own power, I was upon him again, lifting him with one arm into the air, the fabric of his shirt bunching under my grip. "Why does she leave the flower by the bodies?"

"I don't know!" shouted Hughes, beaten and bloody, wriggling in my grasp. "She's crazy! Why do crazy people do anything?"

"Why...?"

I whipped around, Hughes still dangling several inches off the ground. Marcus was swaying on his feet, blood pulsing from his chest wounds, but at a slower rate than before. He held a hand to his hurt and shook his head, his thick black hair falling onto his sweat-drenched forehead. "Why did you want Colquhoun and his son dead?"

Hughes' hands tugged uselessly at my wrists. "Colquhoun was going soft. Getting old. Everyone could see it." He went limp in my grip at last, whimpering. "He was talking about forbidding the sacrament. Forbidding our birthright! Someone had to do something!"

Marcus stumbled toward the living room, his face a mask of misery and pain. "So why not just take out Colquhoun—why'd you go after Aidan, too?"

"Well…" Hughes sighed out the word, his breathing heavy, but his voice regaining some of its strength. "What is it they say? In for a penny?"

"You're so full of shit, Hughes," I snarled, my already wild hair bristling. I dropped the werewolf to the ground, where he collapsed into an unceremonious heap. "This was never about your precious sacrament. This was about power. You wanted it. Colquhoun wouldn't let you have it. So you took it."

Hughes shook his head. "You can't prove any — "

My foot connected with his middle with a satisfying, meaty thud. I waited a minute while the older man wheezed on the floor. Crouching down, my hands hanging loose between my thighs, I demanded, "Why kill me? Mama?"

"Colquhoun left you in charge of the Feóndulf," managed Hughes after a moment, his eyes screwed shut. "I didn't anticipate that. As for Mama, I…I don't know."

Reaching forward, I gripped his chin in my hand, forcing him to look me in the eyes. "What do you mean, you don't know?"

"I never told her to target Mama!"

"Then why is she dead?" I shouted, the wolf in my throat making it sound more like a roar than words, fangs crowding my mouth.

"I don't know, damn it! Revenge?" Hughes struggled out of my grip, scrambling back until his back hit the bottom of the chair. He wiped a shaky hand across his bloody mouth. "I haven't been able to reach Delila since she came stateside. She was supposed to stay in contact, but — "

"She slipped your leash." Marcus' voice had regained its strength, but he was moving slowly, his hand still clutching the wounds on his chest. "Who is she, Hughes?"

Hughes looked from me to Marcus then, heaving a sigh, his gaze fell to the floor. "Delila Pâquerette," he muttered. "Her—her family founded the Feóndulf."

Marcus

"No," I said, coming around the couch and into the living room proper, shaking my head. "You're wrong. Everyone knows Colquhoun and his family founded the Feóndulf."

Beaten and bloody, Hughes still managed a condescending chuckle at my pronouncement. "A comforting fairytale." He shook his head, sneering. "The Pâquerette family founded the Feóndulf."

Grace stood perfectly still for a moment, regaining some semblance of her former composure. She stared down at the wounded werewolf elder, her hands clenched into fists. "Explain. Everything. Now."

Hughes pulled himself across the floor until he butted up against the far wall. He propped himself up into a sitting position, his breathing still labored, his body slowly returning to something closer to human.

"We were living in the Franche-Comté region of France at the time," he began. "It was 1562. The Inquisition courts handed down death sentences daily, for heresy in all shapes and forms. It was a dangerous time to be a werewolf, to take the sacrament, and there were those who believed we should change our ways."

Hughes shifted against the wall, his lips twisting into a frown. "Jean Pâquerette was weak. He had married a human, and had refused to turn her. Their children were mongrels, some born with the gift and some without. They were all weak. The Pâquerettes would've made us abandon our traditions, abandon everything that made us who we are, just so we could blend in. Cower like pups.

"Colquhoun and your grandmother saw that they had to be dealt with," he said, nodding up to Grace, who still towered above him. "Before they brought ruin to the whole den." Hughes tilted his head to one side, his gaze unfocused. "Killing them would've torn the den apart, of course." He shook himself. "So, Colquhoun brought the charge of lycanthropy publicly against Jean Pâquerette and his wife. Your grandmother provided the witnesses. In exchange, she was permitted to break away and form her own den."

I had harbored no illusions about the woman with whom Grace shared blood, nor any about the man who had created the family I served. Or so I had thought. I'd seen firsthand many of the things of which both Mama and Colquhoun were capable, and I understood why no one in over five hundred years had been brave enough to challenge them for control of their dens. But even I had believed there were limits — that there were lines that would not be crossed.

I opened my mouth to speak — to deny, to protest. But no words would come out, my mind reeling with the revelation that Colquhoun and Mama could have done something so contrary to the code of our people. Wolves did not turn on their family. And they certainly didn't involve humans, like Delila, in family business.

If Hughes noticed the turmoil in my face, he didn't show it. In fact, he looked distinctly bored as he continued his tale. "Naturally, as soon as suspicion fell on Jean and Adeline, their sons and their sons' wives were also accused. In a few short months, the whole family had been arrested, tried and convicted." He rolled his eyes. "If their minds hadn't been so clouded by their love for humanity, maybe they would've been able to save themselves from the worst that species has to offer.

"They were all killed, of course." Hughes shrugged, his hand waving lazily through the air. "Burned at the stake, after the requisite torture and purification of their flesh, et cetera, et cetera. But" — Hughes lifted his finger, one of his brows rising in tandem — "for decades there were rumors of a grandchild. Spirited away by a human maid the night of the arrest. A wolf child. But nothing ever came of it. People forget, as people are wont to do." Hughes pointed to himself and smiled a bloody smile. "But not me. I never forgot. And when I needed an outsider with an ax to grind, I knew just where to look."

"And you found this...Delila," I said, leaning against the back of the couch, dropping my hand from my chest at last, tamping down the nausea I felt roiling in my stomach.

Hughes kept his gaze on Grace, pointedly ignoring me. "I reached out to her. I offered her money, prestige, a place in the family...everything your grandmother and Colquhoun denied her." He smirked and shook his head. "She took it, of course. Who wouldn't?"

"She's taking a whole lot more than that." Grace let out a sharp breath through her nose.

"The Council will kill you for this." Disdain dripped from my words, my glare full of unguarded disgust as I looked at Hughes.

Hughes at last looked at me, boredom somehow managing to exude from his very pores, even as he sat there in a shredded three-piece suit. "Oh?"

"You orchestrated the murder of our den leader. Do you honestly think —"

"Do you think they're going to believe you? Either of you?" Hughes struggled to his feet. "A bitten welp and a Nameless bitch?"

There was a loud crack as the back of Grace's hand connected with Hughes' jaw. The man stumbled back into the window, the glass rattling as he collided with it. Grace advanced on him until their faces were mere inches apart. "Get out of my city." She pointed toward the entrance to the suite. "Or I'll kill you myself. Understood?"

Hughes stared at her, comprehension coming slowly. Massaging his jaw, he shook his head. "This is my —"

"Out. Now." Grace took hold of him by the shoulders and shoved him out of the living room. "Go lick your wounds somewhere else."

Chapter Twenty-Five

Grace

Hughes tripped over his own feet with uncharacteristic gracelessness, his hurts obviously taking their toll. He hesitated for a moment on the edge of the room, casting a furtive glance back at Marcus and me. But what he saw must have convinced him to take refuge elsewhere, and he hurried down the hall toward the suite's door, which clicked shut behind him.

After waiting an extra beat to make sure we were alone, I hurried across the room, my hands spidering over Marcus' chest, heedless to the blood that covered us both. "Marcus, shit — are you okay? Do I need to call Kassandra?"

"I'll be fine." He hissed, and pushed my hands away from his hurt. "Are you all right?"

I took a deep breath and leaned forward, my forehead pressing against his cheek. "Haven't been hit like that in a while, but I'll live."

He cradled the back of my head. I felt a huff of breath against my skin. "You know I wasn't talking about—"

"I know." Turning away from him, I collapsed onto the floor, resting my aching body against the back of the couch. I looked up at Marcus and swallowed hard. "Do you think he was telling the truth? About...about everything with the Pâquerettes?"

Gingerly, Marcus lowered himself to the ground beside me. "After everything else he admitted? I don't see why he'd lie about that."

"Jesus." A wave of nausea threatened to overtake me. I drew my hand down my face, shaking my head. "I just can't believe... Why would Mama..." I closed my eyes, allowing some of the exhaustion to seep into my bones as the adrenaline receded from my blood. "Mama always said, you kill another wolf, you do it with your own teeth and claws. You never give them to hunters. Never. How could she do that?"

"How could either of them do that? Colquhoun was—" Marcus stopped mid-sentence, his eyes focusing on something in the middle distance. With a groan, his head fell into his hands, his fingers tugging at his hair. "Damn it. Damn it! Pâquerette. It's French for daisy. That's how Colquhoun knew who was coming for him. That bastard."

What would it be like? To be ripped from your family? I had chosen to leave mine, and I hadn't regretted the decision. But had this woman—Delila—had she always been alone? What would that do to a person? The centuries of knowing that her family had been stolen from her? And that another family, my family, had benefited from this act?

I had grown up, sheltered and safe, because of all that Delila had been denied.

I forced my feet back under my body and stood in the ruins of the hotel suite. "I've had enough of this cat and mouse shit." I crossed my arms over my chest. "It's not my style. Not how I like to deal with things."

Marcus looked up at me, his hand pressed to a cut under his hair. "No...you've always preferred a more head-on approach to conflict." His frown deepening, he stood, his hands falling into his pockets. "Grace, what are you thinking?"

I shook my head, pressing my tongue against the back of my teeth. My mind whirred, and my muscles tensed. Decision made, I dug my cell phone out of my jacket pocket, and began to type out a long message, saying aloud, "No more hiding. No more evasion. If this woman — Delila — if she wants me, I'll show her just where to find me."

Marcus rushed to his feet and strode over to me. "That" — Marcus put his clean hand over my phone and pressed down on it, forcing me to look up at him — "is a supremely bad idea."

"Why?" I dropped my hands to my sides, my phone bouncing against my thigh. "Think about it. She's hunting us. She's damn good at it. But what if we stop acting like prey, and start acting like the fucking predators we are?"

Marcus threw his hands up and turned to walk away, his face twisted in disgust. "And then what, you kill her, or she kills you?"

"Nobody else has to die!" I said, following him step for step. "She has a legitimate claim to head both of our dens. And I don't want to head either of them. We can work something out, something that will give both of us—"

"Grace, you can't be serious!" The younger werewolf spun on his heels, shaking his head and scoffing aloud. "The Feóndulf will never accept that! Neither will the Nameless! This person—"

"Delila. She has a name," I interrupted.

"Delila, Pâquerette, whatever, she's killed at least six people," he said, stressing the number. "This isn't the dark ages anymore. Might does not make right."

I let out a long breath through my nose. "Damn it. Damn it, Marcus... We..." Pushing a hand back through my hair, I shook my head, my voice breaking. "We took her family from her. She's been alone, running, this whole time. She just wants what's hers."

Marcus took my hands in his. His voice was soft and low. "It's not yours to give, Grace."

"Well, I have to do something. If I can talk to her, I'm sure—"

"She'll kill you." He watched me from beneath his brow, his lips a firm line. "She'll kill you, then who knows where this stops. If it ever stops."

"I have to try." I looked into his face and registered his frustration. "I have to try, Marcus! I owe her that!"

Marcus' voice rocketed up into a shout. "You're talking like you're the one who killed her family!"

"I might as well have!" I shouted back, my hand to my chest.

"Don't be an idiot," he snarled. "What Mama did all those years ago has nothing to do with you."

I shook my head. "You can't understand. You could never understand—"

"Why?" demanded Marcus, a growl in his voice. "Why? Because I'm just some bitten mongrel? Not born like you?"

"Yes, goddamn it, yes!" I exploded, pacing the floor, my hands flying into the air. "You have no idea what it's like to have this legacy on your back all the goddamn time and then, then—I find out that it wasn't even supposed to be mine?"

"Oh, go fuck yourself, Grace." Marcus didn't shout. He settled instead for shooting each word at me like an arrowhead, sharp and expertly aimed. His brows were low over his wide, enraged eyes, and he sliced his hand through the air toward me. "I have had it up to here with this woe-is-me, the-burden-of-the-born bullshit. All your life you've been afraid of having to live up to people's expectations, so you ran away to the middle of nowhere and proceeded to be absolutely fucking nobody, all when you could've been so much more." Teeth grinding, he nodded wildly. "You're right, you know? You're right. At least this Delila person has the guts to take you all on. That's something you've never had."

It was true. Every word that had passed between us. He and I both knew it. We couldn't take it back. We could only go forward.

"Like you're any better," I said, my voice eerily calm.

Marcus flexed and relaxed his hands at his sides. "What the hell is that supposed to mean?"

"It means that I don't see you taking what you're owed from the Feóndulf. I don't see you doing anything more than being a good little errand boy." I closed my eyes, my head drooping low between my shoulders. "Even if it costs you everything."

Even if it costs you me.

The unspoken words quivered in the air between us. I turned away from him, holding myself together, my arms wrapped tight around my body. For a long moment, neither of us said anything.

"Point." The 't' clicked off the edge of his teeth. He sounded as miserable as I felt, and I was almost glad of that. Sighing, he collapsed back against the arm of the couch, his hands falling limply between his knees. "If this whole thing doesn't work the way you want it to, you may have to kill this woman. You know that, don't you?"

I rubbed at my forehead. "It won't come to that."

Marcus gave a snort. "Right." He leaned back further, tilting his body so that he was staring up at the ceiling. "Your boundless optimism is inspiring."

I watched him for a moment, my hand falling from my face. "Are you in or not?"

His chest rose and fell. "What do you need me to do?"

Chapter Twenty-Six

Marcus

The nightclub we were in twenty-four hours later was one of the Nameless' own, a front through which the den laundered some of its less-than-squeaky-clean funds. Word that the new head of the Nameless den would be holding a party to celebrate her ascension — mere days after the death of her grandmother — spread like wildfire through the northwest werewolf community. Whether out of a genuine desire to pay their respects, or a need to lay eyes on the wolf brazen enough to host such an event, the turnout was massive.

Putting together the kind of event Grace had in mind at such short notice wasn't cheap, and it wasn't easy. But the Nameless den was full of wolves looking to secure their positions now that Mama was dead, and Grace let it be known that anyone who helped her would have more than just her gratitude. Convincing Kassandra had been the hardest part. Grace and I agreed that it would be best to keep her in the dark as to Delila Pâquerette's true motivations and, for the time being, Lawrence Hughes' involvement in what had happened. We weren't interested in starting a war, but in stopping a killer. Still, I was inclined to agree with Kassandra — using Grace as bait was a bad idea.

For that reason, the Nameless security team appeared to be noticeably absent from the event. Kassandra had left a few low-level officers inside the club, so as not to give the impression of total negligence. But the bulk of her forces were outside, waiting on a signal from a panic button on Grace's ruby-encrusted ring.

I was meant to be outside with Kassandra and her team. Grace had requested my presence there. Whether to keep me out of harm's way, or to keep me out of her way, was unclear. All she had said was that she thought my tactical expertise would be most useful outside the club.

Bugger that.

I swallowed the last of my Old Fashioned then replaced the empty glass on the bar. I watched Grace from across the room, as I had been for the past hour. She was seated in the VIP area, her high-backed booth a half-circle, open to the main floor of the club. A long line of well-wishers and werewolf sycophants had been parading in and out of the booth all night, currying favor, demonstrating their loyalty to the new head of the Nameless — to her. Grace let it all wash over her with the same bland indifference, smiling tightly, nodding, even laughing woodenly from time to time. But I knew she was waiting — waiting for Delila Pâquerette to appear and try to kill her.

I let out a sharp breath through my nose and shook my head, scanning the crowd. The woman wouldn't be able to resist, not a chance like this. But still, I thought she'd pick her moment — she wouldn't be as reckless as the new head of the Nameless.

When I turned my attention back to the VIP booth, my heart clenched in my chest. As she stared at me, Grace's jaw muscles rippled, a clear indication that she was less than pleased to see me.

I plastered on a sickly smile and crossed the crowded dance floor to her table.

"This seat taken?" I asked, already sliding into the booth beside her.

"No." Grace didn't look at me, draining the last of her martini before continuing. "I thought you were supposed to be outside. With Kassandra."

"Well, if you're going to commit suicide with such style, how can I resist a front-row seat?" I asked, pulling my suit jacket down across my chest. "Anything yet?"

"Not yet." Grace shot me a glance from the side of her eyes. She lifted her brows. "Happy?"

"That the psychopath who's already killed six people hasn't taken another stab at doing the same to you?" I tipped my head to one side, still not looking at her. "Ecstatic."

"It's early yet," said Grace, fiddling with the ring on her left hand, the one that concealed the panic button.

"And what if she doesn't want to chit-chat like the last time, Grace? What if she just shoots you? Have you thought about that?" I stared out into the crowd, my jaw clenched. "You may not care if you live or die, but I do."

"I don't need you to take care of me, Marcus." Grace sighed as she leaned forward against the table, reaching for a half-empty bottle of champagne. "So if that's the only reason you agreed to stick around and help—"

My fist slammed down onto the table with enough force to make the glasses clatter. Grace jerked back and stared at me, wide-eyed. I met her stare, my teeth bared.

"I'm here," I growled, "because I'm in love with you, damn it." Struggling to compose myself, I pulled my gaze away from her. "I walked away from you once. I'm not doing it again. No matter how hard you push me—"

An eardrum-piercing wail cut through the noise of the club. The colored lights switched off automatically, and the entire building was flooded by stark yellow fluorescents, leaving partygoers disoriented and deafened.

"The fire alarm?" I shot to my feet, but was yanked back down by Grace.

"It's her!" shouted Grace, one hand over her ear. "It has to be!"

She jammed her thumb against the side of her ring. We waited for a tense moment for Kassandra and her team to appear, but nothing happened. Grace pressed the panic button again and again, looking up at me with the beginning of fear in her eyes.

I whipped around from side to side, searching for any sign of Kassandra or a fire. "We can't chance that it's a false alarm! Where are they, damn it?" I put my hand over hers and pulled her out from behind the table. "Come on!"

We joined the flood of attendees surging for the double-doored emergency exits, but it wasn't until the shouting started that we realized why the crowd had stopped moving forward.

The doors were locked. We'd learn later that they had been welded shut, then chained with silver for good measure. Frantic wolves and humans alike pounded on the doors with their fists, rattling the rigid push bars and slamming their bodies desperately against the unyielding metal portals.

Grace and I fought our way out of the crush of bodies before such movement was impossible, moving back into the center of the club.

"We're not getting out that way," I shouted, still looking from side to side for any sign of Nameless Security. "Where the hell is Kassandra? Where's your—"

A series of explosive bangs joined the general cacophony. One of the overhead lights shattered, sending a shower of glass down onto the increasingly frenzied partygoers. Everyone began to scream as the sound of gunshots reverberated and competed for dominance in the thick, hot air.

I shoved Grace toward the staircase that led to the upper floors of the club. "We're getting you out of here! Now!"

We scrambled up the stairs, climbing until there was nowhere else to go. Moving along the upper balcony, I wrenched open the door to an office, at the back of which was a rickety, disused ladder, and an emergency hatch that could only lead to the roof.

I pulled Grace toward the ladder. "Come on, hurry!"

Grace's expensive shoes slid against the first few rungs of the ladder, making it hard for her to get a firm grip on the rungs, but she eventually made it up. Her strong fingers made quick work of the latch on the roof hatch, and soon we were both climbing out over the tar-covered roof. Wind whipped at Grace's loose hair, and she shivered, her club clothes doing little to protect her from the wet air of the Seattle night. She strode to the center of the roof, her feet splashing through puddles of stagnant rainwater.

"What now?" said Grace, glancing around the wide, featureless space.

I jogged past her toward the far edge of the roof, feeling around the brickwork with my hands. "There should be a fire escape somewhere around here, we can climb d—"

Chapter Twenty-Seven

Grace

Unlike the gunshots in the club, this one was short and muted, like the puncturing of a piece of fabric. The silver bullet tore into my shoulder, spinning me around like a top as I cried out in agony. I clawed at the fresh hole in my body, trying to rip the silver out with my bare fingertips. I collapsed onto the roof, my vision going black.

"Grace!" Marcus was at my side in a matter of seconds, his hand closing over my wound. But he could do nothing to staunch the blood, or to ease the sharp sting of my flesh as the silver burned inside my body.

My vision returning in fits and starts, I looked up, bleary-eyed, into the dark Seattle sky. The moon was high, waning and bright, even against the lights of the city. The vibration of footsteps coming closer made me tilt my head downward. Standing in front of me was the woman who had been hunting me all this time.

"Hello again, Grace," said Delila, her gun held casually in one hand. The breeze took up the exhaust from the end of the barrel and sent it dancing through her loose blonde hair. Smiling, her face striped with shadows from the surrounding buildings, she raised the gun to point at my prone form.

"Delila!" I shouted, the name tearing itself from my throat. I threw my hand up in front of myself. "Wait!"

The assassin's sharp eyes widened with delight. "Oh, we're on a first-name basis now! That is so exciting. I was wondering if any of you dense, denned assholes would figure out what was going on." She shook the gun at me, clicking her tongue off the back of her teeth. "Should've known if anyone was going to, it would be you. You were always the smartest of the bunch. Or at least, I thought you were."

Using Marcus as a handhold, I pulled myself back up onto my feet, pushing through the pain and the haze of the silver. "I—I just want to talk to you."

Delila laughed, her hand coming up to her chest. "Oh, my goodness, is that what all this was for? This whole party thing? Getting me alone so that we could talk?" Her free hand moved from her chest up to her cheek, cradling her face. "Baby, I'm blushing."

"A shoulder shot?"

Rolling my eyes at the sound of his voice, I peered around to Delila to watch as Lawrence Hughes stepped out onto the roof, wiping his hands clean with a handkerchief. "Not like you to miss, Delila." He sneered at me, tucking the bit of cloth back into his tailored jacket pocket. "Surprised to see me?"

"No," I answered. "Not really."

The sneer disappeared. Lawrence blinked, his brow furrowing. "Oh."

"I mean," I continued, blood dripping from between my fingers, "I never thought you'd skulk away without a final 'fuck you' in my direction."

"You're not a subtle man, Lawrence," Delila agreed. "I told you from the beginning—you might as well have just done it all yourself."

"Shut up!" Lawrence snapped, his pale face glowing red.

I snorted out a laugh. The blonde tittered.

"I said shut up!"

"Or what?" I said, the loss of blood and the silver making me lightheaded. "You'll condescend me to death? Come on, man, we were in the middle of something here."

"Kill this bitch. And her lapdog." Hughes glared at Marcus, but there was a smile twisting his thin lips. "Kill them now."

"What's the rush?" said Delila, tossing her hand out toward me and Marcus. "She says she wants to talk."

Hughes barked out a laugh. "What could she possibly have to say to you?"

Delila shrugged. "Thank you?" She turned back to me, nodding her head. "Are you going to say thank you? For killing your grandmother? You're more than welcome. I understand your relationship was...tumultuous, at best."

I swallowed hard. "No." I took the smallest step forward, careful to keep my words measured and clear. "I wanted to say that I understand why you're doing this."

Any hint of joviality dropped from Delila's face. The woman readjusted her grip on the butt of her gun. "You really don't."

"I do. You lost everything." My gaze flickered back to Hughes. "We took everything from you. You've been alone all this time." I straightened, as much as was possible with my injury. "But I can give it all back to you."

Delila shifted where she stood. Her brow furrowed. "What?"

My voice turned desperate, pleading. "I don't want this. The Nameless? The Feóndulf? I don't want any of it." I threw out my hand toward Delila. "You do. You're obviously intelligent, driven, ambitious—"

"—some would say psychotic," countered Delila, a single brow lifting over her green eyes.

"Let me bring you in," I said. "I'll tell the dens the truth about what happened to your family—the truth about what we owe you."

Delila shifted her weight from foot to foot. She glanced away from me, her gaze focused on the ground just beneath her feet. "And...you think they'll listen to you?"

For the first time in days, a small seed of hope settled in my chest. I tried to smile. "Don't you think it's worth a try? You could have a family."

Hughes took a step toward Delila, the color rising in his cheeks as he sputtered, "You can't seriously be considering this—"

Without turning to look at him, Delila twisted her body to one side and fired off a single shot.

The silver bullet hit Hughes in the abdomen. He collapsed in on himself for a moment, stumbling backward until he ran into the hatch that led down into the club. Hand clutching his gut, he stared at Delila, wild-eyed. "You... You..."

"I won't miss the heart next time, Lawrence," said Delila, still not looking at him.

Hughes looked from Delila to me and back again, his face contorted in pain. With a groan, he turned and climbed as quickly as he could down through the hatch, shutting it behind him.

I swallowed down the bile that rose in my throat at the sight of the retreating man. I tilted my head to one side. "Wasn't he paying you?"

Delila cast a bored glance at the now-closed hatch. "Paid me. Past tense." She returned her attention to me, her smile returning, widening, almost running off the edges of her face. "Besides, we both know I was never doing this for the money. I was doing it for me. His resources, his money and contacts, they just made everything easier."

"How did he even find you?" demanded Marcus, speaking for the first time.

"He didn't. Not really." Delila leaned forward and her face was lost in shadow. "I found him."

A siren started to wail in the streets below, the sound mournful and distant, but growing closer with every passing second. Delila moved closer to us so that she could be heard over the sounds of the city. Her gun remained cocked and ready. "I'd been looking for my family for centuries. It was my...reason. The woman who saved my life, who raised me, she died when I was a teenager. But she never told me anything about my parents, about where I came from. She only told me I was 'special'." A bark of a laugh erupted from deep within Delila's chest, so deep it rumbled with the edges of a growl. "That's how she explained what I was. Can you believe that? *Special*. The hunger. The pain. The power. I was special." Her smile flashed off like a burned-out bulb, replaced by an ugly, twisted grimace. "I was a freak. But I wondered if my family were freaks too — if I belonged somewhere."

I nodded. "You do."

"I. Did." Each word snapped out from between Delila's teeth like projectiles. She gestured with the barrel of the gun. "Your people took that from me."

"I can give it back to you," I insisted, my injured arm swinging uselessly at my side. "Isn't that what you want?"

Delila shook her head. "You still don't understand." The blonde woman sneered, one hand coming up to tear sarcastic quotation marks through the air as she spoke. "I don't want to be 'one of you.' I never wanted to be 'one of you'." The glint from the steel of the gun was reflected in her blue eyes as she smiled. "I want to burn your world down. Leave you with nothing. Like I have."

"Grace," said Marcus, his voice barely above a whisper. He started forward, trying to angle his body so that he would end up between me and Delila. "Get beh — "

The black barrel of the gun, unnaturally elongated by a silencer, jerked in Delila's hand. Marcus stumbled back as if he'd been punched in the chest, collapsing down onto the roof.

"I was talking!" Delila stomped her boot-shod foot like a child, a pout stealing across her plump lips. "God, some people can be so rude."

I heard someone shouting far away. It took me a moment to realize it was me, shouting Marcus' name. I started toward the fallen wolf with sharp, jerky steps.

"Uh-uh!" chided Delila, cocking the hammer back for emphasis, the sound bringing me to a halt. "We're not done."

I looked into Delila's eyes and saw nothing. I saw what centuries of loneliness could do to a person, how it hollowed them out and left them a vessel for dark and hungry things. Delila smiled and squeezed the trigger.

There was a click. A thunk. And nothing.

Clicking her tongue off the back of her teeth, Delila brought the side of the gun close to her face, fiddling with the firing mechanism. "Ugh. Silver bullets, you know? I make my own, and sometimes they just jam up the works."

I returned my gaze to Marcus. I let my eyes linger on his body, let them pour over him. He was still. So very still.

There was a clatter. At this strange and unexpected sound, I looked over. Delila had discarded the gun on the wet rooftop. She grinned, her teeth elongating in her maw, her blonde hair growing wild as she began to tap into the wolf within. "Guess we'll have to do this the old-fashioned way."

Like a calm sea whipped into a storm, my mind began to spin, my emotions flooding through me. I had lost everything. I had no home, no family, no love — I was alone. But wasn't that what I had wanted in the end? To cast off all the vestiges of my former life? To be normal? It had all been a monkey's paw wish — a sick, universal joke.

I wasn't laughing. And I wasn't going to let it end like this.

I planted my feet in a wide stance. My words came out in a low growl. "And you just expect me to lay down and die?"

Delila stared at me for a moment. Then, she laughed, a long high-pitched cackle that grated on my eardrums.

The teeth in my mouth began to lengthen and grow crowded. My hair all over my body bristled, and my senses, already sharp, felt honed enough to slice atoms. "Shut up and fight," I spat.

Without further preamble, Delila threw herself at me, howling.

Focusing on the bullet wound on my left shoulder, Delila clawed and snapped at my injury, intending to worsen it. It took all my energy and focus to keep her attacks from landing, but that also kept me on the defensive, never giving me a chance to strike back.

With a single-mindedness that I almost admired, Delila drove me toward the edge of the roof. Stumbling, I attempted to move around her. But she was too fast, and my ploy to flank her failed. Delila grabbed hold of my left forearm and yanked at it, trying to rend it from my blood-slicked elbow. The pain was incredible and my vision blurred. I took the low ground and rolled, ending up in a heap on the roof behind her.

Spinning around, Delila pulled back, her hand ready to come down in a deep, gashing stroke of claws. I saw my first, and perhaps only, opportunity. Crouching, I swept my leg out, and managed to break Delila's foothold on the roof. The older werewolf landed on her backside with a thud, and before she had time to recover, I lunged at her, my fangs aimed for her throat.

I had forgotten how close we were to the edge of the roof.

Delila caught my torso on the bottoms of her feet and lifted, sending me flying through the air and out into the nothingness between buildings.

I landed on the floor of the alleyway, my fall softened by several bags of trash piled high next to a dumpster. I was strong and hard to kill, but not impervious to pain. When I hit, I lost consciousness with all the abruptness of someone pulling the plug on an old TV. One minute the picture was sharp and clear, the next, the screen went black.

In a rush of sensation, I came to a few moments later. The bags beneath me had burst like cushions, a scattering of refuse blanketing my still partially transformed body like snow. With the claws of my right hand dug into the scales of a discarded fish head, I spat the skin of a rotten tomato out of my mouth, and the smell of putrefaction assaulted me. My eyes watered, even as they struggled to focus well enough to pick out the ugly neon yellow sign of the night club.

I looked up to the roof and caught the flash of a face pulling back from the edge.

Staggering onto my feet, I careened toward the street. A door to my left opened, a shaft of light, steam and noise. Before I could avoid it, a tub of warm, dirty dish water was thrown up my nose.

I coughed the water out of my mouth as I ran, but the stench of it and the trash covering me made catching the scent of my opponent impossible. I glanced behind me just in time to see her land on all fours on the floor of the alleyway, snarling.

Shit.

I turned left at the mouth of the alley and darted down a deserted one-way street, anxious to keep bystanders out of the fray. Scanning the buildings around me, running for all I was worth, I could hear Delila behind me. I skidded to a halt in front of a hardware store and, making a split-second decision, I kicked in the nailed-up boards that protected the front door from vandals. I crashed through what was left of the plate glass, and rushed inside. The lights were dead, festooned with garlands of cobwebs, the empty shelves covered in inches-thick layers of dust. I ran toward the back of the store, keeping low between the shelves, when the unmistakable crunch of glass beneath rubber-soled shoes reached my ears.

"Gracie..."

The first syllable of the word rumbled out in a low bumpy growl deep from Delila's chest. The sound tickled the inside of my ears and sent a cool finger of fear running down my spine. I froze. Still as a Zen garden, I waited, straining my senses to catch any indication of where she was.

"There's no running from this, Gracie..."

It took all of my self-control to not jump at the sound of her voice mere feet from me, on the other side of the shelf which I stood behind. I licked my lips, positioning myself so that my body rested against the heavy, filthy metal.

"No running anymore..."

With a roar, I hurled myself at the shelf, sending it toppling. There was a satisfying yowl of pain from the other werewolf as the unwieldy conglomeration of steel and screws found its mark. As the shelf fell, the stockroom door revealed itself. Scattered on the floor, just visible through the dirt and grime, were a handful of silvery ball bearings.

I ran for the door, but I hadn't gotten more than a few feet before I felt her breath on my neck. Her claws slashed across my lower back.

I turned at once and snapped at the older wolf with my teeth, snarling in pain and surprise. Delila once again used my momentum against me, this time to deliver a tooth-rattling punch to my head, which sliced open the skin above my eye. I stymied the urge to retreat and grabbed onto Delila's shoulders, throwing myself against her and sending us both tumbling down to the floor.

We tangled together, claws rending flesh, teeth puncturing muscle. There was no art in this, no great dance or skill. This was animalistic and ugly. This was life or death.

I sank my teeth into Delila's neck. Her flesh gave beneath my jaws. The other woman spasmed against me, clamping onto me, as if in a lover's embrace, before releasing me as the blood spilled from her carotid artery.

I stopped myself from ripping her throat clean out. I eased my jaws open, releasing my hold on the other woman. Delila fell to the ground with a soggy thud, thick red liquid oozing from her savaged neck. I knelt beside her, my wolf eyes taking in every detail.

"I can see them..." Delila gurgled, blood splattering against my cheek. "My family... I can..."

The twitching of her limbs stilled. Delila went limp. Her open eyes stared into nothingness.

After a moment of quiet, I sheathed my claws and pulled her lids shut.

Blood from the cut on my forehead dripping into my eyes, I walked out of the abandoned building, my legs unsteady beneath me. I dropped, first onto one knee, then onto the other. I sat, my head hanging low. My breath slowed, the wolf leaving me at last.

What was I going to do now?

"Grace..."

I whipped around, not believing my own senses for a moment as they took in Marcus crouching behind me, his hand outstretched.

Chapter Twenty-Eight

Marcus

"Marcus!" Grace threw herself at me. She collided against my torso, sending me stumbling. Her hands danced across my chest and face as she nuzzled into my neck. "Marcus, shit! Thank God! You're alive!" Pulling herself away from me, she stared at me in confusion, tears streaming down her face. "How?"

I let out a huff of air and pulled my ruined dress shirt open, popping off a few buttons in the process. Grace stared through tear-blurred eyes at the front of my bulletproof vest, a deep gouge indicating where a bullet had impacted at close range. I shook my head and tapped the vest with my knuckles, wincing a little as I did so.

"I'm not an idiot," I said. "If you know there might be gunplay, you should come prepared."

Grace let out half a laugh, which turned into a sob. She hung her head low, the tears flowing freely down her cheeks and off her chin. She dug her fingers into my arms. "Marcus, I'm so, so sorry. I could've gotten you killed! I'm so sorry. For everything. I screwed up. She's dead. I screwed up."

"Grace, no—you were right." I shook my head and pulled her close, burying her face in my chest. I stroked her hair with both of my hands, resting my lips against the top of her head. "It was right to try." I sighed. "You were right about a lot of things."

Grace held on to me, and I returned the gesture, gripping her more tightly than I had ever held on to anything. We stayed that way until the sirens started in the distance. Even then, it was I who stood first, pulling us both to our feet. "Come on, you're hurt. We're both hurt, let's... Let's get out of here."

Once we were a few blocks clear of the hardware store, a quick call to Kassandra set the wheels of the great machine that was the Nameless in motion. What followed next was a flurry of texts and phone calls, rides in the back of discreet black cars with tinted windows and heated arguments, all of which stretched into the early morning.

Grace and I were seen by separate Nameless doctors, although they spent far longer with her than they did with me. My few cracked ribs gave the serious-looking young woman tending to me little to work with.

"No punctures, no breaks," she said. "They should heal before morning. You were lucky."

"Lucky?" I stared past her at Grace, who was sitting up on the edge of her bed at the Maxwell, anesthetized as a doctor cut the bullet out of her shoulder. "I was prepared. Is she going to be all right?"

"The silver will need to work its way out of her system. She'll be a little weak for a few days." The doctor, a brunette with short cropped hair, leaned back from her work, wiping her forehead with the back of her hand. "Other than that, I'd say she looks worse than she is. She needs rest more than anything."

"Rest. Wouldn't that be nice?" Grace sighed, the cut on her forehead still angry and red, even if it had stopped bleeding. "There's still Hughes to deal with. Besides—"

"No excuses." The brown-haired doctor frowned. "If you don't rest, you'll get sicker. You need to let your body fight off the silver like it would any other infection."

"But—"

"You heard her, Grace," I said, standing from the desk chair in which I had been sitting. I picked up my discarded undershirt, slipping it on over my head. "Rest. I'll be back in an hour."

"Marcus—"

For once, I didn't let the sound of my name in her voice stop me. I left the hotel room, a singular purpose clear in my mind.

* * * *

Hughes slept fitfully as I watched, the wound in his belly obviously causing him discomfort even as it healed. I wondered how he had explained it to the rest of the Council, or if he had. If he had dug out the silver slug himself over the polished porcelain sink in the Four Seasons hotel bathroom, bandaged himself up and put himself to bed.

It really was lonely at the top.

Hughes rolled over onto his side and his eyelids fluttered open. Perhaps he had caught my scent and been urged to wakefulness by the fact that he was not alone. He stared at me sitting in a chair at his bedside, his breathing still slow and even.

I let my head tilt to one side, my gaze meeting his. "You look like hell, sir."

The reality of what his eyes were seeing seemed to crash in on him all at once, and he attempted to scramble into a seated position. "How in the hell —!"

"You pick things up when you're a detective," I said, sitting back in the plush easy chair. "You should really use the deadbolt when you stay in a hotel, you know."

With labored breaths, Hughes managed to get himself mostly upright in the sea of blankets and pillows, one arm slung around his bandaged stomach. He glared at me once he'd found a position to settle in, disgust dripping from his green eyes. "Get out, Bowen."

"She's dead." Swallowing the bile that rose in my throat as discreetly as possible, I kept my gaze fixed on him, unblinking. "I thought you'd want to know."

A confused parade of emotions rushed across his pinched face. "Holtz?"

I shook my head. "Your precious psychotic, Pâquerette. She's dead." Toying with the gold bracelet I wore on my right wrist, I grimaced at him, baring my teeth like a chimp in a cage. "Grace Holtz is very much alive, despite your efforts."

He nodded slowly, not even bothering to look at me now, his gaze focused somewhere on the floor. "What...what is she going to do?"

"I haven't the faintest idea," I answered, rising from my seat. "And even if I did, I wouldn't tell you."

This, at least, got his attention. Silver hair falling into his eyes, he jerked his head up to bark at me, "I don't think I like your tone, boy."

"Good." I propped my foot on top of the metal briefcase that lay discarded beside the bed. Smiling, I stared down at the older wolf, my hands slung in my trouser pockets. "I'm done being your boy, Hughes. I'm done doing the dirty work of a bunch of supercilious, unctuous, two-faced, backward-thinking bastards like you and your inbred Council."

Rearing back, Hughes reached up and slapped me across the face.

I slapped him back without hesitation, my knuckles cracking across his jaw and digging into his teeth.

The still-injured wolf collapsed back into the bedding, a thin trail of blood trickling from the corner of his mouth, the most delicious expression of disbelief on his thin face.

"This is what is going to happen," I said, resuming my former posture of relaxed ease. "I'm going to submit a full report to the Council, detailing everything about your involvement in the deaths of Colquhoun, his son, Mama and the attempted murder of Grace Holtz."

Hughes swallowed blood, sneering. "They'll never believe you."

"I don't much care if they believe me or not." Leaning down until our cheeks almost brushed against each other, I then spoke into his ear. "After I do that, I intend to submit the same report to the Nameless."

He stilled next to me. The defiance was lacking from his voice when he shakily insisted, "Bowen, you can't—"

"Now, what they'll do with the information I provide, I can't rightly say," I continued as if oblivious to his growing panic. "But Delila is dead, and you're alive. I imagine the Nameless will want someone to pay for what happened to their matriarch. I also imagine that the Feóndulf won't be too keen to start a war over you, particularly when they learn that you've been organizing dog-fighting rings in Nameless territory, just to foment conflict in the region."

I pulled back, noting with deep satisfaction the way his hands gripped the sheets under him, the wide, glassy stare he fixed me with and the understanding I saw reflected in its depth. He licked his lips and opened his mouth to speak, but no words came out.

I reached down and picked up the glass on the bedside table, swirling the amber liquid that remained in it around and around.

"I'm sure we can come to some kind of understanding, Bowen," said Hughes at last. He shook his head. "There must be something you want, something you need that only I can provide."

I sniffed at what was left of his large, expensive whiskey and downed it in one gulp. "You have nothing I need." I replaced the glass with a clatter and turned away from him, heading for the door to the hotel suite. "If you're going to try to run...I suggest you start packing now."

Chapter Twenty-Nine

Grace

The morning dawned clear and bright. Another perfect Seattle summer day. I didn't wait for Marcus to come back to the Maxwell Hotel. I didn't rest either. There was too much to do—too many arrangements to be made. By nine, I had made my way out of the hotel with a bandaged shoulder and my luggage. By ten, I had finished telling the saga of the previous night's adventure to Lily, who listened attentively from the employee side of the meat counter in her shop.

"Sounds like a hell of a party," she said when I had concluded my tale. She straightened from where she had been leaning against the counter. "Sorry I missed it."

I mimicked her movement from the other side of the glass, shaking my head hard. "No, you're not."

"No, no, I'm really not," admitted Lily, puffing up her cheeks as she let out a large breath, rubbing her hands together. "So, den leader. What's next? Heading to London to get a handle on the Feóndulf?"

I smirked. "Ah, no — very much no." I shoved my hands into my hoodie pockets, shifting my weight onto my back foot. "I've already talked with the Council — what's left of them, anyway — and officially abdicated my position as head of the Feóndulf. As for the Nameless..." I sighed, my gaze flitting around the room. "I'm confident Kassandra will do an excellent job running things. Especially since she has Sylvia to help her."

"Oh?"

I rolled my shoulders back, grimacing. "You know I never wanted to be in charge of anybody. Not like that, anyway. This little adventure has only convinced me that den politics are way too messy for someone like me."

Lily nodded. "Back to Klamath Falls, then."

"I don't think so," I said.

The human woman fixed me with an unimpressed stare. "Well...aren't you just full of surprises this morning?"

I smiled and shrugged. "I guess, it's just... I spent so long thinking that I had only two options — be what Mama wanted me to be, or be the exact opposite of that. Either be somebody or be nobody. But now I'm thinking, maybe I should take some time to figure out what it's like to just be...me."

Lily smiled. "What about being normal?"

"Eh, normal," I repeated, waving the word away with my hand. "It's just a word, right?"

"Right." The butcher nodded and picked up a towel, throwing it over her shoulder. "Well, wherever you go and whatever you do, you always have a place to land here. And I feel a lot better this time knowing that you won't be going alone."

I furrowed my brow. "What? What are you talking about?"

Lily nodded toward her front windows and, with the hair on the back of my neck rising, I spun around. The only thing I could do was stare at the man that I most, and least, wanted to see. Crouched down on the sidewalk in front of my new car, his face was partially obscured by the kisses he was receiving from a very excited Sadie, whom I had left tied to the parking meter. After a moment, the werewolf separated himself from the affectionate animal, stood and started walking toward the front door of the butcher's shop.

I jerked back toward the counter, my blood pounding in my ears as I gritted my teeth.

"You didn't think you'd get rid of him that easily, did you?" teased Lily, smiling.

I rubbed at the back of my neck, rolling my eyes. "No, I guess not."

The bell on the shop door jingled, and Marcus stepped into the small shop, waving. "Good morning, ladies." Marcus smiled broadly. "You're both looking radiant today."

"Marcus, good morning!" answered Lily with equal brightness. "How about I go get us all some coffee?"

"Sounds wonderful, thanks," he said, nodding as he stopped to stand beside me.

With one last smile directed at me, Lily bustled through the back room and up the stairs, leaving Marcus and me alone in the shop foyer. With all the casualness I could muster, I glanced over at him.

Marcus fixed me with an appraising stare, crossing his arms high over his chest before speaking. "You know, if you were trying to avoid me, stopping here before heading out of town was probably not the smartest idea."

"I wasn't trying to avoid you," I started, my nose wrinkling.

"Oh, really?" He scoffed, his arms swinging down to his sides. "I guess I just assumed when you checked out of the hotel without waiting for me to come back — "

"You're the one who left in the first place," I pointed out, frowning.

"You were supposed to be resting!" Marcus brought a hand up to his forehead. "Or did I just imagine you getting shot with a silver bullet?"

"And how are those cracked ribs doing this morning, mister?" I countered, poking him in the chest.

He batted my hand away, scowling. "That's not the point, and you know it."

We stood in silence for a moment, each glaring at the other. My heart started to thud hard in my chest. I scratched at my ear and admitted, "Okay. Okay, the truth was, I wasn't sure you'd want to see me off."

"Off?" Marcus swallowed and stared at the space just above my head. "So, you are heading back to Klamath Falls, then?"

"No," I said. I enjoyed the way his eyes widened as he jerked down to stare at me, but I changed the subject nonetheless. "What about you? I'm guessing that the Feóndulf want you back in Cardiff, now that everything here is cleared up?"

Marcus grimaced, shoving his hands into his trouser pockets. "They may. But I'm not overly concerned with what the Feóndulf want, at the moment." He met my eyes at last. "I resigned."

I looked back at him blankly. "Resigned."

"From the police," he said. "And the den." Marcus rocked backward and forward on his heels. "I am officially unemployed and unaffiliated."

"Marcus!" My mouth hung open for a moment before I nodded in encouragement. "Wow. Well...congratulations, I guess. What are you going to do now?"

"No idea," answered Marcus brightly. "But I think I'm done taking orders for a while. Everything with Hughes, with Colquhoun... I used to think that loyalty to the den was everything. But now, well. Being loyal to your family is all well and good, but it's only as good as that family is. I'd rather save my loyalty for something that deserves it."

I stared at Marcus. I felt compelled to say something profound, but I settled for reaching forward and tapping his shoulder with my closed fist and smiling. "Good for you, pal."

A blush tinted Marcus' neck and cheeks. He looked away, rubbing at the stubble on his chin. "Yeah, well..." Clearing his throat, he proclaimed, "No Klamath Falls, eh? What will the bank do without you?"

"Credit union," I corrected out of habit. I wiggled my head. "They'll survive. I was actually thinking about doing some traveling. There's a whole world out there that I've only read about in books, you know? Might be worthwhile to see some of it."

Marcus nodded, frowning in mock seriousness. "Sounds like a solid plan. It's just...poor Tim will be devastated."

I frowned. "Tim?" So much had happened in the last week that I had temporarily forgotten the name of my former coworker. The man's existence came back to me in a flash, and my confusion deepened. I scowled. "What the hell—?"

Marcus tutted, loosening the knot of his tie. "The way he looked at you? He was under the sway of your feminine wiles, make no mistake."

"Oh my God," I whined, my face flushing crimson as I winced. "Shut up!"

Marcus laughed, clearly enjoying my discomfort.

I swept past him and headed for the door, not bothering to hide my smile. "Don't be an idiot."

"Sorry, can't help it."

The feel of Marcus' gaze on me was warm, like pulling on a freshly laundered sweatshirt. I realized with a start that I didn't want to let that feeling go. I stuttered to a stop.

"You know…" I closed my eyes and twisted around on my heels. "The car's got an empty front seat. I could use a good navigator."

Silence met my implied invitation. I eased my eyes open to find Marcus watching me through narrowed eyes, his hands on his hips. He tossed his head toward the animal waiting outside. "Isn't that what the dog is for?"

I relaxed into a toothy smile. "Sadie? She can't read a map for shit." I bent forward at the waist, lifting a brow. "I'd even let you pick the music. All that eighties crap you love."

Marcus tilted his head to one side. He pursed his lips. "Hmm. Well, I suppose it could be interesting. I always did want to see more of America."

My heart pounding hard in my chest, I attempted a nonchalant shrug. "Here's your chance."

Marcus scratched the back of his neck and sighed. "All right," he said. "You've got yourself a deal." He offered me his hand to shake.

With an undisguised spring in my step, I walked back and clapped my hand into his. With a sharp tug, Marcus pulled me close. He snaked his free hand under my hair and gripped the nape of my neck as he kissed me with a reckless abandon that left me breathless.

Releasing my lips, Marcus rested his forehead against my own, his eyes shut tight. "You didn't really think I was going to let you get away again, did you?"

I breathed out a laugh. "I wasn't sure."

"Idiot," he said affectionately, brushing another kiss against my hairline. "You're stuck with me now."

"Damn," I answered, burying my face into the crook of his neck and shoulder. "I suppose I'll just have to get used to it."

"So" — Marcus took a step back, smiling wide — "where are we headed to first?"

Want to see more like this?
Here's a taster for you to enjoy!

Hell Hath No Fury: Scorned
Angela Addams

Excerpt

"Are we going to get some street meat or what?" Ruby gleefully shouted as she slung one arm out, pointing her finger in the direction of sustenance.

"Hang on, friend. I need to grab some cash." I tugged Ruby's other arm toward a side street where the bright glow of an ATM beckoned me.

It was late — or early, depending on what side of the moon you were on. Two a.m. and greasy sausages from the vendor down the road was top priority after a night of tequila shots.

Ruby was tanked, and I was feeling a nice floaty buzz, which gave me a perma-smile that hurt my cheeks and made my lips ache.

"Maybe I'll crash at your place tonight," Ruby slurred as she slumped against the wall next to the ATM, her body like a limp noodle. "Take a vacay from my life."

The city streets were wafting some pretty heavy heat after the scorcher of the last few days. Summer was dying, and we were all paying for it. The patios had been full when we'd gone to grab dinner earlier, and the bars had been packed when we'd done a bit of hopping from one dive to the next. It had been fun, but I reeked of other people's sweat, and I was ready to go home.

"My place is hardly a vacation destination." *Understatement of the century.*

My place was a dump, with its hundred-year-old cracked plaster, peeling wallpaper and rusty pipes. But it was *my* dump, and I had been lucky to find something in the heart of Toronto. I got what Ruby was craving, though—peace, solitude, time away from her boyfriend's two kids under five and her boyfriend, who might as well be kid number three. She wanted to stretch out her night of freedom, sleep until late in the morning. drink coffee that she didn't have to chug and maybe have a bagel and some eggs that she didn't have to eat cold. "I can't promise you five-star anything, but you know my couch is always yours."

"I love your place. It's got so much old-world charm." Ruby hiccupped as she rolled her head toward me, a silly grin making her eyes light up. "What's taking so long? There's a big fat juicy sausage calling to me."

"That's so dirty." I attempted to joke, even though I was frowning at the machine, which had rejected my passcode twice already. "Don't know." I punched my code in a third time then slammed my hand against the side of the machine, because violence was always just under the surface for me. "What the fuck?"

"Here… Let me use my card." Ruby pushed off the wall. "Move out of the way."

"I can't." I was rooted in place. My feet stuck as I stared at the machine that was telling me my bank account didn't exist. *It doesn't exist?* "It won't give my card back."

I punched some buttons, agitation quickly turning to frantic rage. I had money in there. My monthly 'shut up and disappear' money would have gone in at midnight, replenishing the joint account with what I was owed. I slammed my open palm against the panel again, and the sting reverberated up my arm.

"Whoa there, lady." A smooth voice slid out of the darkness, dripping with bad intentions. "That machine ain't done nothing wrong." He stepped too close to Ruby, pulling my attention away from the ATM.

Ruby's eyes went wide. She straightened her back and winced. "Charlie." My name was a squeak that shuddered past her lips. A tremor shook her shoulders.

The hairs on the back of my neck perked up.

He was wearing a gray hoodie pulled up over his scraggly dark hair. That and the shadow shielding his face made it impossible to get a good look at him. "You ladies are going to give me what you've got in your bank accounts." He nudged Ruby, and she opened her mouth like she was going to scream, but he clamped his hand over her face. "Quietly."

A loser holding up two women. *Classy.*

"I can't give you jack," I said with a nod to the machine, which was now flashing a recommendation to call my bank. "This piece of shit just ate my card." He didn't need to know about my other bank account.

He snorted what sounded like a laugh, and I got a waft of something not quite right. I mean, aside from the fact that he was trying to rob us, there was also a jitter about him that was making me think he was tweaked out on something. That, or he was really, really on edge. "I'm taking payment one way or the other."

It was obvious that he had a weapon wedged against Ruby's back by the way she was arching her spine. I didn't know if he was hurting her or if it was fear, but she was contorting as far away as she could get with his hand on her mouth. "You scream, and I hurt you. Got it?"

Ruby nodded as tears spilled down her cheeks.

He lifted his meaty hand away. "You try your card."

She made a mumbly noise then staggered toward me, towing the guy along with her.

I didn't know if he had a gun or knife or if he was just using his fingers to scare the hell out of Ruby, but his eyes were dark and menacing, his pupils pinpricks. He licked his chapped lips as he gave me a once-over. I felt dirty just from his gaze. When he met my eyes again and his lips curled into a smug grin, I knew he wasn't bluffing. The guy liked to make women scream.

I calculated the odds of Ruby getting hurt if I took action.

He was taller than me by at least a foot. Heavier, too. Probably had about a hundred pounds on me, maybe more. He likely had a weapon—cowards like him always did. I'd handled bigger men than him. I'd taken down meaner ones, too. I could deal with a bullet, even a few bullets. Nobody used silver anymore and lead, steel and brass are practically mosquito bites. Stab wounds? They would close with time.

"You do anything stupid, and I'll kill her," he growled like he was reading my mind.

It wasn't me who would get hurt. Ruby was a fragile human—and not just physically. She was riding high on adrenaline right now, but that would crash soon, then she'd go into shock.

She was shaking as she frantically dug into her bag, presumably for her bank card. She was sucking air into her mouth and barely letting any go. Her fear was a rising tide, and she was going to drown.

I lifted my hands—the universal sign for surrender—and took a step back to make room for Ruby in front of the machine.

"I c-c-can't find my c-c-card."

Like a snake, the guy struck, smacking Ruby up the side of her head then threading his fingers into her hair. He pushed her head down toward her chest and shoved her closer to the machine. She choked on a sob.

"Stop fucking around," the thief growled.

My hackles were up, flooding high-octane rage into my muscles. My body bulked. I rolled my shoulders back, cracked my spine, narrowed my eyes and did everything I could to keep the beast inside me under control. If she came out, this guy was going to die, and I didn't want to have to explain that to anyone. "Take your hands off her."

He skittered his gaze to me, tilting his head like I was intriguing him—like he found me amusing. "You ain't calling the shots here, lady."

"I found it!" Ruby whipped her card out but couldn't seem to coordinate herself to slide it into the slot.

I clenched and unclenched my fists, tightening my jaw so my molars were grinding. The tingle of anticipation made my gums burn and my fingers ache.

Keep it steady, Charlie.

For Ruby's sake, I was fighting the primal urge to lash out. If I hurt him, he'd hurt her. I needed to bide my time. Wait him out. He'd make a mistake. They always did.

When she failed to get the card into the slot on her third try, he tightened his grip in her hair. "I said, stop fucking around."

"I'm sorry!" She managed to shove the card in, then worked on punching her code on the keypad. "I can only take out five hundred."

"Fuck," he muttered as he speared me with another disgusting once-over. "I guess that means you two are coming with me for the night." As if that hadn't always been his plan.

We waited as the machine whirred then spit out a wad of cash. He was practically salivating at the sight of it. He let go of Ruby's hair then reached for the money at the same time that I curled my fingers over Ruby's wrist to yank her behind me. The sudden movement startled him. He lifted his weapon.

Not a gun.

One badass-looking knife, though.

"Run," I ordered Ruby as I leapt to block the guy from her. He lunged, and I swiped his face, my fist connecting with a rock-hard jaw and sending bolts of pain up my arm.

"Ow, you bitch!" He swung his curved blade down, reaching out to get a hold of my hair, but I ducked and weaved, nailing him in the side with another punch. This time my fist sank in, missing his ribs altogether, drilling him in the liver instead—or trying to, anyway. The guy was made of marbled meat.

He groaned but not surprisingly, didn't go down. I ducked again when he tried to slam me with his blade but miscalculated his reflexes and took an uppercut to the chin. It sent me reeling backward, lights flashing across my vision.

Ouch.

As I was shaking it off, Ruby screamed. The guy pivoted in her direction.

Fuck.

I'd told her to run, but instead, she was frozen like prey.

I leapt onto this back and wrapped my arm around his thick neck. My fingers, complete with partially distended claws against his jugular, were hidden by his hood.

Blending in meant being subtle with my abilities — for both self-preservation and to avoid unwanted attention. I'd had three years to master my partial shift and was proud to say that Ruby had no idea her best friend was a werewolf.

"Take one more step, and I'll bleed you like a pig," I snarled against his ear. To punctuate my threat, I let my claws poke into his skin, drawing first blood. The smell of it revved me up, making my wolf want to howl and my beast want to rip his throat out. I tightened my hold and leveraged myself closer, clamping down on my predatory urges. My fangs dropped, burning through my gums. I scraped them along his jaw and took pleasure in his whimper. "One twitch and you're dead." My voice was guttural, filled with malice that I knew he understood.

The acrid smell of piss hit my nose. *Oh, how the tables have turned.*

"Drop the knife," I ordered.

It clattered to the ground.

I urged my fangs to slink back into my gums but kept the pressure on his throat with my claws. "Ruby, call the cops."

But really, what this guy needed was a good scare and some beastly tough love.

* * * *

We were at the hospital so Ruby could get checked out. She was obviously in shock, with glassy eyes, mumbling a confusing account of what went down. The police had taken our statements already, but it was mine that made sense, so it was mine that would go into their report, which was better for everyone.

I snuck away while the doctor was checking Ruby out and made a call.

"Well, if it isn't the bitch of the hour," Vince drawled, wide awake at holy fuck in the morning, as usual. "To what do I owe this honor, Charlotte?"

"What the fuck did you do to my bank account?" I growled. Attempted robbery aside, finding out that my money was gone had ruined my night. "Where's my cash, asshole?"

"Whoa, whoa, whoa!" Vince sucked on something, probably a fat cigar, then blew into the phone. "You're acting like I'm the one messing up your life, when really, that's all on you, babe."

"I have a contract and a clan vow. First of the month, money goes into that account." I never wanted the account to be joint, but my stepbrother, Andy, had insisted that it must be that way for the family to agree to the deal. I always transferred it at the stroke of midnight to my own personal account anyway, but tonight I had plans and didn't think it would be a big deal to do it a little later than normal. That, apparently, had been a miscalculation on my part.

"Contract and vow are void," Vince said, like I should already know. "Andy isn't in charge anymore. You are S.O.L."

Whatever was left in my gut bottomed out, and I was suddenly nauseous. "Did they kill him?" That was the only way Andy would step down from being alpha of the clan. "What happened?"

I wasn't going to pretend that I was on any type of lovey-dovey terms with my stepbrothers, but Andy was less of a dick than the rest of them. When he'd taken over running the clan after my dad had passed, he'd struck a deal with me to disappear. I had, happily, and for the last three years, he'd upheld his end of it with a monthly stipend delivered wirelessly at the stroke of midnight.

"He's not dead. He's just…incapacitated."

Fuck! Fuckfuckfuckfuck.

"Where is he?"

"That's privileged information, sweetheart." Vince grunted.

"Who's alpha? Del? Lucas?" Either one of my shithead stepbrothers would run the clan into the ground. Both were vindictive enough to shut my account down and void our agreement.

"You've got it all wrong, babe. Sal is alpha now. And it would be a good idea for you to pay your respects…*in person.*"

"Sal?" *Holy fuck!* "He was ousted." My father had kicked him out when he'd gone on a rampage, blood-raging all over Vancouver Island, and had killed a bunch of tourists on a nature hike. I remembered the day my father had sat us all down at the house and told us our brother, my stepbrother, was ex-communicated. Removal from the clan was the ultimate slap in the face. More than that, it was a walking death sentence to be a wolf with no clan affiliation, and it was supposed to be permanent.

"Lone wolf is back and…sweetie? He's not too happy with you and the arrangement you weaseled out of dear old Andrew."

Yeah, because a guy like that would rather have me barefoot and pumping out little werewolf babies than having a life of my own on my own terms. 'Independent female werewolf' was not in his vocabulary. We only existed to serve men like him.

Plus, if my uncle had blabbed about my werebeast, then Sal was probably hungry for a demonstration. Not many females could turn into deformed monsters like I could.

I was special that way.

"I had a sanctioned deal," I spat, rage burning through my brain until all I could see were flames. *That motherfucker!* I kicked a garbage can, which drew the attention of a security guard, who swiveled in my direction.

"I tell you what, *Charlie*," Vince snarled. "Sal will be at the head office tomorrow. I can pencil you in for a meeting so you can discuss your displeasure with the management of *his* funds. I'll even buy you a ticket to get here."

I closed my eyes, took a deep breath then blew it out. When I opened my eyes, the guard was still looking at me but hadn't come any closer. I turned my back on him as I exited the hospital. "Yeah, fine, book me a ticket, asshole." I hung up before he could reply.

The best way to deal with a dictator like Sal was to get right up in his face, and that was what I planned to do. He didn't know it yet, but he was about to meet a side of me he couldn't control.

About the Author

When Robin Jeffrey isn't checking out books to students at the academic library where she works, she can be found cranking out punchy flash fiction, lyrical essays, and world-rich romances. Her writing has been published in magazines across the country and around the world. She currently calls the Pacific Northwest of the United States home, where she lives happily with her husband and their out of control comic book collection.

Robin loves to hear from readers. You can find her contact information, website details and author profile page at https://www.totallybound.com

Home of Erotic Romance

Sign up for our newsletter and find out about all our romance book releases, eBook sales and promotions, sneak peeks and FREE romance books!

Printed in the USA
CPSIA information can be obtained
at www.ICGtesting.com
LVHW100914230823
755831LV00005B/50